KILLING CHANCE

a JOHN DRAKE satire

Credits:

KILLING CHANCE was written by John Drake

Cover art by Collin Brennan

KILLING CHANCE by: John Drake/Three Ravens
Publishing – 1st edition, 2020

Trade Paperback ISBN: 978-1-951768-08-9

For information about the story, contact;

johndrakewriter@gmail.com

@JohnDrakeWriter on Twitter

FOR MUM & DAD

(Mine, that is, not yours. Although I suppose you can tell them it's dedicated to them if you like, just cover this bit with correction fluid)

About the Author:

John Drake is originally from Liverpool, England but is now an adopted Dubliner. He specializes in the criminally under-represented genre of satirical historical fiction and wrote his first 'serious' line of writing at the grand old age of forty. He is the author of both Making Man – a comedy centred around a Neanderthal with itchy feet and the mind of an engineer – and Cheating Death – another comedy set during the famously jovial Black Death of 14th century Europe. He can usually be found sandwiched somewhere in between a good pun and a thesaurus.

If you can keep your head when all about you
Are losing theirs and blaming it on you,
Or watch the things you gave your life to, broken,
And stoop and build 'em up with worn-out tools:

If you can force your heart and nerve and sinew
To serve your turn long after they are gone,
And so hold on when there is nothing in you
Except the Will which says to them: 'Hold on!'

If you can talk with crowds and keep your virtue,
Or walk with Kings—nor lose the common touch,
If neither foes nor loving friends can hurt you,
If all men count with you, but none too much;

Yours is the Earth and everything that's in it,
And - which is more - you'll be a Khan, my son!

~ If, Rudyard Kipling (ish)

PROLOGUE

Mongol Empire, 1215

Takkan scrubbed the grime from the captain's trousers. It was a messy job, but a good one. A friend of his had been on the dreaded latrine duties for almost three months and it was possible he would never be the same man again. Takkan himself had been forced to work them for a week the previous summer and felt lucky to get to the end of it with his olfactory functions intact, let alone his mental state.

He raised the dripping pants to the sky, studying them for missed stains. Once he was satisfied there was no mark for the captain to use as an excuse to whip him again, he lay them down on the drying stone and reached back for the next garment that required his attention.

They say if you hear an arrow coming towards you then it has already missed. Takkan did not hear an arrow, nor the thudding noise his head made as it bounced off the large boulder and down to the floor, joining his limp body as it did so.

CHAPTER ONE

Mongol Settlement

'I don't know why we have to go through this every day' complained Jochi. 'We should be riding the greatest horses in the world, not firing arrows at a dead ostrich.'

'This ostrich could be the difference between you seeing your next birthday or not' said Mekki. 'You of all people should be here every waking moment, after all. If you could aim as well as you ride you wouldn't be here in our little band of military misfits.'

'No need to get personal' said Jochi sulkily. 'You don't hear me going on about your abilities as a servant.'

'True, but I'm not one of the best servants in the nation. You should be a captain by now.'

'You sound like my mother.'

'I'd rather be cooking it' said Stan, ignoring the familiar talk on the disparity between Jochi's horse-riding prowess and his talent with a bow. 'One morning on a spit with a few sprigs of thyme would do wonders for our spirits.'

'It would do wonders for your waistline, too' said Mekki. 'You should try catching the ostrich in the first place and let Jochi here aim at it for a day or two. You'd be killing two birds with one stone.'

'I'm not going after it with a stone' said Stan. 'I'll use an arrow like any normal Mongol. I'm not the one with the hand-eye co-ordination of a myopic parrot, remember?'

'It's a turn of phrase' said Mekki. 'It means taking one action to solve two problems.'

'Oh, like punching you in the mouth?' said Stan. 'It would stop you talking and would make me feel better.'

'Well, yes, I suppose' said Mekki. 'I stand by my idea, all the same. You could do with losing a few folds from your belly.'

'And you could do with losing a few barbs from your speech. What's wrong with you today?'

'I was just trying to lighten the mood. I thought you'd see the funny side of it. I'm as tired of this archery practice as Jochi is. Plus, I'm sick of doing the same things day after day.'

'It could be worse, I suppose; we could be marching with the Horde' said Jochi. 'I'd far rather practise warfare than practice it.'

'He's at it again' said Mekki. 'Words will be the death of you, Jochi. One day someone with a small brain and a big stick is going to teach you a very different kind of lesson.'

'Maybe you *should* find yourself an adventure. It would cheer you up and give us a break from your ill-judged humour at the same time. You might say it would kill two birds with one stone.'

'Don't start giving him any ideas of adventure' said Stan. 'We have a duty to the Golden Horde. That's the way it is, and that's the way it will always be.'

'That's the spirit' said Mekki sarcastically. 'I'm already dribbling with excitement about the prospect of doing today again tomorrow.'

'I have to go' said Jochi. 'Okatai will be wondering why I've deserted my training for an ostrich, and I don't want to cross him again after that misunderstanding about his bedclothes.'

'Same time tomorrow?' asked Stan.

'Can't wait.'

'Dammit Stan, you're as stupid as your uncle. He was a worthless man and you are no different, you great lump of mutton. Now bring me my dark brown shirt with the light lining, not this light coloured shirt with a dark lining! You're a damnable fool. Honestly, I'm not sure I could make it any simpler for you. Why are you still standing there disrespecting me? Go!'

Captain Sulki dismissed Stan with a wicked slap across his face, forcing his apprentice to stumble back towards the door. Stan turned the stagger into a trot, spinning around to face the open flap of the yurt, tottering through it and into the dazzling cold of the Mongolian winter sun. It was a valiant attempt to hide his weakness in front of the captain, but he could have sung twelve verses of "Pillage The Village" in the Jin language and Sulki would have thought no more of him.

He trudged along his well-trodden path between the captain's living quarters and sleeping yurt. He could never understand how one man required two to himself. Those of a similar social standing to Stan had to make do with a single, small yurt for their entire family; one that was much smaller than either of Captain Sulki's and yet was home to anything up to twelve members of the sweeping horde of Genghis Khan.

As he entered the tent he nodded a welcome to Zabin, the captain's eldest daughter and matrimonial target for every father with boys of a certain age.

'Do not nod at those above your station, servant' said Zabin's shadow; a wiry girl whose thin nose outnumbered her redeeming features. 'What are you doing here?'

Stan ignored her, turning instead to Zabin in a subtle show of defiance that he could spin as a show of deference to the captain's daughter should the need arise. 'Good afternoon, m'lady.'

'M'lady? What do you mean by m'lady?' said Zabin frostily.

'My apologies. It is a greeting used in the far west to give great respect to those who work to keep us poor, lowly men safe.'

'And how would an ignorant rat like you know about that?' said the shadow.

Stan's gaze remained fixed on the captain's daughter. 'I have read stories of such things.'

'Oh, you've read them, have you?' said Zabin. 'Are you sure you weren't simply eavesdropping on a conversation between the captains at dinner? A man of such lowly stock as you does not read, servant. He cleans and he fetches, he does not seek to fill his mind with that which he can never understand.'

Stan ploughed on, unwisely as it happened. There was little opportunity for men in his position to impress those who could lift him from the social dirt, but sometimes it paid to retreat into the role of silent dogsbody to ensure you kept the right number of heads. 'I bought a scroll from a passing merchant while we were sacking the great city of Irksum. It tells of the customs of the west. If we are to reach there with the best possible chance of conquering them then we should familiarise ourselves with their ways.'

'Should we, indeed?' said Zabin. 'What does the captain think of your grand plan? Has he read this scroll too?'

'Well, not exactly. It is... a...' stammered Stan. His speech had run out of ideas and he crumbled under the glare of the most eligible daughter in the regiment. 'Please, I misspoke. Forgive me. I am here for the captain's dark shirt. No, the light one with the dark lining. I think. Or was it the dark one with the light lining?'

'You have a dark shirt over your arm, so I assume you have returned here for the light one. Here' said Zabin, passing him the correct item of clothing.

'Thank you' said Stan.

'I insist you come back here this evening after our meal. There will be much to discuss.'

'You...? There will?' said Stan, stunned at the unprecedented invitation.

'But of course. I am eager to hear what my father makes of your western scroll. I will tell him to expect it by sunset.'

Stan swallowed hard, bowed, and backed out of the yurt. He had precious little time to replace the now-lost scroll, not to mention learning to read and write.

'That's right' said Stan. 'I need you to help me find some paper, and quickly too.'

Mekki rubbed the sleep from his eyes. 'Why do you need it so urgently?'

'I'll explain later, I don't have time now.'

'Anyone who says they'll explain something later as they ask for unorthodox assistance is hiding something. Everyone knows that. Give me the abridged version.'

'I told Zabin I bought a scroll from a passing merchant.'

'Can you unabridge that a little?'

'I called her m'lady and told her it is the way the western people address those in power. When she asked how I knew such information I told her it was written on a scroll I bought.'

'Lord of the Sky, Stan! What were you thinking?'

'If it's all the same with you, can we dissect this after sunset? The story's ending hasn't happened yet and I'd like my body to be as it is now when I retell it.'

'Fine. Let's go to Okatai, I'm sure he'll have something for you.'

Okatai was the man you went to when you needed something fixed, whether that be a tool or a predicament. His father was a fletcher with no other obvious talent, but at an early age, Okatai had learned to solve problems without any assistance from those around him, like a tree flourishing in a mirage. He taught himself how to extract meaning from the few examples of writing that made their way past his yurt and had a way of thinking that seemed to find smooth paths through thorny problems.

He lived on his own, or at least that which constituted being alone in the horde. He had once shared his yurt with a collection of other elderly men who had outlived their peers, but he paid them little heed in their final years and had found ways to dissuade those who would take their place in his ever more spacious tent. His passion was in helping the younger men discover how to learn for themselves. It was his way of creating a continual legacy that had once seemed impossible. His children had, like many before them, died fighting for the Great Khan on the ever-shifting battlefields.

Jochi scurried back along the path connecting his master's yurt with a small lake at the base of a steep hill. He walked with the impatient but deliberate gait reserved for those struggling to prioritise both the speed of their return and the quantity of water left in the jug when they arrive.

He had worked for Okatai for almost a year now, a man whose extreme fairness was comparable only to his rigid adhesion to *the rules*. If the level of water in Okatai's jug should fall below the prescribed mark it would take a herd of yaks to stop Jochi from being on the receiving end of a good wallop. Okatai insisted on marking each of his containers with a fill line, scratched in at such a point he deemed satisfactory. He also insisted on punctuality. Lateness was an aberration, prematurity doubly so. The balancing of these requirements had hurt Jochi's brain more often than the academic tests his captain would thrust upon him at a moment's notice. *Letters are your future* he would say as if an ability to read would achieve anything inside this swarm of swords.

Jochi wobbled his way along the path, choosing the moment he considered to be the sweet spot between antecedence and tardiness to enter the yurt.

'Your water, master.'

'Table' stated Okatai. 'And stop calling me master, you know my rank well enough. *Captain* Okatai. The presence of *captain* insists you address me as such. It's really not that hard, Jochi. It's not as if you need to choose from a dozen different titles, as you would if you were addressing the Great Khan. It has, and always shall be, *captain*.'

'My apologies, captain. I get confused between the military captains and... other important captains. Should I address them both the same?'

'Only concern yourself with knowledge you expect to need. I hold many secrets in my head, but none that are useless to me. It is unlikely you will find yourself in conversation with military captains. That is why you are here, after all.'

'How will I know if I need it until it's too late?' asked Jochi, ignoring the slight.

'Enough cheek!' snapped Okatai. 'Bring me the parchments and get on with your work.'

Jochi handed them to his captain and sat down at his place on the floor, careful not to disturb the writing Okatai had scraped into the dirt in front of him. Another test. He scrunched up his brain and tried to make sense of them. There was no doubt his reading had improved recently but he still dreaded Okatai's examinations, failing more often than he passed. He knew the basic meaning behind the shapes but often had difficulty with the nuance of the more complex ones and had precious little confidence in his translations.

He turned to his captain, who had his back to him, then back to the shapes. Then back to the captain again. Any certainty he could fake evaporated in the answer his mind had offered. Surely he was wrong again? If he was right, though, it could be a defining moment in his apprenticeship. Come to think of it, it would have consequences either way.

He rose onto his haunches and paused, looking back at the symbols in the earth one last time. Taking a deep breath, he rose to his full, inadequate height, tapped his captain on the shoulder, and punched his turning face square in the jaw.

Okatai would have fallen to the floor, had he not been expecting the blow. He returned the punch with one of his own, an altogether more forceful one that sent Jochi violently to the floor, scuffing the writing and knocking him out.

When he came back to consciousness Jochi's vision was filled with the cream coloured roof of a yurt. He turned his head to look for Okatai and winced in pain as a rib screamed for him to stay still. The room was almost empty. He was lying on a woolen bed, deeper and more comfortable than his own, and with an unfamiliar smell about it. Okatai's parchments were not in their usual place, nor were his omnipresent inks. On further inspection, he noticed more boiled leather chest plates than were usually present. One more, to be precise, and it was attached to an enormous bulk of a man whom Jochi recognised instantly.

'You awake now' stated the bulk in the booming tones of a man whose brain was smaller than his fist.

'I'm not sure' said Jochi. 'Is my head still the right way around?'

'I check' boomed the bulk.

The man with biceps the size of a sheep put his hands around Jochi's neck and lifted him clean off the floor, swivelling the head from side to side before letting go while Jochi's feet were a little further from the ground than he would have liked.

'Yes.'

Jochi rubbed his neck as if the action would relieve him of this new pain as it grappled for attention with the old one in his chest.

'Thank you for clarifying, Bataar. You may want to take note that I was making a joke; a light-hearted quip in the face of adversity. Just like I explained to you last week, the week before, and every week for the past seventeen years.'

'I not remember. My brain not hold unf… infum…'

'Information?'

'Yes. Not hold infummation very good.'

'Well.'

'Well, what?'

'Your brain does not hold information very *well*.'

'That not nice. Brother should be nice. Mean brother.'

'I'm sorry, Bataar. I'm a little unnerved. I think I just punched Captain Okatai in the face.'

'You did. He very happy.'

'He's happy?'

'That what he say. *Finally,* he say. He also say *watch him like fur rabbit.*'

Jochi rubbed the bridge of his nose patiently. There was a familiar silence while he translated his brother's speech, a skill he had been forced to develop over several years.

'Ah!' he said at last. 'He asked you to watch me *for a bit?*'

'He say fur rabbit.'

'Well, you've done a splendid job of it, Bataar. How long has he been gone?'

'He go before.'

'Of course he did, thank you.'

Using evidence presented by Bataar to establish the correct course of action was a risky business. His only option was to wait for Okatai to return and await his fate, for good or ill. He slumped back to the floor and stared back at the cream roof.

'Well done, Bataar' said Okatai as he stooped through the yurt's opening. 'You may go and help in the armoury. Captain Padding will be glad of your muscle at the grinding stones.'

The bulk bent as far as his spine would allow, leaving the yurt with a scrape of his back on the roof.

'Sit up straight when I'm talking to you, Jochi! We have a lot of work to do.'

'We do?'

'Of course, we have. Now that your apprenticeship is over you must take on real work, something of worth to the Golden Horde.'

Jochi was spared the embarrassment of asking what he could possibly do that was of worth to the proud army of Genghis Khan by a trample of limbs that careered into the tent, knocking him over and causing a stern look to solidify on Okatai's face.

'What is so important that you feel it acceptable to enter my home uninvited?' said Okatai to the pile of bodies. 'Is the Great Khan ill? Have the horses deserted? Speak!'

Stan looked through Mekki's legs at Okatai's granite features. 'Please accept my most humble apology, Master Okatai. I come to...'

'*Captain*! My designation is captain. Am I the only one here with the wit to address people by their correct title, *apprentice*? Need I remind you our Golden Horde is made up of specialised regiments, all with their own leader to manage its day to day operations? Anything above that does not concern you; remember only that the manager of each regiment is to be referred to as captain. You are now, as I am sure you are aware, speaking with the manager of the Human Resources regiment, and as such you will address me as captain or feel the sharp end of my reed pen!'

'Ah. Of course, my most humble apologies for addressing you incorrectly, *captain*.'

'Good. Now, did you tumble in here to show your adeptness at contrition, or is there something of import that brings you here?'

'Forgive my boldness, Captain, but we're not involved with the Trading Regiment. We're more your general service dogsbodies.'

Okatai took a deep breath, the kind reserved for long-suffering intellectual superiors, and waited.

Mekki lowered the corner of his mouth and whispered to Stan, or more specifically to Stan's elbow, such was their entanglement. 'I think we've misunderstood something.'

'That you have' said Okatai. 'You have misunderstood the importance of education. The *import* I was referring to was that of significance, not trade. The context should have been enough for you to extrapolate its meaning, though I doubt your abilities in that regard.'

He helped Stan from the floor with an outstretched hand and motioned for him to stand on the far side of the yurt. The others followed him, hearing the unspoken order.

'I will forgive your discourteous entrance, Stan, if you explain your arrival with eloquence and efficiency. I am a busy captain of the Great Army and the whims of new men are not a concern that should halt my work. Speak.'

Stan twisted the sleeve of his shirt nervously. 'I come seeking assistance in a most urgent matter, Captain Okatai. I am embroiled in a fragile situation of my own making and need others more skilled than I to free me from its torment.'

'I said eloquent, not sycophantic. Still, you made an effort of sorts and so you may tell me your concern and your requirement. Now, get to the point.'

'In short, I must take possession of a scroll that could be passed off as one bought from a passing merchant. One that details the customs of the west. It is a scroll I have mislaid and I cannot write. That is why I am here; to ask for your assistance in producing such a complex item.'

'You have *mislaid* it? You do not own enough possessions to mislay anything. Are you sure it is not a figment of your imagination? No, of course not. That would take a certain capacity for lateral thinking and you are not the type. When, precisely, must you take possession of this scroll?'

'I must present it to Captain Sulki at sunset.'

'Captain Sulki, you say? How interesting.'

There was a pause so pregnant it may have been having triplets.

At length, Okatai spoke again. 'What did this scroll look like? Were there any distinguishing features?'

'There was a red cross in one corner' said Stan. 'That is all I can remember of its design I'm afraid.'

'It is Sulki who should be afraid' said Okatai enigmatically. 'I will provide you with a scroll, but let me say this now, so that it may make sense to you as you reflect on it in your old age. I see a great future ahead of you all, one to shake the very foundations of our empire.'

CHAPTER TWO

Genghis Khan studied the battlefield. Two enormous brigades of cavalry flanked his left side. His right was bounded by a steep hill, too sheer to allow a surprise attack from its brow and too vast to circle. Dominating the expansive flat ground of the centre were countless enemy soldiers, the front third armed with long spears and the rear with powerful, oversized bows. He was outnumbered and outgunned, but knew better than to think the battle was already lost. He had won every confrontation in this Great War and would not fail his loyal troops at this most critical of junctures.

He readied his bowmen.

'Archers!' he yelled. 'Ready your aim! Cavalry, stand forward!'

A polite cough sounded behind him.

'Not now, Ulfred. Can't you see I'm busy?'

'Apologies, my Lord Khan. Lunch is served in the green yurt.'

'Fine, fine' said Genghis, waving a dismissive hand towards his servant. 'I'll be there in a moment. I need but one minute to defeat the evil Tatars once more.'

'Of course, my Lord' said Ulfred, backing out of the tent to the relative sanity of the outdoors.

Genghis took off a sandal and swiped at the Tatar army, sending the roughly hewn figures flying off the table and scattering them across his orange tent in a cloud of dust.

'Take that, hopeless Tatars! The great Genghis Khan has defeated you once more. Until next time, my old adversaries.'

Scanning the table to satisfy himself that he had, in fact, defeated them all, Genghis left the warm glow of his orange Tactics yurt and made his way to lunch.

The previous summer he had wisely insisted on colouring each of his tents to allow for more efficient transitions between them. Until then he spent a lot of his time apologising to various captains for interrupting meetings about the efficacy of increasing the undergarment washing frequency to twice per month, or on concerns raised by the elders on the proximity of the archery practice area to their latrines. It also gave birth to a rather pleasing visual spectacle. Never before had the yellowy green steppes of his homeland seen such a vibrant display.

He entered his green feasting yurt and sat at the head of the small table, picking up a leg of mutton as he took in today's guests.

'Well?'

Ulfred cleared his throat. 'Master of the Skies, Lord of the Bow, Commander of the Golden Horde...'

'Get on with it, Ulfred. I haven't got all day. Don't forget, we have to go back and burn down that village we sacked yesterday. It won't do any good if we go around pillaging without actually destroying the place at the same time. People expect a good village burning when we're in town and we simply mustn't disappoint. I won't have it.'

'Of course, my Lord' said Ulfred, formally. Not that this was a particularly formal occasion, but Ulfred was unwaveringly predisposed to speak as though a head of state was entering the room with an enormous crown on his head and an army at his heel. 'May I present to you Captain Kontor, of the Cartographic Regiment and his wife, Jone.'

The captain and his wife stood, only to bow their heads lower than they had been while seated, before raising them up again and lowering themselves back into their seats. It was like watching a sleeping seagull bob gently on a moderate wave.

'…and Captain Padding of the Armoury Regiment' continued Ulfred.

The manager of the armoury repeated the same, wavelike motion, and settled back into his seat.

'Can I eat now?' said Genghis in what may have been a petulant tone. It was sometimes difficult to discriminate his petulance from his power.

'Indeed, my Lord.'

'So' said Genghis, waving his fork in the general direction of the cartographic captain. 'Do you have any new cart designs in the works, something with a little more oomph, perhaps? It would be nice to be able to throw a few of our victims over a besieged city's walls every now and again rather than just rocks. It's becoming a little...' He spiralled his fork in the air as he sought the right word. '...*mundane.*'

Captain Kontor froze at the sound of the Great Khan's misunderstanding. He didn't even want to be here. His wife had insisted on accepting the invitation, saying it would be nice to have something interesting to boast about to the other women in the leather stitching circle instead of just the discovery of a river that was slightly less contorted than they had previously thought.

'Not as such, my Lord, no. We tend to focus on the topography of the land in the Cartographic Regiment. We generally leave the catapu... cart weapons to the Ballistics Regiment. We have just discovered a narrow opening through a mountain range that we think will...'

'Oh that's a shame' interrupted Genghis. 'I was hoping to hear of some new weaponry to help us smite those damnable Tatars.'

'We absorbed the Tatars several years ago' said Kontor before his brain could authorise it.

'Did I say Tatars? Ah. I misspoke. I was referring, of course, to the...'

'The Jin?' offered Ulfred.

'The Jin!' said Genghis. 'So, no new terror then? How disappointing.'

'I shall speak with Captain Weeeeee this evening, my Lord' said Kontor.

'Why would you do that?'

'Well, my Lord, he is the Captain of the Ballistics Regiment. He will be well placed to update you on their progress.'

'Of course, yes. Good idea Captain...'

Ulfred whispered something from the corner of his mouth.

'...Captain Kontor' said Genghis, to the great relief of the nervous cartographer.

They each picked up a hunk of meat, despite their nerve-shrunken stomachs, and chewed animatedly for fear of offending their great leader. Genghis called Ulfred over with a nod of his head.

'What's his name again?' he said, flicking his eyes to the solitary captain.

'Captain Padding, my Lord, of the Armoury Regiment.'

'That's right, Ulfred. Well done' said Genghis. He pointed his mutton-filled fork at Padding. 'Tell me, Captain Padding, how many leather breastplates do we have?'

'Forty-two thousand, my Lord. Give or take.'

'And how many men do we have?'

'Sixty.'

'Are you seeking death, captain? Do not take me for a fool! How many men do we have?'

'Sixty *thousand*, my Lord.'

'That sounds more like it. When you have finished this fine lunch you will return to your regiment and instruct them to make eighteen thousand breastplates. No, twenty-five thousand, and any other incidentals you deem necessary to allow sixty thousand men to march to war.'

Captain Padding swallowed a clump of mutton and coughed. 'Twenty-five thousand, yes my Lord. My men will get to work first thing in the morning.'

'No, captain, they will get to work today for we march with the full moon. Time is our enemy until then. Now, have you all finished? Good. Ulfred, I will receive you in the black tent at once.'

'Who is in charge of the population records, Ulfred?' began Genghis without preamble. 'I need the captain of the...'

'Human Resources regiment, my Lord?'

'Yes, him. Bring him to me at once. We have a war to plan, I have been too long in the orange tent and my arms need to feel the pull of a bowstring.'

'*It has been but a single day since we sacked our last village, my insane, bloodthirsty, lunatic khan*' is what Ulfred wanted to say to his master. Instead, he chose 'of course, my Lord' and scurried out of the tent to find Captain Okatai.

Stan stopped at the entrance to Captain Sulki's yurt as a guard lowered his head into the darkness, returning a moment later and opening his body to indicate Stan should enter. He fingered the scroll in his hands as he stepped through the slit, desperately trying to remember what Okatai had told him.

Inside the tent were five people, himself included. The captain sat on a solid wooden chair, softened with wool. On his left was his daughter, Zabin. Two men Stan did not recognise flanked them on either side. They were undoubtedly involved in the military arm of the nation, as almost all men of fighting age were. As was the custom, he waited for the captain to open proceedings.

'Stan, please' said the captain, gesturing for him to sit on the floor at the mouth of the tent. 'My daughter tells me you have been involving yourself with passing merchants. Tell me, what leads you to believe that someone of such lowly stock should feel it is an appropriate course of action. Do you have ambitions above your status?'

'My captain' said Stan, nodding deferentially. 'My ambition is appropriate to my station, I can assure you.'

Stan wasn't sure what that meant, but it sounded like the kind of thing he should have said.

'If my scroll can help the Great Horde take one extra step of land from our enemies then I am glad to have helped in my own small way. May it contain information of use to you.'

'For your sake, I hope it doesn't' said the captain, an evil glint glowing in his eye. 'If you are found to be in possession of intelligence of use to the khanate and have kept it to yourself you may be charged with treason and sentenced to death. What a shame that would be, too. Who would I get to deliver the wrong shirt to me each morning?'

Stan felt the ground beneath him wobble. Only his honour, and to a lesser extent his dignity, kept him from tilting over.

'I can see that you were unaware of such a law, young Stan. May I suggest you retreat to the filthy patch of grass you call home and leave the machinations of power to those in a position to understand its importance? Now, the scroll if you please?'

Stan handed the parchment to one of the guards and lowered his gaze to the floor. The captain scanned it casually, then a little less casually. He looked up at Stan with scrunched eyebrows then back to the scroll, reading it once more just to be certain. His eyes moved to an unremarkable spot on the wall of the yurt and stayed there, locked.

'Gubaar' he said at last, pointing at one of the men at his side. 'Take Stan here to my cleaning quarters and have him bathed. Gather up his clothes and burn them; he is to be dressed in the fine clothes of a better man.' He turned to Stan. 'Are you hungry, man? Yes, of course you are. Some mutton too, Gubaar. We will not have a guest of ours hungry while there is food to be shared. Quickly now, I have more tasks for you when you are finished with our friend here.'

Gubaar hoisted Stan roughly to his feet.

'Gubaar, please! Show a little more respect to our guest.'

'Sorry sir, force of habit sir.'

The guard patted Stan down as if brushing the dishonour away and helped him out of the tent.

'Bankhe!' called the captain to the remaining guard. 'I have an important job for you. The most important of your long and distinguished career in the Guard's Regiment.'

Bankhe knew the captain well enough to understand the flattery was false and loaded with a desperation that he complete whatever order was about to be given. He also knew better than to query the motivation behind his orders. He didn't survive long enough to have such a *distinguished career* by questioning his superiors.

'Yessir! Right away sir!'

'Wait!' said the captain to the departing guard. 'I haven't given you your orders yet.'

'Right sir, sorry sir.'

'Listen very carefully, Bankhe. These are the most important instructions you are ever likely to be given, even if you rise all the way to Chief Latrine Officer of the Khan's Personal Guard. Are you ready?'

'Yessir!' lied Bankhe.

'I need you to find Ulfred and bring him to me at once.'

'*The* Ulfred, sir?'

'No, the other Ulfred' said Sulki sardonically.

'Oh, good. I thought for a moment you... wait, there isn't another Ulfred, captain.'

'Well then you had better bring *the* Ulfred to me, hadn't you?'

'Bugger' whispered Bankhe. 'Yessir! Right away sir!' he said aloud.

Sulki jogged along the outskirts of the horde, being careful to keep to the shadows as best he could. At one point he discretely circled a small hill rather than cut across open ground.

As he reached the cleaning stones his heart sank. There were two men there, rather than the usual one. He crouched behind a bush and waited.

'...so she said maybe I'd be a better husband if I *did* listen once in a while. Bloody cheek of her!' said one. 'As if it was my fault I brought back the wrong pot.'

'Women, eh?' said the other, throwing his head back in mock incredulity. 'I'd like to see how they'd cope being on the wrong side of the defensive hill when the siege begins.'

'Exactly. Don't know they're born, do they? Here we are preparing for a game of chance with our very lives and all they have to worry about is making sure our buttons are fastened well enough.'

'Yeah, and there's the latrine duty. They get away with that, too.'

'Speaking of which' said one, standing up and walking around an outcrop to relieve himself.

Sulki loaded his bow, closed one eye and loosed his arrow.

Thud.

CHAPTER THREE

Ulfred hated coming to the workers' area. He was almost phobic towards *other people*, and there was no escape from them here. It seemed to him that the reproductive rate of the Golden Horde was equitable to that of a common rat, with no more pleasant a result. He picked his way through the detritus of life, careful not to step in anything he couldn't identify. He reached Okatai's tent and took a deep breath. This could prove to be an olfactory experience he would remember for some time.

'Captain Okatai?' he called as he bent his head inside the mud-splattered yurt.

'What is wrong with everyone these days?' cried Okatai. 'They either forget my title or they forget the honour of a man's own yurt. Can anybody remember them both at the same time?' He looked up from his parchments and flushed with fear. 'Captain Ulfred, what a great honour it is to have you visit my humble home. Forgive me, I was acting out a passage I have written for my newly promoted apprentice. He has much to learn of our etiquette.'

'Many do' said Ulfred. 'Come, the Great Khan has requested your presence.'

Genghis slid a wooden token across a small section of his battlefield. 'No' he muttered, and slid it back. His finger tapped quickly on a river as his eyes glazed over in contemplation. A gentle cough sounded behind him, snapping him from his thoughts.

'Captain Okatai' announced Ulfred.

'Please, sit' said Genghis without turning.

Okatai looked nervously around the room. There were no seats. Ulfred gestured for him to use the floor and Okatai lowered himself to it, confusion mingling with his nervousness in a peculiar juxtaposition.

Genghis picked up a battalion of archers and placed them on top of a forest halfway up a hill. 'Yes' he mumbled. 'Height.' The tapping stopped. 'Captain Obadai. Welcome.'

'It's Oka...'

'Captain Okatai came here with all haste' interrupted Ulfred.

'Well, I should damn well hope so! I'm the Khan of the Great Horde.'

'Quite so' agreed Ulfred.

Genghis turned to face his visitor. 'I have a great task for you, captain. Open both of your ears and as much of your mind as you can manage. You are in a unique position to help the Great Army in its most significant manoeuvre since I united the tribes so many years ago. For the moment, that is all I will say, for is it not said that secrecy is the friend of the rampaging warrior?'

Okatai didn't think it was. 'It is, my Lord.'

'Then you will do this for the glory of the Horde. Go to every captain under my flag and have them log their subordinates. I want to know how many there are, what tasks they are assigned, the names of those with notable skills and what their favourite colour is. Bring this information back to me tomorrow. You need not wait for an invitation, I will see you when you are ready, which will be tomorrow I am sure.'

'Your will, my Lord' said Okatai, bowing low.

Genghis picked up a single wooden soldier and moved it around in his fingers. 'Should any captain resist, show them this and point to the head. Tell them the Great Khan will personally lighten the load on their shoulders if they find that to be preferable.' He turned back to his battlefield. 'Ulfred, see the captain is well fed before he departs. He has an interesting time ahead of him.'

Ulfred motioned for Okatai to leave, following the captain as he gulped the crisp, fresh air outside.

'Height' muttered Genghis. 'Ulfred!'

The aide appeared at his master's side in a moment, an action that used to scare the willies out of the great warrior, but one for which he was now grateful.

'How many captains do we have?'

'Two hundred and forty-two, my Lord.'

'*Two hundred and...* why on earth do we have so many?'

Ulfred cleared his throat, a habit formed from years of diplomatic responses. 'It was deemed necessary to separate the regiments into more specialised units. You may remember the beginnings of the process, my Lord. The creation of the Ballistics Regiment, with Captain Weeeee at its head, was a lesson to all of us in the wisdom of your modern thinking. You ordered that should he fail to lead the men effectively he would have his head taken from him. *Removing a man's head is the best way to stop his mistakes* you said.'

'That sounds like something I'd say. How did we end up with so many?'

'Once you had shown the Executive Committee how a wise man constructs a meritocracy you left them to it. Things got a little out of hand after that. It's why you introduced the ban on committees. *They are only capable of producing banal averages* you said.'

Genghis nodded slowly, as if approving of his own forgotten words.

'So now we have a captain for every facet of horde life' explained Ulfred.

'*Every* facet?'

'Well, all the important elements are covered by supremely competent men, such as ballistics, armoury and dice making. The other regiments were left to those less... well, to other competent men.'

'Why do we entrust our regiments to men whose capabilities are merely *competent*? Competence does not deliver victory on the battlefield, Ulfred. Nor does it deliver clean underwear for the men. I would not wish to wear an undergarment that had been washed by *competent* cleaners, no matter how supreme they were at being so. I would be much happier were they exceptional cleaners. Would you not agree?'

'Indeed.'

'Our captains must be competently exceptional, not exceptionally competent.'

The servant recognised the spiralling nature of Genghis' rambling and chose to cut the legs off it before his glorious leader ordered the execution of a tree for bending the wrong way again.

'Shall I instruct the captains to ready themselves for battle, my Lord? We could start with the village burning this afternoon.'

'Yes, yes' said Genghis, waving a hand dismissively. 'Good idea' he added. 'Nothing like a good burning to get the tactical juices flowing.'

'If you will excuse me, my Lord, I will see to it at once.'

'I believe I have already given you your orders, Ulfred. Now leave me, I have important work to attend to.'

Ulfred lingered for a moment, watching his master move his armies across the miniature landscape, before heading out and towards the blue tent, home of the khan's personal messengers.

Had Ulfred been blind he would have found the Posting Regiment's great blue tent no less efficiently. The waft of drink flowing from it was a mist of incompetence, curling into his nostrils as he strode purposefully towards the fastest men in the nation. Had they been the best at following instructions they would have served their khan all the better, but as it was they were the only men prepared to be posted to the far corners of the horde's lands, living in the saddle for days on end to deliver orders to the extremities of the empire. Their captain was Paat, a persuasive man in his own way, despite giving each man the right to refuse a position in his outfit. The alternative was a rather more literal posting of their heads on a sharpened pole and none had yet chosen that particular career path.

Ulfred pulled the large cloth opening to one side and waited. He enjoyed these moments more than most, watching the wave of recognition pass through the boisterous crowd until the clamour slowly morphed into a nervous silence. He twirled his drooping, grey moustache in his fingers.

'Captain Paat!' he called to his audience.

The posting captain emerged from the crowd and presented himself to the Great Khan's left-hand man. There was no right-hand man of Genghis of course, that would have required him to cede a little of his power to an advisor.

A left-hand man, however, could subtly nudge the khan from the shadows without upsetting his ego.

'Ulfred' said Paat, nodding slightly.

'It's *Captain* Ulfred, and may I suggest you remember that if you ever address me in the presence of our great leader. He holds an axe above your head and I have his ear.'

'My apologies, Skivvy Captain' said Paat.

'Let us not play this childish game once more, captain. My regiment, as you know very well, is unnamed and shall remain so until such time as the Great Khan deems it appropriate to reveal. Again, I would counsel restraint when poking at the leader of such an entity. Now, walk with me. There is a matter of great urgency I wish to discuss.'

Paat called over his shoulder to the assembly. 'Don't drink us dry while I'm gone, lads. I'll be back before you can finish three verses of *The Merry Siege*.'

'I wouldn't count on that' said Ulfred.

They left the tent to the sound of grown men roaring chaotically. Ulfred steered Paat towards the centre of their encampment, where the yurts were built closer together and with less formal latrines.

'Tell me where we're heading or I'm going back' said Paat.

'Oh, I don't think that will be necessary, captain. Genghis has direct orders for you and I happen to know you're quite attached to your head. For the moment.'

'Your threats do not perturb me, *Ulfred*.'

'My dear Paat – may I call you Paat? – they are not my threats. Come, there is much to discuss.'

Ulfred led them deep into the unwashed mass of the Golden Horde, occasionally passing women scrubbing clothes but more often passing men asleep in the sunshine.

'Look around you, Paat. What do you see?'

'I won't play your games. Spit out your orders and leave me to complete them.'

'What we have here' continued Ulfred 'is potential. We have the numbers to defeat anyone brave enough to face us, yet it is all we have. We have become lazy. Our men are drifting from village to village, picking off defenceless farmers and frightened women. We must sharpen our tools and rampage across the land as we once did.'

'They are the words of an embittered servant, too old to carry the sword he once swung with certainty, not those of our Great Khan. He would not consider any day but the present as the greatest in the history of our nation.'

'And he would consider that kind of talk as treason' said Ulfred. 'Yet I may not speak to him of your subversion. Now, your orders. You are to send word to every captain of military regiments still within the encampment that we are to return to the village we sacked yesterday to burn it to the ground.'

'I'm not sure a village can be sacked, Ulfred, it is too small a settlement. Pocketed perhaps, but not sacked.'

'Then you will be pleased to hear your final orders. We head east in a month, where every fragment of our nation will throw itself into a glorious expansion. Have your men send word to all corners of the empire. Half of all men of fighting age are to return here at once. The time of the Golden Warrior is upon us.'

The amber flush of dawn had been replaced by the glowing orange embers of the ruined village by the time the last soldiers reached the site.

'We may have overestimated the numbers required here, Ulfred. Don't let it happen again.'

'Of course, my Lord. My apologies.'

Ulfred had, in fact, tried to tell Genghis several times the previous evening that bringing three thousand men to burn a decimated village would be considered by most to be a little on the zealous side of sufficiency.

'Look at that for a sight, though' said Genghis. 'There is nothing I have yet experienced that compares to a flaming roof as it falls to the ground, wouldn't you agree?'

'Indeed, my Lord. It is majestic in its finality. I miss the days of siege and flame, they were such happy times.'

'That's the spirit. Now, let us ride back. I must be in the red tent when Okatai returns with news.'

'You must?' asked Ulfred. He had never known Genghis to be channelled to a particular course of action by another man. Excepting himself, of course. His bending of the Great

Khan's behaviour was as close as anything came to being a constant in the chaotic world of the horde.

'He brings significant news to our meeting. As I may also.'

'Captain Okatai, my Lord.'

'Thank you, Ulfred. Bring a seat for my guest, then leave us.'

'Your will, my Lord.'

Ulfred backed out of the red General Administration tent, returning moments later with a simple wooden chair. It concerned him greatly that Genghis would allow a guest to sit in the red tent. He usually insisted on watching them wilt as the endless meetings drew on; it was one of many unorthodox techniques he would use to establish a man's character.

'A cushion, Ulfred. What good is a chair without a cushion?'

'My apologies, Lord. I shall return with one in all haste.'

'Are you feeling alright, Ulfred? You seem a little unsettled.'

'I am perfectly well, my Lord. Thank you for your concern.'

'Then Captain Okatai here can sit on your shirt. Fold it onto the chair if you would. He has the greater need.'

'Your will, my Lord.'

'Now then, Captain Okatai, I believe you are the leading authority on the make up of our great populace' said Genghis, as if he had not met the man the previous day.

'That is very kind of you to say so, oh Glorious Leader.'

'Please, call me Genghis.'

'...'

'Do you have my report?'

'Of course, my Lord. I took the liberty of storing the information in my head rather than use any of your nation's precious parchments.'

'I am not here to listen to your claims of common virtue, Captain Okatai. Now remove your report from your head before I take a more forceful approach.'

Okatai felt a bead of cold sweat stutter down the side of his face. He took a deep breath and raised his chin.

'There are fifty-eight thousand, nine hundred and twelve men, my Lord. Most are tasked with military matters; armoury, weaponry, horsemanship, and so on. Some are assigned more sedentary roles such as washing, haberdashery, and the general upkeep of the common areas. The less physically able among us use their intellectual abilities to maintain our administrative functions. There are several notable individuals. Tishock, of the Fastening Regiment is said to be able to sew a thousand buttons to soldiers' coats in a single day. Her favourite colour is green. Bataar, of the Armoury Regiment, is of a size as to beggar belief. His favourite colour is mud.'

'How many are in your regiment?' said Genghis, seemingly ignoring the hard-earned report entirely. 'I have a great order for you; an opportunity to mould your legacy in the greatest conquest the world has ever seen.'

'It is just me and my apprentice. *Former* apprentice, I should say.'

'Ah, had to chop his head off, did you?'

'No, my Lord. He has completed his apprenticeship.'

'So just the two of you then? That could make it tricky.'

'We will perform our orders with vigour and determination, my Lord.'

'Genghis.'

'*Genghis*' muttered Okatai uncomfortably.

'You will need more men. Choose two or three to ride with you.'

'Ride, my Lord?'

'But of course, it would take far too long to reach a great Jin city on foot.'

Okatai shifted uncomfortably in his seat. 'Where would you have me go, my Lord?'

'You will ride with the wind to Rhizun and collect information on everything you see there.'

'Everything?'

'Everything. Population size, weaponry, food stocks, political alliances, nap times, everything.'

'Your will, my Lord. I shall make preparations at once.'

'When you have completed your reconnaissance of Rhizun you will return to me with all haste. I will expect you within a month.'

Okatai ran the arithmetic. 'But my Lord Genghis, it will take a week to make the journey alone.'

'Which is why I ordered you to take more men, captain.'

'But that won't... Of course, my Lord. I will return with a great mountain of intelligence for the good of the nation.'

'On parchment will be fine, captain.'

Genghis stood, signalling an end to their meeting. 'Have Ulfred record your report before you go. Leave no detail in that grey head of yours, and tell no one of your orders.'

'If you will allow it, I have a question, my Lord.'

'Yes?'

'How will my men get inside the walls of this great city?'

'I will leave that particular quandary for men of *intellectual abilities* to solve, Captain Okatai. I look forward to your safe return.'

CHAPTER FOUR

'Of course I win' said Mekki. 'A Horse always beats a Sword.'

'Not when a Hill is rolled' said Jochi. 'That gives me the high ground. Only an Archer beats a High Horse.'

'Double Archer' said Okatai, stepping into his yurt. 'You need to roll Double Archer to beat a High Horse.'

Jochi and Mekki scrabbled to pocket their dice, sending dust spiralling into the air.

'You should not hide evidence after the crime, men. It only serves to magnify your guilt. You are lucky there are more pressing matters to attend to. Where is Stan?'

'I haven't seen him since last night, captain' said Jochi.

'Please, call me Okatai. There's no need for such formality now.'

'There isn't?' asked Jochi. 'You said it was the backbone of a hierarchical society. Is it because my apprenticeship is complete?'

'Lord of the Sky, no' said Okatai. 'If we're going to be travelling together we'll have to learn to respect each other without the need for fancy titles.'

Jochi's brow lowered a little. 'Where are we going?'

'Just a quick visit to the Jin city of Rhizun, shouldn't take more than a month or so. I should mention our orders are from the Great Khan himself. We are to make our way to the walls and find a way in.'

'A month!' cried Jochi. 'I can't go away for a month, I have commitments.'

'No, you don't. Your parents are dead and you have no girl to impress.'

'What about my friends?' said Jochi desperately.

'Oh don't worry, they're both coming with us' said Okatai, picking up a roll of parchments and stuffing them into a knapsack. 'Which brings me back to my original question. Where is Stan?'

'Try Captain Sulki's yurts' said Mekki. 'He may still be there.'

'I have a better idea. You try. Be swift, we ride at once.'

Mekki gave a shallow nod and scampered away. Okatai scanned the room. 'Prepare four bags, Jochi. Minimal provisions, we will find sustenance on the road. Fill the bags with our writing equipment.' He roved around the tent like a polite thief, lifting coats and moving chairs. 'Aha! Bring this too.'

'But that's your writing block, captain. It isn't exactly portable.'

'Then you'll have to use your brain, Jochi. I'll be back shortly with the horses. Be ready.'

'Please tell Captain Sulki I wish to see him at once' said Mekki to the guard.

'The captain is unavailable for visitors' said Bankhe flatly.

'Then perhaps you will pass on a message to him?'

'That would be possible' said Bankhe, as if the request was of such complexity as to warrant consideration.

'Tell him I have orders from the Great Khan and any who stand in my way, even for a moment, will see the sun twinkle off an axe's blade before they can say *get the captain at once.*'

The guard chewed on his lower lip. Captain Sulki had been more forthright than ever in his insistence he not be disturbed.

'The captain is not home.'

'I must find Stan at once.'

'He is not here, good day' said Bankhe, resettling himself in his place at the tent's entrance. He repositioned his spear in his hands, just enough for Mekki to take it as a threat, and stared to the horizon.

Mekki gave up, heading over to the captain's sleeping yurt instead. If Stan was nearby, it was likely he would be completing some onerous chore for his dislikable master. As he approached the opening a part of him hoped it was empty. If he disturbed the captain and Stan was not there he would be in more trouble than he cared to imagine. *Not as much as if I fail the Great Khan*, argued the rational part of his brain. He steeled himself and peered into the gloomy interior.

'Stan?' he whispered.

Nothing.

'Stan, it's me, Mekki.'

'Hmmfph.'

Mekki looked around the room but could see no sign of anyone. He stepped inside, breaking a host of honour codes as he did so, and searched for his friend.

'Hmmfph. Hurrumpffpphh!'

Mekki froze. A scuffling noise came from somewhere near his feet but there was nothing there, just an empty space with an old rug covering part of the hard mud floor. Mekki wandered onto it and felt his leg give way. Another muffled noise, louder and shorter than before, sounded below him as his foot landed on something hard. His torso bent over the hole as his feet thrashed at whatever was grappling with him from below. He crawled back up onto the floor and swished the rug away.

Stan. Wide-eyed, bound, and gagged.

He leant down and hauled his friend up. His arms and legs had been tied with leather thread and there was a muddy cloth stuffed into his mouth. Mekki untied the knots, pulled out the gag, and loosened the bonds around his wrists and ankles.

'Out!' whispered Stan, his voice scratchy and hoarse. 'We don't have long.'

'What happened to you?' asked Mekki as they scampered out of the yurt.

'I gave Okatai's scroll to the captain, just like we planned' began Stan. 'Whatever was written on it had a powerful effect; he started being all nice to me. It was the most disconcerting experience I've ever had. He fed me with the most incredible mutton, there weren't any firm white bits on it at all. I swear, Mekki, I'm never going to eat our plain food again if I can help it. There's a whole world of culinary quality out there that I would never have thought possible if I hadn't tasted it with my own head.'

'And was your supper the most significant event of the evening? Did you enjoy it so much you felt it only right to be punished with a nap in a mud pit?'

'Fine. But that isn't the last you're going to hear of that food, I can tell you.'

'Marvellous, something to while away the hours on our adventure' said Mekki.

'What adventure?'

'I'll tell you my news after you've told me yours.'

'Very well. I was well-fed, as I said, and he had me dressed up in these fine clothes.' He looked down at his new, albeit now muddy, tabard and trousers. 'He even had someone else dress me. I would sooner have the mutton than have someone dress me.'

'Stop talking about mutton, Stan. Spit it out.'

'I ate it all, sorry.'

Mekki gave a stern look.

'Right, well' continued Stan. 'He was being unusually pleasant and generous, something that only served to amplify my misgivings. I was sure he was up to something. Whatever Okatai wrote on that scroll had set a fire under Sulki. I decided to find it and memorise the shapes in the hope that I could draw them for Jochi to decipher. I had seen Sulki store it in the pouch on Gubaar's belt. When he fell asleep I tried to steal it. It may surprise you to learn I'm not a very efficient spy. No sooner had I given the belt the slightest of tugs, than Gubaar's hands were around my throat. He put me in that *security pit* while he went off to find the captain. It seems he has been waylaid. To top it all off, the scroll wasn't even there!'

'It seems to me' said Mekki, 'that Okatai has many questions to answer. He has orders from Genghis himself to take us to the very edge of Rhizun, perhaps even inside it. I have a terrible feeling this is the start of a great story we will tell around the fire when it is our turn to be the greyed elders. Come, we are leaving at once.'

Okatai pulled hard on the saddle strap of his horse and hoisted himself up. Mekki was lingering nervously at a safe distance from the horses as Okatai called out to him.

'You will ride Tilly, the chestnut one' he said. 'There's no getting out of this, Mekki. You're a Mongol of the Great Horde, the finest horse riders the world has ever seen. Get up on your steed and learn to act like one.'

'What if he careers away in a frenzy? I'm not very good at steering. Or stopping for that matter.'

'Then now is the perfect time to learn. I don't want to order you, but I will if that's what it takes to get you onto the bloody thing.'

'You *don't* want to order me? Are you quite well, captain?'

'Just get up.'

Mekki studied the contraptions slung over his horse as he approached. There were more loops of leather than he had limbs, which did nothing to allay his conviction that he would choose poorly and fall several times before seating himself correctly. He took a deep breath, picked a spot, placed a foot, and pulled on the horse's mane to hoist himself onto its back. As he was lifting his trailing leg over Tilly's back she reared suddenly, throwing him in a graceless arc towards a half-hidden rock protruding quietly from the ground. He landed he heard a crack, then felt it; a scything pain that engulfed his lower leg.

'Bloody kids' murmured Okatai. 'Get up, boy, there's no time for showmanship. This is not some game of dice we're playing here, we have orders from the Great Khan that must be fulfilled. Get up!'

Mekki was oblivious to the captain's lack of sympathy. All he was aware of was the razor-sharp pain as it morphed into a pounding throb.

Okatai raised his eyes to the sky and sighed. 'See to him, Jochi. Check his leg and help him on to Tilly. Quite how you and he are so friendly is beyond me.'

Jochi knelt beside his friend. 'As if a trip away from the Horde wasn't enough, you've now got two breaks in the same day.'

'Shtup' mumbled Mekki.

'It must be bad if you can't appreciate a bit of humour. How does it feel?'

'How does it feel!? It feels like I've just been thrown from a horse, Jochi.'

'That's more like it, friend. Keep your spirits up and you'll forget about it in no time. Let's get you onto your feet.'

Jochi put his shoulder into Mekki's armpit and lifted him to a stoop.

'Now, ready? I'll let you go after three. One... two... three...'

Jochi stepped to the side, leaving Mekki to stand on his one good foot.

'Come on, boy!' snapped Okatai impatiently. 'Walk back to your horse like a man.'

Mekki placed his foot tentatively on the ground, or more accurately slightly above the ground. A shiver of fear ran through him at the prospect of the pain that would come if he put any weight onto his ankle.

'Five...' began Okatai. 'Four...'

One reason some people live longer than others is their conviction that you should never let a countdown reach zero, whatever the circumstances.

'Fine' said Mekki. 'Just give me a moment.'

He took a breath. Then another. Then he wondered how long he could draw out this mental preparation to delay the pain. Then he saw Okatai's glare. He laid his foot onto the ground without moving any of his weight onto it. In one smooth, graceful motion he leaned slowly to his left, then continued the trajectory as his foot refused the weight, and flopped to the floor with a heavy thud.

'...three...'

Jochi helped Mekki up again and turned to Okatai. 'He can't ride, captain. Even you have to admit it.'

'*Even* me? Watch your tongue, Jochi. It will get you into trouble more often than it will help you escape it. He cannot travel, it seems, but he may still help us.'

Okatai retied his horse and knelt beside Mekki. 'You may stay here, but there is work for you to do. Watch Captain Sulki. Know his routines; where he goes from one moment to the next, what he has for dinner, how many times he scrapes his sword on his sharpening stone. Everything.'

'But I can't remember all that, especially not for a whole month' cried Mekki.

'Then you had better learn to write. Make your own letters up if you have to, I don't care. Just know everything about him. Build yourself a crutch – if he moves outside the common areas, you move behind him in the shadows.'

Okatai looked up at the sound of someone approaching.

'Stan, here at last I see' he said. 'Don't worry, there's one for you.'

'Can somebody please explain what's going on here?' asked Stan.

'No, get on your horse and ride. We head east until sunrise. YAH!' He kicked his heels into his horse and disappeared in a cloud of dust.

The three men exchanged glances.

'Go' said Mekki.

Jochi patted Stan firmly on the shoulder. 'I'll explain on the way.' He hoisted himself onto his steed, Patsi, and trotted off after the old man.

Nobody watched as they left their home behind. The entire nation would see their return.

CHAPTER FIVE

C aptain Sulki paced around his yurt like a fox in an empty chicken coop. Bankhe had been gone too long, even allowing for his brief sortie to the cleaning stones. A myriad scenarios were playing continuously in the agitated space between his ears, returning to the same conclusions each time. Bankhe had either been unable to find Ulfred, or worse still had found him and described too much of the previous evening's events to the most influential man in the horde. If Ulfred was of a mind to stem the flow of such sensational information then it would take no effort on his part to remove Bankhe from the field. Once that was done there was only one place for Ulfred to focus his attention – a thought that sent cold shivers through him.

Ulfred was a man who lived on his reputation. For the most part, the old stories of his ruthlessness would be enough to reduce hardened warriors to crying for a hug from their old Aunty Yog, but every now and again he needed to top it up with a fresh head. In the time Bankhe had been out searching, Sulki had come close to convincing himself that this whole escapade would be better if it was simply swept under a rug. Perhaps now wasn't a good time for the horde to be compromised by such a thunderous revelation. Perhaps now was a good time to maintain an active heartbeat too, for that matter.

Just as he was about to step out of his yurt to find his guard there came a shuffling noise from outside. Bankhe's head poked in from the split in the wall.

'Captain Ulfred of the Great Khan's personal office to see you, my captain' said Bankhe with more formality than Sulki had ever heard from him before.

'Well don't keep him waiting, Bankhe. Invite him in at once!'

Bankhe backed out of the yurt and was replaced a moment later by Ulfred's smothering greyness.

'You are welcome in my home, Captain Ulfred' said Sulki formally, knowing Ulfred would appreciate his adherence to protocol.

'I graciously accept the invitation, Captain Sulki' replied Ulfred. 'Your guard tells me there is a matter of existential consequence to the horde that requires my immediate attention.'

'He said it like that?' thought Sulki out loud.

'Not precisely, but he described the events preceding your orders. Orders, I might add, that you would only consider prudent in the event of a horde-wide emergency. I know your sly ways well enough to know you would not use up what little grace you have with me on something less cataclysmic.'

'It is no little amount of grace I have, as we both know' said Sulki pointedly. 'If any man in this great nation can call upon you for counsel without flames licking the tent poles of the Great Khan himself, it is I.'

'If you have called me here to check our balance sheet then it is now balanced a little more in my favour. I have no time for such low-level power plays, *sheep shearer*. Not today.'

'Then I will leave tradition on the floor and move straight to my motives, if it pleases you?'

'It would please me greatly to get this over quickly. What triviality do you deem so important as to summon the Khan's personal captain to your filthy hovel?'

Sulki bristled at the insult but knew he had, for once, a far greater arrow of his own to launch.

'A usurper hides within the horde. One of such provenance as to threaten the authority of the Great Khan himself.'

'I was afraid you might say that' said Ulfred, in what Sulki considered to be a disappointingly untroubled tone. 'On what grounds do you make such a treasonous proclamation?'

'This' said Sulki, taking the scroll from his belt and unfurling it to face the Khan's aide.

Ulfred took in the writing without emotion. 'I'm afraid you must come with me at once. We have much to discuss.'

That's more like it thought Sulki.

Mekki pressed his fingers into the fleshy part of his ankle again. The pain had eased a little since his friends had left, but he still struggled to last too long on his feet. He had created a simplified form of writing that would allow him to recall Sulki's movements to Okatai when the time came. It consisted of a series of symbols, each representing one of five categories of activity. He would then note ten symbols for each day of surveillance, with the endeavours Sulki spent most time on appearing more frequently than the others. As it turned out, he didn't need them at all.

His friends had been gone for less than a day before boredom began to bite. Within a few long, drawn-out hours he felt like a soporific lion in a pit of sleeping rabbits. Sulki, he soon learned, led a staggeringly dull life.

Mekki took up a position beside the turnip boiling pots with his swords and sharpening stone and settled down for a day of amateur espionage. The sun was beginning the arduous dip from its zenith when he saw Ulfred striding confidently towards Sulki's yurt. A short while later the khan's personal captain stepped out and to the side, letting Sulki pass, before holding up a halting hand to Bankhe and falling in behind the captain of the sheep shearing regiment. Even Mekki's below-average spying skills were honed enough for him to see the dynamic. Ulfred was a man for whom striding confidently in front of subordinates was an important show of superiority, so to see him behind a captain could only mean he wanted to keep a watchful eye on the man. Mekki picked up his tools and jogged painfully to store them in his yurt.

He followed the two men at a polite distance, stopping now and again to rotate his ankle with his hand, as if that was going to help ease the throbbing pain. The mass of people thinned out to a mere bustling crowd as they edged closer to the Great Khan's personal complex of brightly coloured tents. At last Ulfred and Sulki passed by the heavily guarded entrance between two unremarkable tents and disappeared from view.

Captain Sulki's mind woke before his eyes, the hard ground beneath him nudging it towards the memory of the previous evening. Ulfred had brought him to Genghis' private camp of rainbow tents, to what Sulki assumed was to be an exhilarating discussion full of intrigue, secrecy, and leverage. Instead, he was shown to an empty yurt and ordered to remain there until summoned. Three guards were posted to him, two outside the opening and one outside the opposite, cloth-walled side; a touch that Sulki felt was both unnecessary and offensive based on the knowledge Ulfred had of his motives. They were, of course, completely necessary to anyone with a fuller knowledge of them.

His eyes opened at the sound of clanking metal. Ulfred strode in powerfully without waiting for an invitation.

'Now, what was it about your message that made treachery so appealing to you?' asked Ulfred, as if their conversation hadn't been interrupted by a night of sleep.

Sulki ruffled his hair and squinted the drowsiness from his eyes. 'Its content speaks for itself, does it not?'

'It does not, captain, and that is rather the point. All I see is an ambiguous and fantastical theory, whose only value lies in its contortion by those desperate to breach the inner circles of the nation's power. Remember, cousin, I have spent enough time in your devious presence to know that altruism is beyond your wit. You will forget about this irrelevance and return to your own, I am sure the sheep will be wondering why they are still fully clothed.'

'It seems you have forgotten your past transgressions, *cousin*, for only a fool would recall them and dismiss my petition.'

'I recall them as well as you do, but our entanglement does not reach the doors of treason. I would sooner sacrifice myself than my Khan, as you well know.'

'Then I will go directly to him and be damned with protocol. He will learn of the revelation that threatens his khanate. He will see the loyalty in my action and the disloyalty in yours. The days of you having his ear will be over.'

Ulfred bristled, then steeled. He made himself taut, stretching his back to straightness and his head to the roof of the yurt.

'Then you have delivered me onto a road neither of us would choose. Reflect on that in the time that is left to you. Captain Sulki of the sheep shearing regiment, I hereby arrest you for the crime of high treason against the nation and its Great Khan. You will be confined to this place until such time as the opinion of the Great Khan warrants an investigation of your actions. You will be given only the sustenance required to keep you from starvation during this time and you are forbidden from shortening your hair or nails. If your trial has not been completed before the arrival of the sooty tern from the east then you will have your head shaved and your nails given a good trim. The penalty for conviction, or of cutting your hair or nails, is death. This includes peeling your nails with your teeth. May you be spared an itch as they grow.'

Ulfred made a note to update the official arrest wording at the earliest opportunity.

Sulki knew better than to challenge his cousin. When it came to conducting a cost-benefit analysis on incendiary subjects, Ulfred was the Alpha, the Omega, and all the letters in between that no one other than lonely librarians ever remember, rolled into one thin, grey vessel.

'You shall be notified of any progress that may be made in your case. Until then, you are to remain in this place without agitation' said Ulfred. He backed out of the yurt, staring through Sulki's skull as he did so, as if to indicate an ever-present eye watching over him.

'What did you write on the parchment, Okatai?' asked Stan, stretching his saddle-weary arms to the sky.

They had ridden in silence for almost an hour, Okatai steadfastly refusing to answer the myriad questions of the two young men until they reached a point he deemed far enough away from the camp. They dismounted on the far side of a bleak hill, tying their horses together with a complex network of leather straps that kept them still despite the barren landscape.

'The Great Khan has given us our orders' said Okatai, answering an entirely different question. 'We are to document every detail of the great Jin city of Rhizun. When our work is complete, we will return home.'

'And the parchment?' pressed Stan. 'Whatever you wrote sent me to an earthen prison. Not that you seem too concerned about my disappearance.'

'There are greater forces at play, Stan. You are but a pawn in a great play.'

'That may be so, Captain Okatai, but this particular pawn is rather interested in the plot. What was so damning that Captain Sulki felt it necessary to remove me from the board?'

'He said we should call him Okatai' said Jochi.

Stan looked at his friend, then to Okatai. 'Is this true?'

'Yes, yes. A minor incidental' said Okatai dismissively.

'I respectfully disagree, *Okatai*' said Stan. 'You are more bound by etiquette than anyone in the Horde. If you wish us to address you so informally then you need our help more than we need yours. Whatever the catalyst for our little adventure, we have a pivotal part to play. Tell us everything you know or I'll saddle up Daisy again and head straight back home.'

'To your *earthen prison*?' said Okatai pointedly.

'Jochi will go with me' said Stan

'Hang on a minute now' said Jochi. 'I just aided the escape of a criminal. I'm not going back any time soon.'

'I'm not a criminal! I'm just an apprentice who delivered a message written by this man' said Stan, pointing a tense finger at Okatai.

'If only that were so' said Okatai enigmatically.

'You gave me the message yourself, old man. Enough chicanery. Answer our questions or we will leave you to journey alone.'

'I cannot tell you all I know, for to do so would be to compromise our objective.'

'You sound like a military captain, not some...' said Stan, trailing off as he failed to find a polite ending to the sentence.

'I may not be in a military regiment, but the art of war is painted on many canvases' said Okatai.

'Can you be a little less poetic?' asked Jochi. 'It doesn't suit a man of the Administration Regiment.'

'I am not in Administration!' roared Okatai, standing up as he did so. 'I am the captain of the Human Resources Regiment, and many other things besides. Hold your tongue, dogsbody, for we have a long month ahead of us and it would be far better for all concerned if we could get along. I am reluctant to resort to violent discipline, but not so much as to eliminate it from my options altogether. You would do well to control that flapping tongue of yours too. It is a greater weakness than you realise.'

'Tell us your secret and we will move on from this petty squabble' said Stan diplomatically.

'There are some secrets that should remain in the shadows.'

'Just tell us why we are going to our enemy's door' cried Stan, impatience bubbling in his chest.

'Oh, *that* secret? Well, yes I suppose I could tell you that much. Firstly, they are not our enemy. Not yet.'

'Anyone outside the nation is our enemy' said Jochi with practiced monotony.

'What use is a nation if it cannot include others in its make up? The more diverse our population, the broader our skills will become. The new world will be born from the womb of the Great Horde, Jochi, and we four will be the catalyst for the absorption of the proud Jin dynasty.'

'Bring it down a level or two, Okatai' said Jochi. 'You are speaking with the common folk now, where plain speaking wins out over eloquence, no matter how much you may revel in it.'

Okatai rubbed the bridge of his nose, then stared at the floor for a moment before taking a decisive breath.

'Men' he began. 'Genghis Khan himself has entrusted me to perform a reconnaissance of Rhizun. He ordered me to bring trusted men to assist me in documenting every aspect of the city, from the foundations to the flags, and to report back within a month. As it is, I must make do with you. Why he wants the information is his business, but I am sure we will all draw the same conclusion.'

He took a glug of cold water from a goatskin flask, wiped his face with his sleeve, and looked at Stan, tossing him a hunk of greasy mutton.

'The message you delivered to Captain Sulki is of such a... *delicate* nature that nothing would compel me to disclose its meaning here, even if my secrecy forces you to return home and forfeit both my orders and my head. Your capture was unfortunate, Stan, but not something we should dwell on. You have escaped, for the moment. Be satisfied with that blessing and do not ask me again.'

The absolute finality in Okatai's tone was understood by both men, if not the reasons behind it.

'How long will it take to get to Rhizun?' said Jochi, changing the subject.

'If we ride hard each night and are not waylaid we should reach it within five days.'

'Each night?' said Jochi. 'Don't tell me you expect us to ride in the darkness. It doesn't make sense, the horses could break their legs!'

'Then ride carefully. Must I remind you so soon into our journey that we carry the orders of Genghis Khan? We remain a valuable prize for the Jin warriors, no matter what the reality may be. They will be on their guard but I would wager they are not at such a level of readiness that they feel the need to scout after sunset. We will each take turns standing guard during the day and will ride the steppes under a cloak of shadow. Come, there is a darker gloom to the south, a small forest I would say. We will head there and make camp.'

The old man tied the flask to his knapsack and mounted his horse.

'Bring everything with you, including the detritus of your meals. There may be men here before sunrise and I will not be caught for the sake of a discarded chicken bone.'

He turned his horse and kicked, spurring the animal on towards the gloom.

'Do you have the faintest idea what's going on?' asked Jochi.

'I'm beginning to think we shouldn't ask too many questions' said Stan. 'If he won't explain why one of us was kidnapped and held in a secret pit by a captain of the Great Army, then I don't expect him to reveal the less dramatic details of an administrative sortie to the Jin.'

'Are you sure that's what we're doing?' said Jochi. 'If this was an ordinary expedition, why the sudden haste? And why would he insist we address him without his title? I know him well enough to know that he would see that as abhorrent in the extreme. He is a man who holds etiquette in higher regard than his own mother. He's hiding something else, I'm sure of it.'

'Then what should we do?' asked Stan.

'There's nothing we *can* do, other than to follow him to the edge of Rhizun. If we make it inside we'll get him drunk and persuade him to give up his secrets.'

He hauled Okatai's writing block back onto Patsi's back, swung his knapsack over his shoulder and lifted himself onto his horse.

'Last one to the gloom is a Jin latrine!' he called, giving his mount a sharp kick and careering away.

CHAPTER SIX

Rhizun
Jin Empire

Lah Fing scratched his head absent-mindedly. The view that filled his day was almost flawless in its monotony; the hill-distorted horizon being the only focal point for miles around. The cold winter sun was tantalisingly close to the peak of the western hills. Once that perfect yellow circle was breached his shift would be complete and he could return to his warm quarters for the sleep he had been battling for the last hour.

Then, much to his chagrin, something happened.

A small pack of animals crested a hill and zigzagged their way to the flat grassland. He squinted as the group came to a stop. What may have been three men dismounted, unslung their shoulder bags and began fiddling on the floor with their belongings.

There was a change in the light to his left. A hill had ruptured the sun and Lah considered ignoring the travellers. He could make his way to the sentry office with false ignorance and let the relieving watchman deal with the volcano of reporting protocols that was about to erupt. If he was caught, however, the number of logistical hoops he would have to jump through would keep him busy until his hair turned grey.

'Mord Lin! Here! Something's happening.'

'What is it?' said Mord from fifty paces away. 'I'm not walking all the way over there just to see another bird picking at a dead rat.'

'It's a band of men. I'm not even lying this time.'

Mord repositioned his bow onto his other shoulder and stared at his fellow watchman for a few moments.

'Fine, but if this is another of your practical jokes I'll spear you like a sheep and the birds can pick at you instead.'

'You need to work on your people skills, Mord. Life needn't be a sequence of black and white decisions about whether a problem should be solved with a good spearing or not. There is quite a large space in between for things like negotiation, compromise, pleasure, games, art, and culture. You should try them out, it might help with your anger management issues.'

'I'll compromise your ability to walk if you talk to me like that again. Now, what is it I'm supposed to be seeing?' said Mord, knowing better than to voice his true feelings about the way life in the city had changed in recent years.

'There' said Lah, pointing. 'See those shapes in the landscape that were never there before? I'd say that's probably something you should report to Captain Sikhing. What with you being a noted Watchman of the great Jin city of Rhizun and all.'

'I am no fool. I can see them as well as you. I can also recite every rule of the Watch and I'm sure you don't need to be reminded of rule number forty-two.'

'I don't think chicken sacrifices are quite necessary, Mord.'

'Don't play with me, Lah. If you are as astute as you are unprofessional you will know that rule forty-two states that whichever Watchman first identifies a possible threat must report said threat to the captain of the Watch as soon as they can find relief from their position.'

'But I've only just been and I haven't had a drink since.'

'You see, now you are trying my patience and that is not a characteristic for which I am famous.'

'No, that would be...' began Lah before trailing off for a moment. 'That would be... ah, look! They're doing something.'

Mord formed a tube with his hands and raised it to his good eye. 'They're lying on the floor, you damnable fool!'

'Well, then they *are* doing something. See, I can be as professional as the next man.'

'Not while you're standing there you can't. Go and find relief for us both, we must report this to the captain at once.'

'That's right, captain. Three men with three horses' said Mord with striking professionalism.

'Nine horses must be quite a handful' said Captain Sikhing, stroking his long, thin beard thoughtfully.

'My apologies, captain. I must not have been clear. They have one horse each, totalling three horses in the group.'

'Ah, well. That makes more sense. Why would they need nine horses if there are only three of them? Come to think of it, how would they keep them all under control. Not even the Mongols could control three horses at once. They could bolt at their leisure and be roaming the steppes like common rodents. The horses, I mean. Very large rodents, admittedly, and with a bigger appetite. Where do you think they find their food? I've never seen a wild horse eating, have you? Perhaps they eat the smaller rodents. How many rats would a horse need to fill its belly do you think?'

Corporal Tsensible of the Watch let out a familiar sigh. 'Lots. Now, my captain, we must report these findings to Roo Ling. May I suggest I go in your place? There are pressing matters here that require your attention. You must double the Watchmen on the western wall and have runners send back reports at regular intervals.'

'Ah right, yes. You there! Who are you again? Nord, that's it! Tell those Watchmen just off duty they are to return to the wall until sunrise.' He turned to Tsensible. 'You may go to Roo Ling, I will look after the *urgent matters* here.'

'As you wish, captain' said Tsensible, backing gratefully out of the Watchroom.

'Wait' called Sikhing. 'Before you go, remind me where I left my pants. Never run a Watch without your pants, that's what my dear grandmother used to say.'

'They're on your head, sir.'

'So they are! Thank you, Tsensible. What would I do without you?'

Who bloody knows thought Corporal Tsensible, who bloody knows.

CHAPTER SEVEN

'**A**re you having trouble with your ears, Jochi? The instruction was most clear. Perhaps I should nick your lobes with my dagger as a reminder. You may have completed your apprenticeship, but a man never completes his learning.'

'You asked me to write a simple sentence about our journey and I have done so; *I know nothing that can help me to answer this question.* That I have minimal intelligence in this regard is down to you more than I.'

'You do not have *minimal intelligence*, you are of moderate intelligence at least. A boy does not leave his apprenticeship behind without intellect.'

'If twisting my words pleases you, Okatai, then you can use what I have written to find a meaning that fits your instruction.'

'Then I will test you in a different way. This time I will tell you what to write.'

'And what will that prove?' asked Jochi. 'You already know I can write ably.'

'Indeed I do, and yet it will still be a formidable challenge. Please write *how can you answer this question?* in the ground in large letters.'

'And that is a challenge, is it? I've had enough of this nonsense. I'm not your apprentice any more, Okatai. I am free to do as I please.'

'Then you would do well to see past the labels of apprentice and teacher. I have much to show you still, not least of which is the humility to know when you are ignorant. Now, write it out in Jin letters.'

'Jin!? But I don't know Jin letters.'

'Quite so, Jochi. You are unacquainted with them at the very time you are to step into Jin lands and have given no thought to their value. Do you think they are so confident of defeating the Great Horde that they have not learned ours? There is your ignorance, young man. I suggest you replace it with knowledge.'

Jochi sagged. 'Fine. How do they write *how*?'

'I will show you. Once.'

Okatai scratched at the ground with a sharpened stick in a series of short, angular lines. When he was satisfied with his work he handed the stick to Jochi. 'Now you try. Make each word thirty paces long.'

'I say, Quentin, that was marvellous' said Jingo.

'Quite so, quite so' replied his brother. 'Say what you like about those filthy men, they know how to feed their horses.'

The two beetles lay on their backs at the top of the steaming mound of manure. Neither spoke for a time, both keen to enjoy the uncommonly soporific feeling.

'That one looks like a tree' said Jingo.

'That one what?' asked Quentin.

'That cloud.'

Quentin scanned the blue and white canopy above them. 'Ah, I see it now. Looks more like a pig to me. That one over there is a bit like Uncle Farqhuar.'

'I'd give a hundred balls of dung to see the look on his face if he could see us now. He wouldn't be so sure of himself then' said Jingo with a satisfied sigh. 'This is the life, what?'

'Wouldn't that be something? *Going off on your own will only lead to trouble*, he said. Well, if this is trouble then sign me up!'

'No more picking scraps from the undergrowth for us, brother. It's warm, fresh dung from here on in.'

'Rather!' said Quentin. 'I could die a happy beetle knowing we were right.'

As luck would have it, he was *right* sooner than he may have hoped.

'It is done' said Jochi, throwing the stick to the ground and slumping next to Stan, impaling an unsuspecting beetle as he did so.

'You have only just started' said Okatai with an uncharacteristically cheerful tone that did nothing to allay Jochi's anxiety. 'This is the future of warfare!'

'Warfare!?' said Stan, snapping his head up from the ground. 'Who said anything about a war?'

'You may not be as competent as your peers, Stan, but you remain a member of the Great Horde. War is not a condition that comes and goes like a leaf on the breeze; it is a permanent state of being for our great nation. That I have to say that out loud only compounds your failings.'

'Now, listen here!' said Stan, raising his body from the dirt and his voice from the depths. 'I am... I am...'

'Precisely. Now, gather round men, we have much to discuss. You will play your part in the Great Khan's glorious victory, despite your flaws. The walls that lie between us and our mission are an imposing physical barrier that we cannot hope to breach with force.'

'You've just noticed that, have you?' asked Stan bravely.

'Hold your tongue!' snapped Okatai. 'I am aware that even you will have concluded that one man and two upstarts could not hope to defeat an entire Jin city in a traditional battle, but our fight will be like nothing this place has seen before.'

'I'm not fighting' said Jochi. 'I have a bad back. My uncle says it's a sign from the Lord of the Sky that I am needed elsewhere when the swords clash.'

'If you would let me get more than one sentence out at a time you will discover there is no benefit in delivering excuses before the test is revealed.'

'A battle is a battle, Okatai' said Jochi. 'What hope do we three have of defeating such an enemy?'

'None' said Okatai flatly. 'Unless you listen to my orders and follow them like men. We are the future of warfare, pioneers of a new military breakthrough.'

'Right!' shouted Stan. 'That's enough. You've said that more times than I can count but not one morsel of detail has left your lips. Speak plainly of our plan and without ambiguity, or I'll turn my horse to home and face the consequences.'

Okatai's face flushed with angry impatience. 'The consequence for desertion is death, boy. I know you are not *that* stupid, so I will forgive and ignore your poorly judged ultimatum. It is prudent for you to be better informed now the city is in sight, however, so if you would be so good as to keep your ramblings to yourself for a moment I will enlighten you with the more pertinent elements of the plan.'

The two men sat still and quiet.

'Thank you' continued Okatai. 'As is bludgeoningly obvious to all, there is no hope of us winning a city in a traditional battle. We wouldn't even reach the wall before an arrow took us, so you may rest easy on that front at least.

We will bury our weapons here and approach the city walls unarmed, once we have...'

'Unarmed!?' squealed Jochi. 'We had no chance before but at least we may have escaped with our lives. How can we expect to achieve anything without so much as a dagger in our sock?'

'...once we have assurances from the prefect that we will not be harmed' continued Okatai pointedly.

'And how do you plan on gaining such an assurance?' asked Stan. 'Will you ask him nicely? Perhaps you intend to compliment him on his new hairstyle.'

'I do not expect you to understand the minutiae – that means the small details, Stan – of my great plan. That is why I am leading and you are not.'

'Spit it out then, man' snapped Stan. 'Tell us how we will breach the wall of a Jin city with nothing sharper than Jochi's jockstrap.'

'There are more points than those on a blade' said Okatai. 'The sharpest weapon in the battle to come is not made of metal, nor stone. Our wit – *my* wit – will see us to a great victory. I will have them open the gates and greet us as warmly as if we were coming home.'

'*By?...*'

'By giving them no choice but to open them. The Jin are an intelligent race, born of insatiable curiosity. It is my opinion that this curiosity will neutralise their intelligence. They consider it to be one of their greatest strengths, but we will twist it into a decisive weakness.'

Okatai picked up Jochi's writing stick and dragged it through the dusty ground.

'Your punishment was no such thing, Jochi. Look at my letters, what have I written?'

'Precisely what you asked me to write' said Jochi.

'Indeed. We have given the Jin a great riddle: *How can you answer this question?*'

A silence stumbled into the gathering and settled down for a doze. The two mens' eyebrows contorted themselves to varying degrees. Then, after an uncomfortable few moments, Jochi cleared his throat.

'They can't. It'll confuse the buggers into thinking we must be Jin, on account of the letters being Jin ones. They're not the brightest lot, are they? I've heard they wash their teeth every week without fail. Their *teeth*, by Gods!'

Okatai closed his eyes slowly. 'Stan?' he asked with a sigh. 'Do you have something less... blunt to offer?'

'Well' began Stan as he chewed on a reed. 'You said their curiosity would be their downfall, so it follows that they would be so curious to know the answer as to invite us in to discuss it. I'm not sure it's a good plan in reality, but I believe that answers your riddle well enough.'

'I'll give you marks for pointing the horse in the right direction, but I have to take them all away for your lack of confidence in my abilities. It is progress, though. Well done.'

Stan flushed.

'They will be too curious to resist, as you say' continued Okatai. 'But there are steps we must tread carefully before we see an open gate. Our riddle will get us to the door, but our wits will see us through it.'

CHAPTER EIGHT

Roo Ling, prefect of Rhizun, placed a blue vase gently onto his writing desk and took a step back. He pushed his lips to one side of his mouth in thought and stared at the display. Something wasn't right. His impossibly neat pile of valuable paper was in the centre with the ink jar to its right. The vase was where it should have been; at the back of the desk and dead centre. On the wall was a small tapestry of colourful fruit.

He turned to his bed. It was pressed into the corner of the room, just as it should have been. His bedside table was empty, excepting a small cup of water. The only window framed a view of his lands perfectly, the pleasingly tree-speckled panorama stretching out to the unmoving horizon.

But something was wrong.

'Feng!' he called out to the walls.

A shuffling noise preceded a discreet knock on the door.

'Enter.'

Feng crept in and waited.

'Something is wrong' said Roo Ling, secreting a question into the statement.

Feng looked about the room. 'Here, master' he said, pointing at the chair. 'It must be placed under the desk for the room to be in balance.'

'Then how can I get to my desk?' asked Roo Ling. 'I have important messages to send to the Emperor.'

'It is allowable to move it when in use, master.'

'Did you just make that up? Seems a little convenient. How am I to keep myself balanced if there are rules I am not aware of? I could be compromising the entire exercise by stubbing my toe on a table leg or sneezing in the wrong direction. My most senior advisors assured me that Feng's Way was the balancing foundation upon which a successful city must be based, but I'm beginning to wonder at its effectiveness. So far all it has achieved is to send my humour into a spin.'

'Master, I can assure you that this is the defining quality of your great city. When we are wholly aligned there will be a feeling of peace to permeate every nook. It will give birth to a grand tranquility that will consolidate our position in the great order of the world. A serene mind frees the body to accomplish the grandest of deeds.'

'And you're absolutely sure about this?'

'Oh yes, master, quite sure. Is it easier to work at a desk overflowing with the detritus of your meals, with bones and grease compromising the sanctity of your station? Or is your mind better able to perform at the high level it demands when it is devoid of such distractions?'

Roo Ling raised a single eyebrow.

'When the villagers of my youth followed my teachings and removed the burden of chaos from their souls' continued Feng, 'we were able to grow the most enormous vegetables.

I can remember soybeans the size of fists and cucumbers as big as thighs.'

'Save your exaggerations for those with less wit, Feng. Tell me, are the blacksmiths in the pits nudging their anvils to balance themselves, or are they still to reach that particular stage of enlightenment?'

'They are learning, master. They have much to balance and, as you say, less wit for the task.' Feng gestured to the wall behind the desk. 'May I?' he asked. Roo Ling gave a small nod and stepped back. Feng moved the table away from the wall slightly, just enough to allow his thin frame to squeeze into the gap. He adjusted the tapestry, walked back around the desk, and put his hand to his chin thoughtfully.

'No, no, no' he grumbled, and made his way back to the wall. He moved the hanging back to where it had been a moment ago and retraced his steps, pushing the desk back against the wall and holding his chin once more.

'Yes, that should do it' he muttered to himself.

'Hang on a minute' said Roo Ling dubiously. 'It's exactly as it was when you entered the room.'

'And yet it is not, my lord. Please, sit again at your writing desk and allow the perfectly aligned energy to flow through you.'

Roo Ling gave a sideways glance of doubt before pulling out his chair and sitting down.

'Wait outside' he ordered.

As the door closed he looked about him; at the perfect pile of papers and the ornamental vase, at the tapestry and the view through his window. He closed his eyes for a moment, letting out a large and rather satisfying sigh as he did so. When he opened them again it was as though he had been transported to a different place entirely. Everything was where he *felt* it should be. Nothing was interfering with anything else. He picked up his writing stick and scratched out a message to Emperor Aizong.

Your Imperial Majesty, Your servile city of Rhizun exults in your honour, showing such a bloom as befits a great city of your empire. The people humbly praise your benevolent and merciful rule each day. May the shadow of time pass through you and on to your enemies, oh immortal leader.

I must insist again, dear cousin, that we dispense with such a flowery introduction to every letter I address to you. It is a waste of ink, both in its construction and my protestations against it. That said, I am glad to hear that you remain in your rightful place at the heart of this great dynasty.

Now, to business. It is with both pride and comfort that I can report only positive testimonies from this most distinguished and loyal city. The quandary with the latrines I highlighted in my previous missive is now resolved and those peasants living closest to the flood are recovering well. The pigeon mating in the Sun Tower has abated at last and Captain Win assures me his regiment is now working night and day to ensure The Tests will not be affected by this unexpected delay. They will be of such a scale as to reverberate into the consciousness of our descendents. Elsewhere, the construction of your living quarters is almost complete, and as requested I have arranged for every stone in its construction to be adorned with the image of a one-legged flamingo.

My anticipation rises at the prospect of your arrival, your Imperial Majesty. May the wind be at your back as you journey to grace us with your eminent presence.

I remain your loyal servant,

Roo Ling, prefect of Rhizun

'Here!' called Roo Ling.

Feng glided back into the room at the summons.

'The Emperor must receive this before his departure' said Roo Ling as he dried the parchment with a graceful waft.

'I will take it to the Messaging Tower and instruct Captain Wing to deliver it with all haste. I will impress upon him more urgency than is required, master, and will return only when I see the horses' dust settling on the threshold with my own eyes.'

'I should make you Chief Communications Officer' said Roo Ling. 'You have a way of answering unasked questions. It is a fine trait for a man in high office.'

'I am but a humble servant of the great Roo Ling. Your will is my deed, master.'

'You see? Any man who says flattery is a bastion for the sly is wrong. It serves you well, whether you believe your expressions or not.'

The prefect curled his silken moustache thoughtfully.

'I will send word to the Lord of the Scrolls' he continued, 'instructing him to add your name to the list of officers. It will be a new position, dealing with all matters concerning... *audible aesthetics*. You will speak for me when there is something to be said to my people and you will be sure to paint a glorious picture of our great city. You can deal with the difficult questions too, I've never enjoyed them very much and you would make a better job of it in any case. Well, not better obviously – I am the prefect after all – but you'd come close I'm sure. You will travel with me when we march on those filthy Mongols and ensure the men are free from distractions when the swords clash. A man with your skills should not be left behind a desk when there is glory to be had in the battlefields. You will be my first Public Relations Officer, Captain Feng.'

Feng shifted from foot to foot uncomfortably. He had never understood the appeal of hurling oneself onto an enemy sword, though he would never voice such an opinion. 'I am here only to do your will, master. It will be a great honour' he replied, despite the swirling dread in his stomach.

'Marvellous. Now, bring me something to eat. All this talk has given me an appetite.'

Feng bowed low and backed out of the room, closing the door behind him and sliding to the floor as his brain calculated his new life expectancy.

Bugger, he thought.

CHAPTER NINE

Genghis Khan was not a man prone to introspection, particularly when it came to decidedly non-military matters. Give him a varied landscape, a hated enemy, and fifty thousand or so men and he would be happier than a thrill-seeking leaf in a tornado. Ask him to explain the nuances of teenage romance, however, and you would be as well to ask a herd of stampeding yak to move ever-so-slightly to the left. Somewhere in the middle of these two extremes was a quandary his subconscious had been grappling with for months and had now decided it was high time it let the more conscious parts of his brain deal with it. His subconscious was not happy about this at first and had argued back and forth with itself before coming to the conclusion that it wasn't its problem to deal with, and anyway, the consciousness never seemed to pull its weight these days. It nudged the idea over and retreated back into its safe, predictable space in a dark corner of his mind.

The problem in question concerned who would come after him. He had no children and had killed the brothers he once had as he climbed to the throne of the khanate. There was no man in his nation he could rely upon to be as infallibly untrustworthy as a khan needed to be. It was not so much that he was trying to fit a square peg into a round hole, it was more that he had no pegs at all and couldn't find the hole.

His subconscious rolled its metaphorical eyes and nudged his consciousness again.

There would be no answers found inside his private complex, he thought.

Genghis stood then and called for Ulfred.

'Yes, my Lord' said Ulfred within a moment.

'I need some old, ragged clothes and no questions.'

'Yes, my Lord.'

Ulfred returned a few minutes later with a matted coat and a pair of worn trousers, stolen from a huge stable boy who was instantaneously and chronically self-conscious as he stood in the stables without so much as a belt covering the parts of him he would never deliberately reveal.

Genghis pulled a hood over his head and looked at his reflection in the bowl of clear water. It felt strange to see himself in such a way as this, disguised in clothes not even a corporal would consider.

He stepped out of his yurt, pulled at the uncomfortable coat, and headed towards the great mass of people that thronged the landscape. His landscape. His people. But not *his* people. For all his power, he was toothless when it came to his succession. It was a certainty that he would be dead when the time came to decide who would continue in his footsteps, and if he knew one thing it was that the dead are not influential negotiators when it comes to matters of such significance. The memory of a late relative can determine whether or not you wear your lucky sheep's foot going into battle, but their opinion is rarely referenced when it comes to grand matters of practical importance to the nation.

He was a young man the last time he walked freely about his people away from the battlefield and as he passed them now, unrecognised, it rankled with him that they were neither friendly to the stranger, nor supplicant to their leader. Was there anyone in this rabble of violence who could take his mantle? He ploughed on, stepping over sleeping soldiers as he went.

After a few minutes he was surprised to discover he needed to build up some courage to make conversation with one of these nameless pawns. Not because of a fear he would be recognised, but rather that the nuances of speaking with commoners were now a mystery to him. He picked an arbitrary woman sitting alone, cross-legged as she wove buttons onto a jacket.

'Woman!' he said.

She looked up from her work at the overdressed stranger.

'I haven't done anything wrong' she said instinctively. 'I was given these coats by the captain himself, so don't you go trying to get me thrown into the pits. My husband was on the front line at Xhakina.'

Genghis, already a long way out of his comfort zone, was thrown a little further afield by both the content and the frostiness of the woman's speech. Xhakina was, at least, a topic he could converse on. He had masterminded the victory after all. 'Was he indeed? Then he is a worthy man.'

'Was' said the woman flatly.

'Oh, I see' said Genghis, omitting the required apology with impressive ignorance. 'What did he die of?'

'Xhakina.'

'Well, that's something then.'

The woman's forehead creased. 'Something? What *something* is it, precisely?'

'He died with honour for the good of the nation' said Genghis without irony.

'Oh, that' spat the woman. 'He died because our incompetent leader is quite happy to destroy his people with the wave of a sword from behind a wall of iron.'

Genghis' brain caught the violent eruption of power rising in his throat just in time. He took a deep breath.

'What would you say to him if he was here?'

'I would tell him how much the children miss him, and how his murder was on the soul of the khan, not himself.'

'Not him, me!' snapped Genghis.

'You?'

'I mean *him*. The Great Khan.'

The woman twisted her face slightly. 'I'd tell him to bugger off back to his rainbow yurts and never bother us normal people again. That's what I'd tell him. Not that he'd pay any attention of course. He's famously out of touch with his people on account of him having none of his own, isn't he?'

'Is that what they're saying?'

'*They*? Who are you?'

'You wouldn't believe me if I told you' said Genghis.

'Try me' said the woman.

'Another time, perhaps.

The wind changed direction, whipping the woman's buttons from her lap. Genghis made no attempt to help her collect them, mostly because his nose was screwed up behind his hands.

'What is that bloody awful smell' he managed.

'It's fine, I'll get them' said the woman. 'Who asks that kind of question anyway?'

'Someone whose nostrils may never recover' said Genghis. 'It smells like... like... Oh Lord of the Sky, no!'

'You are a strange man indeed' said the woman. 'A powerful man too I would say. Perhaps even the *most* powerful.'

'Why would you say such a confounded thing?'

'Who else would not recognise the stench of an open latrine? There is only one man in the nation who spends his days far enough away from them to have forgotten their stench.'

'I have an old war wound' lied Genghis. 'I cannot smell as well as most, but even I can smell that. It must be worse than usual.'

'Must it?' asked the woman in the unbelieving tone of one who has raised four children.

'Yes, it must. And another thing' said Genghis, wagging a finger. 'If I was the Great Khan your head would be on a spike by now with talk like that. We should be careful not to be overheard, I hear he has a lupine temper.'

'You'd know, I suppose.'

Genghis had heard enough. If this woman knew his identity, suspected even, then his power was already waning. He needed to cement his succession, and quickly.

'I will leave you to your buttons, woman. If I ever meet the Great Khan I will keep your assessment of him to myself, for fear of losing my flawed nose for your loose tongue.'

'Bye then, oh Great Khan' said the brave woman with a smirk.

Genghis turned and made to walk away. His first step was into a worryingly brown puddle whose contents splashed up Genghis' trailing leg as well as onto the face of the woman.

'I don't know how you people live like this' he said without apology and left the woman to her buttons.

Two dragonflies zigzagged around each other in the clear blue sky. To anyone looking their way they were a predictable picture of whimsy and wonder; a flittering ray of beauty in the cultural cesspit of the Mongol horde. Anyone listening to them would have experienced something altogether more surprising. A little known characteristic of these majestically fragile beings is that they possess a voice box that creates a sound akin to slate grinding on a rock. It puts them second on the list of the world's most irritating sounds, just behind that of a spoilt child who has just had their favourite toy taken from them because Great Uncle Kukkoo was on his way over to tell them all about the time he rescued the village elder from a particularly aggressive marmot.

'Bugger off!' screeched Bikka. 'I found it, so I'm keeping it.'

'You only saw it because I had the bright idea of hunting in the puddles near the big folk' scratched Akka.

'If your hunting skills were as good as your thinking we'd be feasting on the finest mosquitos this side of the great hill by now.'

'I could say the same for you and your lateral thinking.'

'I don't even know why I still fly around with you' said Bikka tersely. 'You're the most unpleasant dragonfly I've ever met, and that's saying something.'

'Nonsense! What about Old Tiktik. He could spend all day decimating your character and still think he let you off lightly.'

'Well, that's old ones for you. They think they can say whatever they like just because they've been around long enough to see a season change. Bloody pompous oafs!'

'Watch what you're saying. My father is a *bloody pompous oaf*. Are you saying he's unpleasant too?'

'All I'm saying is that everyone turns into cantankerous old dragonflies as soon as the weather changes. Why don't any of us try to glide gracefully into old age with polite compliments and constructive advice?'

'So you're having a go at the whole dragonfly community now, are you? And *you* think *we* could do with being more polite? You should look at your reflection before you go and cast such aspersions on the entire population.'

'You see, that's exactly the kind of thing I'm talking about. You could have said "Oh yes, Bikka, you've got a point there. Let's discuss it and weigh up the pros and cons of such an innovative idea. If we all got along a bit better we might even be more productive." But no, you had to go and stick the needle in, didn't you?'

'Now who's sticking the needle in?'

'That's not the point. At least I'm trying to be a little bit self-aware.'

As Akka prepared to hurl the perfect response to his hunting partner, the argument was concluded with undeniable finality as the finest boot in the horde splashed down through their puddle, crushing them both and saving them the trouble of changing the course of dragonfly socioeconomics forever.

CHAPTER TEN

Corporal Tsensible rocked gently from foot to foot. A meeting with Roo Ling was like one of Madam Pi's bread puddings. The prospect of one was gut-wrenching, but the reality was often pleasantly painless. Another similarity was that you sometimes threw up shortly afterwards.

He was saved further excruciation by the arrival of a Guard of the Prefecture, their garish red outfit, and white plumage giving them the look of a recently stretched radish. Tsensible stood, brushed himself down, and waited to be given direction.

'Your audience will now be heard' announced the radish formally. 'Follow me.'

Tsensible was drawn along labyrinthine corridors. Some were furnished with doors at regular intervals, implying a mundane and unremarkable series of tasks being completed inside. One showed no break in the stone for almost a hundred paces before being interrupted by an unremarkable doorway that did nothing to appease his feeling of dread.

'You're lucky' said the radish. 'My last... *guest*... went through that doorway. The door was open, of course, but I'd say he could fit through the keyhole by now.'

'Really?' managed Tsensible, despite the rising nausea. 'How... *interesting*. I won't take up too much of the prefect's time. Just a quick message to deliver and I'll be gone.'

'Yes, I imagine you will be' said the radish. 'Ah, here we are.'

The floor reached a series of uneven steps leading to a large wooden door with sweeping designs covering every space. Lanterns lined the walls, coating the entrance in a thick, honey-coloured sheen. The radish skipped up the stairs as a leaf would ride a gentle breeze. Tsensible's legs, however, stammered up them gracelessly. He had been this way only once before – a rare and confusing meeting with the prefect on the subject of planting pots – and on that occasion he had tripped on the very first step, sending him and his scrolls to the floor in a predictably ungainly manner. His attempts to woo the onlooking granddaughter of the Master of the Purse ended at that moment too.

Tsensible clambered breathlessly over the final step at last, to the patient relief of the guard.

'Compose yourself' ordered the radish, before pulling on a thick rope that hung from a gap in the ceiling.

The action seemed to achieve nothing, though the guard was now content to stand motionless nonetheless. Tsensible wondered at the ability of such men to petrify themselves for such long periods each day when he himself could not remember the last time he was still for more than a moment.

The enormous door opened slowly and Tsensible's eyes were gradually assaulted by a room lined with guards in unnecessarily colourful liveries. More frivolous personalities than his had long since labeled these as The Vegetables. Some wore the radish-like outfit of Tsensible's guardian, while others wore greens, oranges, and yellows of an equally biocomparable nature. He was ushered in and encouraged to proceed down the only route open to him; past the rainbow warriors and towards a large dais. Sitting there, on a carved, wooden seat was Roo Ling, Prefect of Rhizun.

Two caricatures of masculinity stepped in front of Tsensible as he reached earshot of the prefect. He stopped suddenly and waited. And waited.

Leaders of men the world over are owners of extraordinarily location-specific skill sets. They master only those tasks deemed essential to clamber to the top of their own political pile. The leader of the Akapundi Tribe in Western Africa, for example, no more needs to understand the intricacies of ice tunnelling than an Inuit angakkuq would need to know how to bring down a giraffe. They do, however, share in glorious unanimity an ability to hold large gatherings to complete silence without the slightest feeling that they should get on with whatever it is they're about to say. A mere baker would have filled the air with wistful proclamations on how the seasons weren't as distinctive as they used to be, with phrases like: *"that isn't real snow young man, and I should know – I lived through the great storm of 1198 when there were snowflakes the size of chickens and we had to eat frozen pinecones for breakfast, lunch, and dinner. You young ones don't know how lucky you are..."* and so on.

Tsensible waited. He watched Roo Ling call an aide over and whisper something into their ear. No doubt some important instructions to ensure the safety of the city, or the method of Tsensible's execution.

'What's on the menu for dinner, Ettiket?' whispered Roo Ling.

'Pickled soybeans, master. With fruit parcels to follow.'

'Oh marvellous, I do like a fruity parcel. Has he fixed the supply problem with the peaches?'

'The thief has been identified, master. I have our best men on the case and expect an apprehension presently.'

'Well that is good news. You can't have a fruity parcel without peaches, isn't that right, Ettiket?'

'It is, master.'

The aide resumed his statuesque position at the prefect's right hand, satisfied that he had carried out his duties flawlessly.

'Corporal Tsensible. I believe you have news from the watchtowers.'

'I do, master.'

'Have you come here to invite me to a guessing game, or do you plan to reveal more information before you are incarcerated for withholding intelligence?'

Tsensible swallowed nervously. 'There are men on the western plain, master. They have horses.'

'How many?'

'One each, master.'

Roo Ling rubbed the bridge of his nose slowly, an action that did nothing to quell the rise of bile in Tsensible's throat.

'How many *men*, corporal?'

'Three, we think, sir.'

'Think? You *think* there are three men? I would say that the size of a Mongol scouting pack would be in the '*Definitely Know This Before Troubling The Prefect*' category, wouldn't you?'

Tsensible's voice barged past his brain for a brief, life-changing moment. 'I didn't say they were Mongols, sir.'

Roo Ling froze, then slowly raised himself from his heavily carved chair to stare down at the now-panicking corporal.

'Would you care to repeat that?' said the prefect in a menacingly flat tone.

Not really thought Tsensible.

'My apologies, master. What I mean is that it is awe-inspiring to see an intellect such as yours calculate the... the... undisclosed details of my... of *our* report. Our report, yes. They are, as you say, Mongols. Naturally.'

'Naturally? Why, Corporal Tsensible, is it so *natural* for them to be Mongols?'

Bugger thought Tsensible.

'Well, I mean... it has to be them, doesn't it?'

'Why?' asked Roo Ling firmly.

'Well...'

'If you start another sentence with *well* I will put you down one for a week. Now, why are they so naturally Mongols, man? Be quick!'

'Yessir! They had to be, because... because they came from the west.'

'*And...?*'

'And the Mongols are to the west.'

'And why could it not be anyone but the Mongols?'

'Because they are inhuman, blood-thirsty animals with a crazed leader and a penchant for destroying everything in their path?'

'Precisely! Now, let's get down to business. What else do you know about this advanced party?'

'With respect, I don't think they're having a party, master. There are only three of them and they seemed a little bored, if anything.'

Roo Ling let the ignorance slide, it would only have taken longer to explain and he had a fruity parcel to see to.

'Was there anything remarkable about them, other than their horses?'

'Yes, master. They wrote something in the dust, large enough for us to see from the ramparts.'

Roo Ling squeezed the metaphorical stone a little more, finally seeing a drop of red appear.

'And...?'

'It said: How can you answer this question?'

'Did it, indeed?' said Roo Ling, pulling his strapped hair over his shoulder and stroking it mindlessly.

Two of his aides exchanged a rare, wide-eyed glance. One gestured to the other with a subtle nod of their head and moved in towards the prefect. The motion seemed to snap Roo Ling from his reverie. He slung his hair back over his shoulder.

'Enough, gentlemen.'

The aides backed into their positions and waited with tensed muscles.

'Allow them into the city, corporal, and bring them to me at once' announced the prefect, before sweeping across the dais and through a door at the back.

The radish took Tsensible by the arm, spinning him around and pointing him towards the entrance.

'Come' he said woodenly.

They made their way back through the maze of walls before Tsensible was finally untethered from his guardian. As he reached the crisp air outside he stopped, leant against a cold, stone pillar, and closed his eyes. He slumped to the ground slowly, muttering childish profanities to himself as he considered the sharp downward turn his day had just taken.

'You don't think I was a little too mean to him?' said Roo Ling. 'He looked a bit anxious, wouldn't you say?'

'It was not menace on display master, but authority' said Ettiket, a short yet thin man whose facial features seemed to triangulate to a point just below his chin. 'Those less familiar with power are not as discerning in the understanding of its nuances as those who control their destiny.'

'A simple yes or no would suffice' said Roo Ling. 'Perhaps just once you could speak plainly. It is tiring having to play our conversations back in my mind to be sure we were discussing the same thing.'

'I live under the yoke of your wisdom, master. Your will is my existential compass.'

Roo Ling paused. 'So that's a yes, is it?'

'Indeed, master.'

'Right, well you clearly have a long way to go on that front. Please ensure you practice. My brain is tired of your contorted piffle.'

'I am humbled by your...' began Ettiket, before stopping to screw up his face. He was experiencing an altogether alien internal scruple that had temporarily escaped his mind and camped out in the creases of his face. 'Indeed, master.'

'That's better. Now, when the Mongols arrive I will greet them in the Great Hall. From there they will be given a tour of the city. Ensure they are sent to my War Chamber on their return. I have a surprise or two that will sweep their certainty from them.'

'The War Chamber, master? I will arrange for the tactics map to be moved to a secret location, the armoury reports too.'

'There will be no need for such precautions, Ettiket. I intend to reveal all they desire. They will believe us to be defeated, yet it is we, the Jin, who will stand on the corpses of the horde as we build our eternal empire.'

'And we will do this by revealing our secrets and neutralising our advantage?'

'Indeed we will. It is the last thing they will expect.'

It will be the last thing we expect too, thought Ettiket. 'Indeed, master.'

'I say we get the watchmen to do it' said Captain Sikhing. 'I'll be damned if I'm setting foot outside the walls while the Mongol Horde bays for blood.'

'They're not really baying though, are they?' said Tsensible bravely. 'They're more sort of... lingering. Plus there are only three of them, hardly a horde. With respect, of course.'

'Then it's settled, you will go with them' declared Sikhing gratefully. 'Take the two spotters with you and invite the marauders in. Send word to Captain Snu Zhi to make rooms ready for them before you go. Oh, and Corporal Kan-Tor will need to be told of the horses.'

'Your will' said Tsensible with reluctant deference. 'I will see to it at once.'

'Now, has anyone seen my pants? They're sneaky little buggers. Always hiding from me.'

Tsensible pointed blankly to his captain's head and wondered, not for the first time, how this man came to outrank him. He left the room and headed for the stables.

Captain Khi slid the last of the wooden planks from the city gates and signalled to his men to push them open. A great screech came from ancient hinges as huge sections of wood parted, allowing the sunlight to conquer the darkness at the entrance floor. Three men cast new shadows, each of them shuffling subtly backwards as if being at the back would save them from the three rampaging Mongol warriors.

'I'm surprised you haven't come out with an inappropriate quip yet, Lah Fing' said Mord Lin. 'Have we finally found a limit to your immaturity?'

'We'll find a limit to your breath if you don't pipe down' said Lah without moving his attention from the landscape through the gateway.

'Gentlemen, please' said Tsensible placatingly. 'Keep your hearts red with fire and your heads cold as ice. That is how we will defeat them.'

'Perhaps you could recite them into submission?' suggested Mord.

'Perhaps I'll leave you to execute this sortie alone' countered Tsensible.

Captain Khi watched on nervously. He was never at ease while the gate was open, and even less so when there were Mongols prowling. He nodded towards the open exit and in a moment four muscular gatemen heaved on the doors, beginning the labourious closing manoeuvre. The three men of the expedition exchanged worried glances before stepping forward onto the defenceless plain.

Corporal Tsensible stepped from the shadowy gateway and into the glare of the winter sun. 'Let's get this over with quickly' he said, striding to the front of the group.

'Settle down there, corporal' said Mord Lin. 'I saw them first so I'll lead this little raiding party, thank you very much.'

'You seem to have forgotten your rank, Watchman, and mine too for that matter. I am a corporal of Rhizun, a rank that rarely carries any gravitas. As with all ranks, however, it is superior to that of a lowly lookout.'

'A corporal worth his stock would be familiar with the regulations concerning scouting sorties, particularly rule seventeen. For clarity, I will quote directly' said Mord, grateful for the opportunity to show off one of his few practical talents. *'During reconnaissance missions where the principal discovery individual is present, they shall take command of said mission for so long as the integrity of the party is sustained.'*

Lah Fing listened with curiosity. His default position was one of danger avoidance, but a dim noise was calling to him from the distant haze of his subconscious, just around the corner from his evolutionary survival instincts. It occurred to him that leaders of daring missions survived to tell the tale, more often than not, and those left behind on the battlefield were usually the insignificant pawns, sent forward to blunt the edges of the enemy's sword with their skulls. He wasn't sure whether it applied to groups of three, but if there was the slightest chance it would increase his life expectancy he was going to leap on it like an eagle on a rat.

'Thank you for the reminder, Mord. We wouldn't want to go against regulations now, would we?' he said.

'Precisely' said Mord. 'Now, fall into line, men.'

'I believe it is my line to command, watchman' said Lah, stepping in front of Mord and striding out onto the plain. 'After all, I am the *principal discovery individual*.'

'Ah' said Mord.

'A-ha!' said Tsensible, claiming victory despite his loss.

'Follow me, gentlemen!' called Lah, exhausting his knowledge of how a leader should behave as he did so.

Mord and Tsensible trotted behind their undeniably legitimate leader as he strode purposefully away from them and towards whatever peril the small Mongol scouting party held in store.

They marched in silence for a time, as is often the case with small reconnaissance teams with little in common, until Lah's gait changed almost imperceptibly. After a few moments, he stopped and turned to the others with a look of anguish on his face.

'What is it?' asked Mord. 'Have you sighted the enemy? Are they readying for battle?'

'Not quite' said Lah through stretched lips. 'It is a problem of an altogether different nature.'

'Is it an antelope? Tell me it's not an antelope' said Mord in a rare show of genuine emotion. 'I don't trust them.'

'You don't trust them?' asked Tsensible incredulously. 'What is there to *not trust*?'

'Their antlers for a start. What kind of animal has spiralling antlers?'

'Goats' said Lah. 'They often have spiralling antlers.'

'I think they're technically horns' said Tsensible. 'Antlers fall off.'

'Aha!' exclaimed Lah. 'Then antelopes don't have antlers at all. They have horns. See, Mord, there's nothing for you to worry about.'

'So it is one' said Mord, backing slowly away from the as-yet-unconfirmed antelope.

'It's no such thing' said Lah.

'Goat, then?' asked Tsensible.

'It isn't an animal at all, it's nothing of the sort' said Lah. 'I have a pressing call of nature that must be seen to at once. If you wouldn't mind turning your backs for a moment.'

Tsensible rolled his eyes. 'Is he always this unsuitable for leadership?'

'He breaks new ground every day' said Mord.

'There! All done' said Lah cheerfully. 'Now, as you were men. We'll be on top of those wretched sheep-eating Mongols before you can say *mutton grease on a summer's day*.'

CHAPTER ELEVEN

Why do some birds go to all the trouble of finding a solitary worm buried beak-deep in the hard ground when they could gorge themselves on the very leaves they sleep amongst each night thought Stan as his sentry shift wore on drearily. Perhaps they're fussy eaters? That would explain them passing on the leaves, but not their preference for worms. Maybe worms taste like the finest roasted boar and their appearance is a deterrent to those who would consume them to extinction. I wonder if that's why there are so many lizards around here? He looked up at a shadowy movement in the distance. That's probably one there. Big blighter, too. Or is there more than one? Yes, three I think. We should test them out for dinner. Actually, if they get any bigger we'll be having them for breakfast too. They're a little more upright than I would have expected. And those arms look a bit... army. Oh bugger!

'Men!' he yelled. 'Men!'

Okatai and Jochi bolted upright.

'What is it?' asked Okatai.

'There are men coming straight for us from the east. Three of them.'

'Gather up our things and remember your orders.'

'What orders?' asked Stan. 'You haven't given us any. All we've heard so far is that everything's going to be fine if we just be nice to them.'

Okatai cocked his head. 'Then be nice.'

The three men arranged themselves into a military line. Okatai adjusted his breastplate, straightened his back a little, and took a single step forward. The blurry outline of the approaching figures sharpened into three Jin men dressed in similar yellow outfits. They stopped twenty paces away from Okatai and waited, as did he. After a short time, and with a premonition reserved for those who hold etiquette in the highest regard, Okatai and Tsensible walked towards each other.

'Stay where you are, corporal' said Lah Fing. 'I'm in charge here.'

'Of course, you are, watchman' said Tsensible without breaking stride. 'I am merely putting myself forward to protect you from any unexpectedly fatal violence.'

'Ah, well. Yes. Of course. Carry on then corporal, carry on' said Lah.

Okatai and Tsensible stopped a pace apart. After a brief period of politeness, Okatai cleared his throat.

'I am Captain Okatai of the Golden Horde; servant of the Lord of the Sky and vessel of the immortal Genghis Khan in this life and the next.'

'I am Tsensible, servant of our glorious Prefect Roo Ling and officer of the Watch of Rhizun' lied Tsensible. Now was not the time to admit to being a mere corporal.

That sort of truth can get you into real trouble. 'I am curious to learn why a band of Mongol vagrants have violated the lands of the Emperor. Are you lost? Or are you here to surrender?'

'Neither' said Okatai. 'We come with true hearts and honest intent. We seek refuge in your learned city. We are men of words and ink, not warriors.'

Lah Fing whispered to Mord Lin from the corner of his mouth. 'Turds and stink, more like.'

Tsensible snapped his head to face the watchmen and glared. Then he didn't. His expression changed from anger to pleasure in a few confusing moments, before turning to face Okatai again.

'What colour is the sky?' he asked.

'It is grey now, but it was a vivid blue yesterday' answered Okatai.

'What is that?' asked Tsensible, pointing at Okatai's water skin.

'It is a water skin' answered Okatai.

'And that?'

'That is a horse.'

'Which of these men is shorter' asked Tsensible, pointing to Lah and Mord.

'That one' said Okatai confidently.

Tsensible nodded slowly. 'It is rare indeed to find such a small group of your people so close to one of the great cities of our empire. Rarer still to find one who speaks our tongue. Why are you here, wordsmith?'

'I am a man inspired by knowledge, friend. Not for military gain, nor territorial advantage, but rather to help me on the path to enlightenment. Is it not said that a man may beat a drum for many reasons, but the greatest of all is to hear its echo?'

'No.'

'Ah, well it is said by my people, and may that be the first of many gifts I hope to bestow upon the great inhabitants of Rhizun.'

'In return for...?'

'I ask only for a short period of shelter while I learn of your customs.'

'And your men?'

'Indeed, though they are only beginning their intellectual journey. This is to be their great epiphany; a life-changing experience to set them on the path to harmony.'

'Tell me, Captain Okatai, why should a cultured man of Rhizun take a filthy Mongol at his word? My people also have mottos, and there are many that would be appropriate. It is said that a cook cannot change his pots. It is also said that an enemy who covers your head in fine silk remains an enemy with an interest in your head. Perhaps they are not as graceful as yours, but their messages are delivered effectively enough, nonetheless.'

'What I offer you now is as close to treason as I am prepared to travel, even allowing for the distance between here and the heart of the Great Horde. My nation is one of warriors; a vast, matted rug of ignorant violence. I yearn for more enlightened times when the divided factions come together to share knowledge and improve lives. Your people are masters of invention, of intellect, and of culture. My people are strong; unmatched in the saddle and patriarchs of warfare. There is so much that could be done if we learned from each other. For my part, I am a captain of the Mongol Horde, but one who covets the Jin's thirst for intellectual advancement. There is nothing more I can say to counter many years of brutality from my people. I will bend to your decision.' Okatai finished his cajoling negotiation with a small bow.

Corporal Tsensible wasn't used to this at all. He was usually the one to be told what to do. That an enemy captain would venerate himself at his feet was both exhilarating and a little uncomfortable. His brain was also trying to rationalise the oxymoron of a Mongol vagrant speaking his language with eloquence.

Flattery won out in the end, as it always does. There was also an opportunity to improve his chances of a much-coveted promotion in the confusion. They were, after all, ignorant of his orders to bring them in. He would shroud them in a cloth of complicity and keep this captain in his debt.

'Come with me, captain. You are now bound to me until I claim back this great favour, for I will gift you an audience with the prefect himself.'

'Enter' called Ulfred.

His guest slipped in and walked to a table on one side of the yurt. He leant on it casually in an uncommon show of indifference to both the rank of his host and the honour of his home. Any other man of the Golden Horde would have stood stiffer than one of Captain Padding's breastplates in front of Genghis' left-hand man, but this visitor was not like the other men. He only had one ear, for a start. He was dressed entirely in the darkest of brown clothes and wore a strap of leather over his head to cover his missing ear. He was extraordinarily lean and appeared to be made entirely from taut muscle. It all combined to create a distinct impression that efficient violence was permanently just a moment away. He was also a most unlikely expert in all things ornithological.

'I have news' began Ulfred. 'Please, sit.'

The guest didn't. He rarely did anything he hadn't suggested first. He was an unequivocal master of unilateral decisions; the antithesis of a committee in a singular, human form.

'You may stand if you prefer.'

Bugger, thought the guest. *Now what do I do?* He chose to lean a little more casually on the table, somewhere between sitting and standing. It gave the impression that he was trying to reach something with his foot without ever quite catching it.

'A delicate matter of the most significant importance has arisen, one that requires a swift, flawless resolution. It is my belief that it will take a man with your unique... skillset to ensure the job is completed to the satisfaction of the Great Khan.'

The guest adjusted himself on the table.

'I require an oath from you to ensure the information I am about to relay remains in your memory and does not find its way to less loyal and incorruptible people. I will then give you your instructions.'

'I will stand for an oath' said the guest, finally. 'But don't expect me to promise something I can't deliver. If your orders prove impossible to accomplish then I will not be bound by an oath given without full disclosure of the facts. It is against National Regulations.'

Bloody National Regulations, thought Ulfred. Genghis' committees had a lot to answer for, and empowering the people with rules was the greatest of them all. Ulfred was a believer in the old ways of doing things and was yet to find a regulation he couldn't navigate around with a few well-chosen threats.

'I believe there is a new family of red-footed falcons in the great conifer. It is heartening to see such fragile creatures taking shelter among so much military might. It would be a shame indeed if they were to go the way of so many of our enemies.'

The guest resisted. 'Your threats are just that. I understand your techniques well enough to know you have no intention of harming them. I will complete my orders to the extremes of my abilities and will keep your secrets safe, but do not expect me to take an oath for something I cannot foresee.'

'As you wish, Lo-Ki. I'll have your legs cut off instead' said Ulfred flatly. 'Guards!'

Two vast bulks strode into the yurt and drew their swords.

'Fine!' snapped Lo-Ki.

Ulfred dismissed the guards with the wave of a finger.

'I will take your oath, but it won't change how I operate. They are only words, after all.'

'My poor man' said Ulfred, thick with condescension. 'Words are the keys to our future. Men of your disposition will be cast aside as intelligence wreaks a new destruction across the land.'

CHAPTER TWELVE

C orporal Tsensible arrived at the base of the irregular stairs again. This time he treaded efficiently, making it to the summit without embarrassment. He turned to the gathering below him and wondered how this would play out. It was surely to be a comical show of poorly executed diplomacy. None of them, as far as he knew, had the wit to compete with the prefect of Rhizun when it came to political chicanery, and the meeting was guaranteed that dynamic at least.

'Watch out for the stairs' he called. 'They're tricky little buggers.'

The statuesque radish was waiting for them as they congregated in front of the enormous wooden door to the prefect's audience chamber. His little finger twitched faintly, betraying his feeling of extreme anger at having Mongols pass his sword undecapitated. He repeated the calming mantra his grandmother taught him as a young boy in his head and remained commendably motionless.

Lah Fing was the last to arrive at the door. 'Lovely day for an intimidating meeting with an enemy leader, wouldn't you say?'

In a remarkable show of patience and respect, the radish waited for the silence to die down a little before pulling on the heavy rope. He was exceptionally good at waiting. It was just one of the benefits of his preference for internal ruminations over the company of others.

The group also waited, suffocating in the awkward tension that comes when people who, under normal circumstances, would never raise an eyebrow in greeting to each other but are forced into painful small talk in a confined space.

The radish twitched. The unidentifiable command to open the great doors had been relayed to him and a moment later they were released from their current discomfiture and into another, more portentous one. They filed past the rainbow warriors and stopped in front of the great dais. Roo Ling made a point of not noticing them for a few power-filled moments, choosing to cleanse his tabard of an unauthorised speck of fluff instead.

'Ah' he said at last. 'You must be the brave invaders. Tell me, have you realised yet that you are in mortal danger?'

This was one of those questions asked only by those so bored with power that they have to create their own entertainment, like an elderly cat with a ball of sheep's wool. Roo Ling knew they hadn't the faintest notion whether they should answer or not, gifting him the high ground of the conversation and setting the tone for what was to come.

Tsensible had lured himself into the beginnings of an unlikely alliance with the enemy. The more favours he did for these filthy Mongols, without seeming to do so by his allies, the greater the repayment would be when the time came. He notched another onto the tally as he took a pace forward.

'These men were spotted this morning by the Watch, master. They appear to be an advanced party from the Mongol Horde.'

'This morning!? It's way past lunchtime, corporal. Why am I only seeing their rat-infested faces now?'

'Our watchmen reported their sighting with the speed of an eagle, master' said Tsensible, desperately trying to steer the conversation away from any parts that involved the prefect.

Roo Ling turned to his aide, standing dutifully by his side. 'I thought eagles were more renowned for sight than speed. Is this not the case, Ettiket?'

'It is, master' replied Ettiket faithfully. Nobody in the room felt the need to suggest that they were also, in the grand scheme of things, fast.

'I will not ask you again, Corporal Tsensible. Repetition, as rarely as it is required, is not in my nature. Tell me all you know of how these men came to be inside the walls of my city.'

Because you invited them in, oh gloriously incompetent leader is what Tsensible would have liked to have said. He wisely chose a slightly less fatal answer. 'They were some distance away when Private Lah Fing here spotted them at the foot of the western hills. He reported the anomaly to Captain Sikhing who...'

'Dammit, man! I don't want to hear every how every link in my chain of command failed in their duty to protect my city from an invading enemy. Cut to the chase and save us all from your wearisome tale. I don't have time for every last detail, I am a man of many responsibilities. Today is bath day, for a start, and I'll be damned if some rancid Mongols are going to stop me from cleaning myself, even if the concept is yet to present itself to them. I wouldn't be surprised if these specimens here have never let water into their jockstraps. Filthy buggers.'

Roo Ling paused and turned to Ettiket once more, lowering his voice to a whisper. 'Am I going on a bit?'

'A little, master' said Ettiket.

'Well, Tsensible?' called Roo Ling. 'Why are they here?'

Tsensible took a deep breath before joining Ettiket at the guillotine of truth. 'You asked me to bring them here, master.'

'Did I?' asked Roo Ling thoughtfully. 'Did I, Ettiket? It doesn't sound like something I'd say.'

Ettiket hadn't moved from the prefect's side. He was experienced enough to know this was going to be a conversation that required his constant presence at his master's ear.

'I believe you did, in fact, give the order to bring them to you, master.'

'Well, well' said Roo Ling. 'Fascinating.'

He sunk into a thoughtful trance, leaving the rest of the room to squirm through an uncomfortably long silence. At length, he spoke again.

'Well, they're here now. Let's see what brings them to Rhizun. Guards! Prepare the dungeon.'

Ettiket leaned forward. 'May I respectfully remind you of your earlier decision to use the War Chamber, master? As you said, it would be a better venue for any follow-up conversation with these animals. They hold invitations in high regard and it would be wise to have them lower their guard before we strike. They may have vital information in our battle to vanquish them from our lands, too.'

'Good point, Ettiket, good point' conceded Roo Ling, clapping his hands together. 'Right, where is Captain Merang? Somebody inform him there will be a feast for...' he nodded his head at each of the men in front of him. '...the usual people plus six. And Feng is to oversee the table settings.' He clapped his hands again, causing several of the rainbow warriors to bump into each other in their eagerness to do their master's bidding. Roo Ling stood, bowed to his guests, and left.

Those still in the room sagged their shoulders with a collective sigh of relief. Tsensible looked about him, realising with a resigned feeling that he had been left to deal with the Mongols alone. Lah Fing and Mord Lin were already halfway to the door.

'This way' he said, waving his arm towards the opposite end of the great hall. 'I may as well show you the sights while we're waiting.

'We'll start at the Mai Lu' said Tsensible. 'It's the selling road so should give you a feel for the place. We have a saying here; *A man's motivation is in his shopping.* If you know what we spend our money on then you will know what we strive towards.'

The Mongols ignored him, choosing discretion over a display of ignorance. Instead, Stan turned to Jochi.

'Do they have spices?' he asked. 'Something I haven't seen before, perhaps?'

'How would I know?' said Jochi. 'Ask him yourself.'

'Fine. What's the Jin word for spice?'

'It may surprise you to hear that I'm yet to learn their culinary vocabulary. He may have learnt ours, however. Try him out.'

Stan skipped to the front and tapped Tsensible on the shoulder. 'Spice?' he asked, putting four fingers of one hand into his mouth in an attempt to ensure an understanding.

'Spice?' asked Tsensible.

'Yes, do they sell them here? I would like some with my dinner.'

'You want spice for your dinner?' said Tensible, incredulity dripping from his tone. 'We are not animals here, Mongol. None here would eat spice, no matter how hungry we were.'

Okatai interrupted. 'I think there has been a misunderstanding, gentlemen. Corporal Tsensible here is a fine master of our tongue, but alas it appears he has confused *spice* with *mice*.' He turned to Tsensible. 'The little furry rodents with long tails and an ability to scare away elephants are called *mice*. The colourful powder you use to enhance the taste of your meals is called *spice*. An easy mistake to make.'

'Ah' said Tsensible. 'Then I can tell you there are spices in such variety and abundance they will lead to a waste flood experience you'll never forget.'

After a brief moment of concern, Okatai let out a grateful sigh. 'You mean a *taste bud* experience we will never forget?'

'No.'

'Oh.'

'Here we are!' announced Tsensible cheerily as they turned a corner. 'The Mai Lu.'

A blitz of colours assaulted them. There were silks of all hues, from deep reds to pale greens, sunset yellows to midnight blues. Okatai and his men were rarely exposed to anything outside of the brownish-green range and it widened their eyes to see such gaudy effervescence.

'Sorry about the smell' said Tsensible.

Only then did the Mongols notice it, a thick stench of life that was a shock to their olfactory senses. They were used to stomach-emptying smells, which was rather the problem. They had unknowingly lowered their resistance to pungency with just a few days away from the Great Horde. They were now paying a high price.

'Bloody frogs!' exclaimed Stan.

'I thought you called them *bogs*?' replied Tsensible.

'We do' said Okatai. 'Stan here was using a Mongol phrase to show his... surprise. Is it the latrines we can smell, then?'

'Heavens above, no! That's Ul-suh's boiled kidneys. They're quite the delicacy, you should try them. A little word of advice; if you do, be sure to compliment him on their quality. He has a rather skewed muscles-to-patience ratio. He's also rather opinionated when it comes to... *outsiders*.'

'Perhaps tomorrow' said Okatai diplomatically.

Stan couldn't contain himself any longer. He trotted ahead to explore the exotic foods on offer, bouncing quickly from one to the next as his attention was caught by strange sights and alluring scents. He stopped briefly at an inviting aroma radiating from a stone doorway before lurching inside.

'Where's he off to?' said Jochi.

'His downfall, by the looks of it' said Tsensible, rushing after him.

Tsensible sprinted towards the doorway, suddenly aware of the responsibility he held to protect this rabble of uncultured foreigners. He leapt over the threshold, waving his arms wildly as if corralling an escaped horse, then stopped dead. For a moment he wondered if he had entered the wrong building, but it was definitely Ul-suh and he was definitely holding a non-violent conversation with Stan.

'He's with me!' cried Tsensible in an attempt to defuse a situation that didn't exist.

'Calm down, corporal' said Ul-suh. 'This soiled Mongol here is a fellow enthusiast of the culinary world. Men of our disposition are able to put outward differences aside for the betterment of our art.'

'You are?' said Tsensible incredulously. 'I thought you said the Mongols were an unintelligent vermin on the landscape and we should smite them with all the power in our arsenal.'

'They are, and we should. That doesn't mean I can't appreciate a like-minded soul when I meet one, even if they are disguised in the shape of a steppes-rat.'

'Hang on a minute' said Tsensible, struggling to maintain a grip on the conversation. 'When did you learn to speak their tongue? I seem to remember you skipping those classes to work on *more useful* skills. Ones with more arm swinging and head bashing.'

'A secret talent is more useful than a boasted one, corporal.'

Tsensible shook his head in confusion. 'Bugger this' he said, and left the room, calling back to Stan as he did so. 'We're heading up to the garden wall at the top of the road. We won't wait long for you.'

'Sorry about him' said Ul-suh. 'He can get a little uptight about things. Comes from his father, I think.'

'That's quite alright. It takes all sorts, doesn't it' said Stan, rolling his eyes in mock superiority.

'I'm sure he's very good at his job, whatever it is' said Ul-suh. 'Now, tell me how you would roast a goat's leg. Do you let it dry a little first, or do you prefer the juices to soak through the meat as it cooks?'

Stan had waited his whole life to have a conversation like this. 'Well that all depends on when the goat was slaughtered' he began.

CHAPTER THIRTEEN

Genghis stared at the orange-blushed figures on his battlefield again. *There must be a way through* he thought. The Tatar infantry filled the valley floor, flanked by their cavalry, and protecting the opening to the steppes behind them. Their archers lined the hills on either side.

There was no way through.

The leader of the Great Horde looked about him and his wandering eye was caught by something at his feet. It was a stone, smaller than his fist but big enough. He picked it up and tested its weight with a couple of low tosses into the air. It would do. He stepped backward a pace and twisted his torso back and forth, practising the move that would destroy the evil band of vermin that stood in his way.

He was ready.

He swung his arm, building up an enormous power, before unwinding himself and launching the rock into the valley. Dozens of Tatars shattered into myriad pieces. Shards of painted wood flew across the tent as Genghis pointed triumphantly at the Tatar leader, now no more than a collection of splinters on the table.

'Nothing stands in the way of the great Genghis Khan!' he roared.

A familiar throat-clearing sounded behind him.

'What is it, Ulfred? Can't you see I'm busy?'

'I have important news, my Lord.'

'And you think my Tactics yurt is the best place for that, do you?'

'No, my Lord. I am here to escort you to the yellow yurt.'

'The Provisions tent is hardly any more appropriate. What has come over you, Ulfred?'

'With respect, master, the Provisions yurt is more of a peach colour. The yellow Diplomacy tent, however, is ready for your arrival.'

'Well come on then' snapped Genghis. 'My leadership will not be compromised by the ambiguous colour pallet of a greying elder.'

Ulfred led them across the grassy space at the centre of Genghis' private complex and up to the entrance of his master's Diplomacy yurt. A large table took up most of the space inside, though its top was unusually bare. Genghis took his seat at its head and looked back at the open flap of cloth.

'Come.'

'My Lord' said Ulfred as he entered.

'Please' said Genghis pointing to a large padded chair on the opposite side of his table. 'What news of the reconnaissance?'

'Nothing as yet, my Lord. Their return is not expected for some time.'

'Shame' said Genghis.

Ulfred waited for his khan to elaborate. He was particularly adept at it. A disproportionate amount of his days were spent waiting patiently in front of Genghis. Had there been a Lingering Regiment then Ulfred would undoubtedly have been its Lieutenant-Colonel.

'Where are my plans?' Genghis asked, noting the empty table. 'Did I not order them to be left here for my convenience? What if there is an urgent campaign that requires my attention?'

'I thought it best to hide them away from prying eyes, my Lord. Our meeting does not require maps or models and I have a man waiting to join us.'

'Who will succeed me?' asked Genghis at last.

'Succeed you?' parroted Ulfred with disbelief.

'You know, who will come after me?'

'I haven't given such a terrible concept the slightest thought' lied Ulfred. 'Your highest ranked officer, I suppose.'

'There are so many regiments these days there will be a civil war before my eyelids have closed. No, there needs to be another solution. One with more... *undeniability*.'

'Like something hereditary?' asked Ulfred.

'No. Not *like*. It must be infallible.'

'May I take a moment outside, my Lord?'

Genghis nodded absent-mindedly. Ulfred stepped out into the crisp air, taking in a deep lungful in a vain attempt to clear his head. He had spent most of his adult life nudging

Genghis this way and that; the hidden power behind the ego. Now, in the space of two days, a thus far wholly ignored matter had raised its eyes above the parapet twice. The issue of succession had been pencilled into his plans some way down the line, when the grey hairs of his master outnumbered the black. Now it was front and centre, with an emphatic scroll and a khan with too much time on his hands and a knack for precision timing. He would always have preferred to deal with it later, but the schemes of the subservient are only as reliable as the whims of their masters. He dismissed his obsolete guest, took one last breath, and stepped back into the yurt.

'I believe I may be able to assist you' said Ulfred.

'I knew you would' said Genghis. 'I can always rely on you to solve the most ardent of riddles. So, what do you have in mind?'

'This' said Ulfred, taking the scroll from inside his shirt and placing it on the table.

Genghis' eyes bore into Ulfred's mind. 'What is this?'

'The solution to your problem.'

'The same problem to which you haven't given the slightest thought?'

This is why he shouldn't be allowed to think freely, thought Ulfred. 'I have not had time to digest its content, my Lord. Your ruminations spiked my memory, that is all.'

'The succession is not a matter to *ruminate* on, Ulfred. It is to be *resolved*.'

'I believe this may be its resolution' said Ulfred, moving the conversation along as best he could.

'What does it say?' asked Genghis.

'I would have to look at it again to be sure. May I?'

'No, you may not' said Genghis, swiping a hand to grab the scroll from the table.

He tapped it in his open palm a few times, deep in thought. Ulfred lingered masterfully.

'What is the gist of it?' asked Genghis, unfurling the parchment.

'As your private captain, I take modest pride in my ability to control the information that swirls around your people. On this occasion, however, I must place myself at the feet of your justice, for some news has reached me before I knew of its existence.'

He waited for Genghis to react. He had learned long ago to gather as much evidence on his master's mood as he could before ploughing on with any proposal. The silence found its way through Genghis' trance and snapped his consciousness back into the room. The scroll's revelation had sent him back into the mists of his memories; of simpler times away from the focus of leadership.

'The hilltop village' stated Genghis.

'Indeed, my Lord.'

'Then it was all true.'

'It would appear so' said Ulfred, despite owning the knowledge for a lifetime.

'Boy?'

'Yes.'

'Good' said Genghis. 'Who is Takkan?'

'His brother. Half brother, to be precise. Someone has closed that particular door already it seems, his body was found at the cleaning stones with an arrow in its back. He is no longer involved.'

'Is the boy here, in the horde?' said Genghis, unfazed.

'He was.'

Genghis stared fiercely at an unremarkable wooden pole in the wall of the yurt.

Ulfred waited.

'How did he die?' asked Genghis at last.

'*Die?*' said Ulfred. 'My Lord, he is not dead. He is very much alive, in fact.'

'Does he know the power he holds?'

'No, my Lord. He knows nothing of his heritage, nor his potential.'

'And how did you come to learn of this development?'

Ulfred was too wily a man to lie too often to the great Genghis Khan. He was rather attached to his head for one thing. 'Captain Sulki came to me with certain evidence he had procured by unknown means. He intended to extort me – *us* – to further his career.'

'What is his current position?' asked Genghis.

'Sheep Shearing Captain, my Lord.'

'Ah. Understandable then' conceded Genghis. 'Still, we can't have this sort of information floating around unchecked now can we, Ulfred?'

'Indeed, master.'

'Bring the boy to me. I will deal with him first.'

Ulfred took a breath. 'I'm afraid he is not here at the moment. He was sent with Captain Okatai to Rhizun.'

'Then you had better get him back, hadn't you?' said Genghis with just a hint of a questioning tone.

'Indeed, master.'

'Send Sulki. It can be the first part of his punishment.'

'As you wish.'

'You had better have a trial too before you tell him his punishment. We don't want to be seen as unfair.'

'Yes, my Lord' said Ulfred, bowing low and stepping towards the exit.

'Wait!' said Genghis, staring thoughtfully at the scroll.

Ulfred waited.

'Where are my armies?'

'I have sent word with Captain Paat. They will be here any day now.'

'When you have dealt with Sulki, bend all of your efforts to readying the nation to march. When Paat returns I want him in my presence quicker than he can quaff a jug of Old Kahzi's special dancing juice.'

'Your will, my Lord. I will ensure the military regiments redouble their efforts in preparation, too.'

'There is no need for that, Ulfred. We do not ride to battle, we ride to the future.'

CHAPTER FOURTEEN

Okatai and Jochi followed their Jin guide out of the Mai Lu and into the relatively fresh air of the residential streets. Not that it would otherwise have been considered so. It was only *relatively* fresh in the same way that a whistling arrow is *relatively* benign while plunging towards someone else.

'There are gardens at the end here' said Tsensible, pointing towards a distant wall. They were built by our ancestors many years ago to please the growing population.'

'What's a garden?' asked Jochi.

Tsensible searched Jochi's eyes for evidence of mockery but found none. He had never had a need to define a garden before and stuttered as his brain tried to find the words for something so self-evident.

'It is a place full of grasses and trees. Flowers too.'

'All of that stuff surrounds the city for miles around. Doesn't make much sense to me to have any of it on the inside. Couldn't you just go for a walk beyond the walls instead?'

'Well, yes but it's… you know? Ah, there's a bench. You don't get many of those on the steppes. It's in a convenient location, too, right next to the residential quarter' said Tsensible, struggling to cope with Jochi's petulant but irrefutable logic.

'Sounds like they just forgot to build something there – a guard house perhaps. Maybe when they realised they had run out of stone and were one building short they told the people it was a garden, not something *for guarding*. What do you think, Okatai?'

The ever-greying Human Resources captain glared at Jochi. 'I think you should widen your vocabulary. I am sure the intelligent people of Rhizun can tell the difference between a garden and a forgotten patch of wasteland. I also think it would be best if you kept your mouth shut, at least until such times as our safety in this fine, awe-inspiring city is assured. Show more respect to our generous guide here, please.'

Jochi swallowed. 'Yessir!'

'And don't call me that here. I am Okatai, remember?'

'Yessir Okatai.'

'Anyway, here we are!' announced Tsensible with false cheeriness. 'This way please, gentlemen. I am sure the reality will salve your doubt.'

He led them through a narrow stone archway to their left and into an expanse of colour so striking it brought them to a standstill. Red flowers dangled nonchalantly from deep green branches. Swarms of yellow and orange carpeted the ground in large, perfect squares.

Two worms concertinaed their way through an apple.

'You'll never guess this one' said Pippin, a worm with an inflated opinion of his mimicking abilities.

'You're right, I won't' said Cox. 'I never do, on account of you pulling the same face every time.'

'This one's a good one, though. Watch.'

Pippin strained his muscles and contorted his features in such a way as to convince himself he looked exactly like a chrysanthemum.

'Are you being a worm?' asked Cox. 'Because you look exactly like a worm, just so you know. You also look the same as when you were doing a golden larch.'

'You have no imagination, that's your problem' snapped Pippin. 'Our days would pass a lot more pleasantly if you played along.'

'They'd pass a lot more pleasantly without your impressions. It's time you faced up to it, Pip; you're a worm, and worms are not natural entertainers. We're more your reliable, predictable, vegetation-processing types.'

'We are only limited by our own boundaries' said Pippin haughtily.

'And what's that supposed to mean?' asked Cox.

Pippin hesitated. 'I don't know, but it sounds like the sort of thing I should say when someone challenges the meaning of life.'

'*The meaning of...?*' said Cox with incredulity. 'You're a worm, not an emperor!'

'Who says I can't be emperor if I want to be? I have just as much right to be emperor as the next worm.'

'You're right. You're absolutely right.'

'I am?'

'You have exactly as much of a right to be emperor as the next worm, which is no right at all.'

'No wonder you never get anywhere in life' said Pippin petulantly.

'I'll get to the other side of this apple and that's all I need concern myself with. You could do a lot worse than sticking to what you're good at. Remember what Granny Smith used to say? *Ambitious worms get plucked by the bird.* Keep your head down, mulch the food, and live long enough to see another sunset.'

'That's the spirit' said Pippin. 'I was being a chrysanthemum by the way, not that you seem to care.'

Cox was spared the tedium of explaining the meaning of worm life to his brother again. Unfortunately for Cox it was because they were both eaten by a passing Mongol.

'Does every step in this city have a gaudy surprise lurking around the corner?' asked Jochi, plucking an apple from a drooping branch and biting into it without looking.

'It is fabulous, is it not?' said Tsensible proudly.

'No. It's giving me a headache' said Jochi. 'I can see why they put a wall around it.'

The Jin were a proud people by nature, but Tsensible was a man whose pride was outweighed by both his practicality and his impatience. If the gardens would not turn their heads then he needed to lower the cultural bar a little.

'Perhaps that is enough for the moment' he said. 'Come, you are to have a private audience with the prefect. I will show you to your rooms so you may ready yourselves.'

'Ready ourselves?' asked Jochi.

'Your dinner clothes will be laid out in your rooms, of course' said Tsensible.

'Dinner clothes?'

'Enough, Jochi' said Okatai. 'There's no need to repeat everything you hear.' He turned to Tsensible. 'Thank you. We will retire there for the moment to await our summons.'

'Retire?' echoed Jochi. 'I've only just finished my apprenticeship.'

Okatai ignored him, holding out an arm towards the archway. 'We will go there at once, Tsensible. Thank you.'

'Let's take a different route back to save your nostrils from the Mai Lu. It will give me a chance to show you the great pavilion of Bans Tand too.'

They followed Tsensible, crisscrossing the unappreciated fauna and heading out through an identical archway on the opposite side of the gardens. The streets here were wider, with smooth ruts flattened into the earth. The buildings were taller too, with openings high up on the walls and roofs so elevated that their peaks were hidden from view.

'This is a rather dull part of the city, but it is a quicker way to the pavilion' said Tsensible. 'It is used for storage of those items we produce in great numbers. They are mostly maintenance items and unused weapons; squared rocks, timber, arrows, catapult stones, rope. Nothing too engaging I'm afraid.'

When there was no response he turned to the Mongols. They had stopped a little way down the road, staring in awe at the towering structures.

This is what they're struck by? Thought Tsensible with disbelief. A bloody warehouse?

'Can we get inside?' asked Okatai.

'Erm…'

'I've held an interest in storage logistics ever since my great uncle was killed by a poorly stacked wall of tent poles' lied Okatai. 'I won't take long, just a quick look will be enough to see how your city solves a problem we cannot.'

'I suppose it couldn't do any harm' said Tsensible, stepping forward and loosening the large, iron bolt that held the doors closed.

Okatai peered inside. It was an enormous vault, five men high and countless wide. Most of the items were pressed against the walls, leaving a wide, bare floor that seemed to go against all reason. He scanned the room for weapons, making a quick approximation of their quantities.

'And this is the only storage for the entire city?' asked Okatai, folding an explosive question invisibly into a banal one.

'It is.'

'Then it is impressive indeed to do so with such a space left in the centre. Is there a use for it?'

'It's mostly used for The Tests' answered Tsensible. He was never sure why, but then there were a lot of things he didn't understand, now more than ever. A feeling of social saturation came over him. 'If that is all, captain, we should make our way directly to your accommodation. The pavilion of Bans Tand can wait for another day.'

'Right, well, I'd better be off' said Stan. 'I'll come back for that liver and sage pudding before I leave the city.'

'Be sure that you do, friend' said Ul-suh. 'It has been a surprising pleasure to speak with you.'

Stan stepped out onto the Mai Lu and froze. It wasn't clear to him how much time had passed, but it was certainly enough to be sure that his friends had abandoned him, for the moment at least. Tsensible had said something about guarding a wall at the end of the street so he headed that way in the vain hope they had waited there for him. It took no small amount of will power to pass by the alluring foods, though his lack of bartering material made it a little easier.

Had he a gold ring he would have happily exchanged it for some mysterious crimson fruits that seemed ubiquitous among the stalls.

He made his way through the residential street without seeing anything that could be described as a wall that would require guarding. He passed by a stone archway that gave him a glimpse of the vivid colours so popular among the Jin people. On he went, along the long street until it stopped at another running perpendicular to it.

He had a choice to make. Either way, he concluded, it would be an arbitrary one, so he turned to the right. The sun would then be on his back, at least.

He stayed on this road until it too reached an end; a huge wall that Stan presumed was the city limits. Turning right would take him back to the Great Hall, the one place he assumed his friends wouldn't be, having just left there, so he turned left and headed into a maze of streets whose walls seemed to loom more the further in he travelled. He was used to vast, open spaces and felt as though the encroaching buildings were brushing his head and crushing his breath. An unfamiliar feeling of dread rose up in his stomach and he began to panic. *This is like the river tree incident all over again*, he thought, as his walk turned into a trot and through the labyrinthine laneways.

He was now completely lost and fear was building in his throat. His reasoning battled with his paranoia in an attempt to keep his wits about him but it was a losing fight. Strange eyes darted at him from behind large wicker baskets full of roasted crickets, while every window seemed to hold a furtive threat.

A stout figure stepped out suddenly from a doorway, planted its feet wide apart, and folded its arms aggressively. It may have been a woman, but the leathery, aged skin gave no conclusive evidence in that regard. It shouted something incomprehensible; a series of syllables whose exact meaning were a mystery to Stan but whose message was clear. *Bugger off back the way you came,* they said.

A tomato splashed onto his chest. He looked up at a sinister window just in time to receive an apple to his forehead. Slimy fruits and vegetables of varying ripeness hailed in on him from more and more disgruntled residents until he could do nothing but slip on the gloopy mess at his feet.

'Wait!' he called to the enlarging crowd, now evolving into a baying mob, or at least an irritated one. 'I am lost. If you could point me in the direction of the Guarding Wall I'll be out of your hair at once.'

Those at the front of the mob looked about them, whispering from one to the next until a ragged line of heads parted at the back of the crowd and rippled towards the front. An excruciatingly short man with a wide, bald head spewed out of the gathering and wobbled to a standstill in front of Stan. 'Smahtarz' he announced.

'Well, there's no need for that' snapped Stan despite his predicament. 'My name is Stan, of the Golden Horde, and I am lost. If you could direct me to the Guarding Wall I will be on my way.'

'My name is Smahtarz' said Smahtarz.

'Ah. I see' said Stan. 'My apologies, I thought you were... never mind.'

'You are look for Garden Wall?'

'Looking' corrected Stan instinctively.

'Bad language not allowed here' said Smahtarz with a wagging finger. 'We may not have coin but we have pride.'

'No, no. *Looking*' said Stan, raising his voice and exaggerating the movement of his mouth to help the Jin man understand. 'I am *looking* for the Guarding Wall.'

'You look for Garden Wall' stated Smahtarz. 'I show you.' He walked past Stan, tugging at his arm as he did so. 'This way, Mongrel.'

'Mongol' said Stan, an instant before promising never to correct a Jin man again.

'We call you Mongrels because you breed like rats every place you go. There is no purity to your race. No refinement.'

'You speak as though purity is something to covet, yet diversity is what keeps us strong and grows our empire.'

'That is willy' said Smahtarz.

Stan resisted the urge to correct him again. *Let him think his willy is silly,* he thought. 'Why were they throwing food at me?' he asked.

'You are in the Lu Hen Cha – the poor road as you would say. Even some Jin are not so brave to walk here. A visiting Mongrel is like a snake in a mousetrap.'

'Then why did you save me?'

'I speak good Mongrel tongue. That is how I got my name.'

'I don't understand' said Stan coyly.

'*Smahtarz* is an ancient Jin word. It means man of useless knowledge.'

'Well, you may have to change it now. Thank you for saving me, I was beginning to feel a little disturbed in the...' He stalled, concentrating. 'In the Lu Incher.'

'Hen Cha.'

'The Lu Hen Cha.'

A widening of the buildings signalled an end to their journey through the slums of Rhizun.

'I will travel alone from here' said Stan. 'Thank you again for your help, I will not forget it.'

'Nor will I' said Smahtarz, raising one thin eyebrow. 'Your head is sure to be worth many coin. No more talk now, I take you to Prefect Roo Ling.' He pulled out a wooden stick from his pants and struck it against Stan's back. He then twirled it around slowly, revealing a small, curved blade at one end. 'Go! If you stop I will use this the right way.'

CHAPTER FIFTEEN

Ulfred swept into Sulki's yurt with the confidence of an untouchable man.

'Your punishment has been decided' he began without preamble.

'Hang on a minute, I haven't even been tried yet.

'Ah yes' said Ulfred, disappointed that his prisoner had noticed. 'Your trial has been held and you were found guilty on all charges.'

'*All* charges!? There was only one!' cried Sulki.

'We added a few more, just to be sure. Don't let that concern you though, I have arranged for you to receive a lenient sentence.'

'Now listen here, I'm all for the idea of keeping my head where it is, but I demand to be given the chance to defend myself.'

'Oh I wouldn't worry about that, I'm sure you'll have to defend yourself quite a bit in the coming days.'

Sulki froze as he sorted his potential punishments into an order of preference.

'You are to follow Okatai and his band of men to the gates of Rhizun. I know you are not a skilled warrior like other captains, so I have arranged some protection for you on the road. Bataar will travel with you – more than enough protection for one man, even you. Once there you will locate them and order their return. They are not to be harmed, by Genghis' own request. In the unlikely event that you fail to carry out these orders, you will be held responsible and dealt with accordingly, as will your head. I strongly suggest you find them and keep them safe.'

'When you say *his band of men*, who are you referring to exactly?'

'I do not know their names' said Ulfred with a snort. 'Three nameless men. Find Okatai and you will find them.'

'And you're sure all three set off with him?' said Sulki, now panicking a little more.

Ulfred gave Sulki a look that bordered on respect. 'One has remained behind' he said, 'but then it seems you already know this.'

Sulki gulped. 'Your eyes reach far indeed. I shall release Stan and take him with me.'

'Stan? My dear cousin, it is Mekki who remains behind.'

'So you do know their names?'

'Their names are an irrelevance. Just bring them back, or I will break yours.'

It had been a full day since Sulki had disappeared into Genghis' private complex of yurts. Mekki was desperate to return to his own but knew better than to lose his mark. For all he knew, his friends' lives were on the line and no amount of internal debate could steer him away from that train of thought, much as he tried. He packed up his turnip boiling pots, added a log to his small fire, and rummaged through his bag for his sharpening stone. He drew his dagger up and down in slow, smooth lines, found a focal point at the trees in the far distance, and let his mind daydream the interminable minutes away.

A movement to his right snapped him back to reality. Sulki was leaving the complex unguarded, staring straight ahead with a glazed look in his eyes. He trudged through the crowd, bumping others' shoulders without consideration and trampling on whatever detritus his feet found as he moved. Mekki stamped out his fire, threw his dagger and stone into his bag, and set off to follow the loathsome sheep shearing captain. He walked parallel to him and a few paces back so as not to catch his attention until at last, they reached the captain's yurt. Mekki took a few backward steps to give himself a little cover near a thin bush. He watched Bankhe being summoned inside before leaving again, returning a few minutes later with Bataar. The two men disappeared once more into the yurt. Over the next few minutes, he watched Bankhe go back and forth between Sulki's two tents, delivering a range of unremarkable items from the sleeping yurt. Mekki watched him with mild curiosity until the guard passed by the sleeping tent and on into the great maze of life beyond.

When Bankhe returned he was carrying something that sent Mekki hobbling towards his own yurt to gather up his things and ready himself for a long, and almost certainly very painful journey. It was just a small metal pot, but Sulki had thought enough about it to send his guard away to find one. Mekki recognised it from the few military sorties he had been unlucky enough to find himself on. It was a standard-issue foot soldier's cooking pot, designed specifically for those with little food and lots of land to cross. Whatever was going on between Sulki and Ulfred, the sheep shearer had clearly been ordered to travel far from the horde.

Back at his own yurt, Mekki gathered up as many items as he could carry, fastened them into his leather bag, and returned to his hiding place near Sulki's home. In the same moment he settled on the floor, Bataar and Sulki emerged, turned their backs, and set off on their journey. Mekki followed them, for good or ill.

'Where is your horse?' asked Sulki.

'Me not ride good' said Bataar. 'Too many flat horses.'

'Well, I'm not waiting around for you to catch up. If you want to travel with me you will keep up with my pace or be left behind for the ravens to feast on your belly.'

'But Captain Ulfred said you not want to be dead?' said Bataar before scrunching his eyes in concentration. 'He say... he say... *you must keep him safe and not make him dead, Bataar. He not a warrior and will die.*'

'Then it seems the Great Khan has spoken once more and I have no choice. Come, we have a long journey ahead of us.'

Sulki mounted his bay horse and gave a gentle kick with his heel. Bataar slung an enormous knapsack over his shoulders and took the first of many giant steps towards his brother. Nobody was there to say goodbye, as is often the case with convicted criminals setting off on a journey of redemption.

It occurred to Sulki that he must be the instigator of any conversation, no matter how stunted it may prove to be. There is a natural balance between the amount of silence one can handle when travelling with a solitary companion and the time spent bouncing thoughts around one's own head. When that head belongs to a narcissist with a superiority complex, the contractions between outbursts are significantly reduced.

'What happened to you to make you so stupid?' asked Sulki. 'Were you dropped on your head as a child?'

'Yes' said Bataar honestly.

'Oh' said Sulki. 'Did it hurt?'

'I not remember.'

'Right... right' said Sulki, already close to retreating into his own head for the day. 'So what is it you do, exactly? For the nation, I mean.'

'I push stones for Captain Padding. He nice man.'

'Marvellous!' said Sulki, misjudging the excitement in his tone a little. 'Enjoy it, do you?'

Bataar's forehead concertinaed in concentration. 'Yes. It help Great Khan. Bataar... *enjoys* helping.'

'*I* enjoy helping' corrected Sulki.

'Good. We same then.'

'No, no. I mean you should say *I* enjoy helping.'

'I confused. Why you say same thing two times?'

Sulki sighed. 'For the moment I'm going to assume you can understand speech better than you can execute it...'

'Ah, I good at executing.' Bataar grinned a little maniacally, revealing large brown teeth that pointed in all directions. 'It is best word I know. When I little boy Captain Neknik said I could be best executing man in horde if I walk hard. Me not know why walking help but I not clever like Captain Neknik.'

Sulki stared at the horizon for a moment. 'Work!' He said at last. 'You could be the best executioner in the horde if you *work* hard.'

'That good advice too' said Bataar.

'This is going to be a long ride' thought Sulki aloud.

'I walk' said Bataar.

'Yes, Bataar. You will walk hard, I am sure.'

CHAPTER SIXTEEN

'Here we are, gentleman' said Tsensible, opening a plain, narrow door at the end of a dimly lit corridor. 'I trust this will meet your requirements.'

Jochi stepped inside first. 'Oh bugger!'

'What is it?' asked Tsensible, afraid that some detail had been missed. 'Are the trousers too yellow? Are your beds not to your liking? I'm afraid I must confess Captain Snu Zhi has limited knowledge on the bedroom needs of your people.'

'I should hope so!' said Okatai, blushing slightly.

'Oh my! I didn't mean... I meant, well, other needs. Furniture and so on.'

'There are three beds' said Jochi.

'Of course there... oh bugger' said Okatai.

'Ah.'

'Indeed.'

'I'm going to find him' said Jochi.

'I'm afraid that won't be possible' said Tsensible. 'The prefect expects your attendance in the War Chamber presently. It is not an invitation you should ignore if you wish to maintain the current distance from your chin to your toes.'

'What about Stan? He's probably still in the shop discussing the right way to boil a cabbage. We could go straight there and get him.'

Tsensible knew when to intervene in a problem and when to abstain. It was one of the reasons he had made it as far as his twenty-fourth birthday. 'I will go and get him. You two stay here and get ready for your audience with the prefect. If you move from this room I'll... I'll... I'll feed your friend to the pigs.'

Okatai nodded. 'We will stay, but hurry. He must be here for our audience. It is of the greatest importance that we see your ruler together as one.'

Tsensible closed the door and made his way briskly along the hallway. *One job* he thought. *One bloody job.*

As he made his way along the streets of Rhizun towards Ul-suh's shop he considered the punishment he might receive for losing such a prize for the prefect. If Roo Ling saw Stan's behaviour as an escape, then Tsensible was in almighty trouble. *I may be one head short now* he thought, *but it could very well be two by the end of the day.*

He stepped through an archway into the great garden that separated the commoners of the Mai Lu from the privileged few, slamming his knees straight into the nether regions of a scurrying little man as he did so.

'Watch where you're bloody well going!' cried the man as he crumpled to the floor. 'I have important business with the prefect and he will be hearing about this, I can assure you...' He looked up for the first time and scanned his assailant's fine clothes. His newly-crimson cheeks suddenly drained themselves of all colour. 'Sir' he said deferentially. 'My apologies, I thought you were a common beggar.'

'A beggar?' said Tsensible. 'Are you saying I look like a beggar?'

'No, no. Of course not, sir. Had I laid eyes on you before my disrespectful outburst I would, of course, have said you were... Oh, I don't know. Something better than a beggar I suppose.'

A figure darted from behind the shortest man in the city and sprinted off down the road.

'Stan!' shrieked Tsensible. 'It is I, Corporal Tsensible. Come back!'

'Corporal?' said Smahtarz incredulously. 'You're only a bloody corporal?'

'For now' said Tsensible and hurtled off after Stan.

Two mosquitoes hovered outside an open window.

'So he says to me' began one, '*all I did was have a quick look at his back.* Now, I told him not to go poking around those lizards, but you know what *that lot* are like. No respect for their elders.'

'Oh, I can imagine' said the second. 'It isn't like it was in our light. Things were brighter then, including us. Now things have gone a bit darker, the young ones think they can fly around as if they own the place and stick their proboscis in any bit of flesh they fancy. No refinement, that's their problem. It'll be the death of them, mark my words.'

'Oh, it will, Gladys. They'll find themselves impaling the wrong arm and before you know it they'll see the flat end of a Splatter.'

'You're right, Flo. You're absolutely right. One minute they'll be swanning around like a king on a thoroughbred and the next they'll be a flat red stain in a forest of hairs.'

'Just like Miriam' offered Flo.

'Oooh yes, just like Miriam' agreed Gladys. 'She was a case, wasn't she? No consideration for others. I heard she used to fly out in a light rain just to find an unsuspecting victim, and her with two hundred and forty-seven hungry mouths to look after. It's immoral.'

'It is, Gladys. It is. I heard she tried to bite off more than she could suck. Got trampled on by a goat, I heard.'

'Yes, I heard that too' agreed Gladys. 'Serves her right too, the little…'

'Now, now dear. I won't stand for any bad language while I'm here. It isn't proper.'

'I was going to say mosquito' offered Gladys weakly.

'Well that's fine then' said Flo. 'Now, where were we?'

'We were on our way to this shelter' said Gladys as they buzzed into the room.

'Lovely spot' said Flo.

'Yes, lovely spot' agreed Gladys.

'Look at all these bright colours. They remind me of the ones we used to get when the light was brighter. Remember them?'

'I do, Flo, I do' said Gladys, flying in for a closer look.

'Wait! There are Splatters here! Get out!'

Gladys heard the cry, but unfortunately for her, they were the last words she ever heard as a Splatter came down hard on her back.

Bugger this, thought Flo and zipped back out of the window.

'Where are these clothes we're supposed to wear?' asked Jochi, slapping an itch from his arm.

'I fear these may be them' said Okatai, raising up a vivid pair of yellow trousers. 'The Jin are a little more flamboyant than I expected.'

'Well I'm not wearing this' said Jochi, delicately picking up a lilac waistband between two fingers as if it would bite his arm off. 'What's wrong with good old browns and greens? Are they expecting to be ambushed by a battalion of easily distracted children?'

'Unfortunately, as you well know, we have no choice. Dressing like a rainbow is a trial we must endure if we are to learn their secrets. Keep our orders to the forefront of your thinking, young Jochi. It is the only way we will defeat them and their petty games.'

'I'm not sure they're playing, Okatai. Look at what Tsensible is wearing, I think they dress this way on purpose.'

'Either way, we must co-operate. Hold your nose, grit your teeth, and slip quietly into that sky blue shirt. It is for the good of the nation.'

'It had better be' said Jochi. 'If my dear departed father could see me now I'd be whipped from one end of the empire to the other.'

'I told you, no family talk while we're on this mission' snapped Okatai.

'You said nothing of the sort' said Jochi. 'You told us nothing except to call you Okatai and keep our wits about us. If you're going to add rules in as we go then may I suggest you get them all out in the open before we break any unspoken ones on the correct way to address a chicken.'

'I'm sure I was quite clear. Family is not to be mentioned again, under any circumstances.'

Okatai cursed his slip. He had been full of tact and subtlety since setting off from the horde but these Jin people had unhinged him slightly.

'How do I look' he said, changing the subject.

'Like a summer's dawn, but not in a good way' said Jochi honestly. 'How about me?'

'You would be well hidden in a trough of gems. Also not in a good way.'

The two men lay down on their beds and sighed. Jochi turned to Okatai. 'Do you realise we may well be displaying the least Mongol-like behaviour in the history of our nation?'

'We have been doing that since the day we left' said Okatai. 'The clothes are just a bonus.'

Okatai leapt suddenly from his bed and drew a dagger from his belt. Tsensible stepped into the room, took in the scene, and quickly made a choice between commenting on the Mongols' clothing and removing the dagger that pointed at his nose. He chose the dagger.

'Captain Okatai, please' he said, raising two open palms in placation. 'There is no need to be anxious while you are here; your safety is my most pressing priority. I must, however, kindly request you leave your weapons here while you meet with the prefect. He is rather against the idea of having enemy blades within an arm's length of his ribs. In any case, I have done you a great favour and captured, I mean *returned*, Stan to you.'

'I thought we were to be unarmed?' whispered Jochi.

'Not now' said Okatai.

Stan stepped through the doorway. 'Nice of you to abandon me in a strange city. I nearly drowned in tomato juice.'

'Stan!' called Jochi, jumping out of his bed and clasping his friend's shoulder. 'What happened to you?' He sniffed the air tentatively before lifting one of Stan's hands to his nose. 'Looks like it was more than tomato juice. What is that terrible smell?'

'Let's not squabble over the details' said Tsensible, keen to keep the identification of the liquids dripping from Stan's fingers a mystery. 'What's important here is that Stan bathes quickly and dresses for our meeting. It is not advisable to keep Roo Ling waiting. That's his job.'

'A bath?' cried Stan. 'Don't you try and impose your strange ways on me. I'm a member of the Great Horde, not some common sheep. I do not bathe.'

'Fine' said Tsensible. 'How about just a quick wash to get the worst of the slime off you? Once you change into your new clothes I'm sure we'll hardly notice the pungency.'

Stan looked at Jochi and Okatai properly for the first time. 'Lord of the Sky! You two look ridiculous. I'm not lowering myself to such fancies.'

'But you must all be present at the meeting. It is vital' said Tsensible desperately.

'Then you will agree that my presence is more important than my attire' said Stan.

Tsensible stiffened. 'It is important for us to respect your traditions. I will allow you to wear your traditional clothing, but on one condition. You will change into Jochi's old clothes. They do not come with such an accompanying stench.'

'But he's half my size.'

'Then breathe in, or wear the finery we have so graciously prepared for you. That is your choice to make.'

'Fine. Jochi, hand me your pants.'

CHAPTER SEVENTEEN

A tired looking guard looked up wearily at the approaching group. *More work* he thought drearily. He was caught in the no man's land between having an easy, well-paid job and having one that allowed his day to pass faster than a daydreaming elephant. The upshot was that he spent his day grumbling about everything, mostly to himself.

'We are here to see the prefect' announced Corporal Tsensible. 'Please tell him we have arrived.'

'Who is *we*?' asked the guard.

'Tsensible of the Watch' replied the corporal who wasn't an officer.

'And your friends?'

Tsensible tilted his head in incredulity. 'They are Madame Floaty's Butterfly Ballerinas.'

'All right, no need to get all silly about it' said the guard. 'One can't be too careful these days.'

'And what is so special about *these days*?' asked Tsensible.

The guard rankled. 'Well, you know. *These days* are always a cause for discretion. Mustn't let just anybody into the War Chamber.'

'You're quite right, of course. Tell me, what are your exact orders concerning visitors to the War Chamber today?'

'I am not to let anybody into the War Chamber' said the guard monotonously.

'Unless...?' coaxed Tsensible.

'Unless they are Corporal Tsensible and three filthy Mongrels.'

Tsensible shivered at the mention of his rank. 'Do not show such discourtesy!' he snapped, scrabbling to deflect from the disclosure. 'They are honourable soldiers of the Great Mongol Horde. To refer to them as anything else is to dishonour their traditions. I will not stand for it.'

'Right you are, Corporal. Wait here' said the guard, prising the large door open and slinking through the gap.

He reappeared a moment later. 'Roo Ling, prefect of all Rhizun, Lord of blah blah, etc., etc., will see you now.'

The three Mongols followed Tsensible through the door and into a serious-looking room that could only be described as *heavy*. Everything inside was on a grand scale, from the enormous stone steps leading up to the central table to the metal braces whose sole purpose appeared to be the storage of thick crystal goblets. What little light there was centred on the table, at the far side of which stood Roo Ling, prefect of all Rhizun etc., etc., and his omnipresent aide, Ettiket.

'Welcome, gentlemen. Please, sit. We have much to discuss.'

Okatai sat across from Roo Ling, with Stan on his right and Jochi to his left. Tsensible sat diplomatically between the two groups.

'I see you declined our generous offer of clothing' said Roo Ling to Stan. 'Does all of your army's attire fit so snugly?'

Stan stood up to reply, stretching Jochi's leather breastplate further. Several stitches snapped, opening up the entirety of his right side and causing the leather to point at a jaunty and unflattering angle.

'This is your army, is it?' asked Roo Ling, raising an eyebrow to Okatai. 'I am white with fear.'

'Forgive us, prefect...' began Okatai.

'*Master* is the correct title, captain. Please do me the courtesy of using it' interrupted Roo Ling.

'...master' continued Okatai, nodding respectfully, if a little reluctantly. 'There are nuances to your customs that are unfamiliar to us. One of these is the requirement to change clothing with the wind. Stan here had a need to change his and must make do with Jochi's for the moment.'

'Was the fine clothing we offered unsuitable?'

'It's too bright. I like a good brown, master' interjected Stan. 'It suits me.'

'It suits you?' said Roo Ling, taken aback by the boldness with which he was being addressed by a mere... whatever he was. 'Name and rank, soldier' he demanded.

'I am Stan, master. My rank is...' he cast a desperate look to Okatai.

'He is a cog in the future of our nation' said Okatai.

'He is?' said Jochi.

'I am?' said Stan.

'If I may be so curt as to explain our motives for arriving in your fine city unannounced?' said Okatai in a questioning tone.

'You may not' answered Roo Ling. 'You are here in my War Chamber at my request, not the other way around. I had heard you Mongols were emphatic to a fault when it came to honour and respect, yet it seems I may have been misled. Let it be recorded that I am to show grace beyond requirement in allowing your indiscretion to pass without consequence. Rest assured I will not be so merciful should you choose to test me further. Now, Stan, do you consider it acceptable to arrive at an audience with the prefect of the greatest city of the Jin empire in ill-fitting and manifestly displeasing clothes?'

'I do, master' replied Stan.

'You *do*?' said Okatai incredulously before gathering his wits. 'Stan, please! Perhaps you should leave the diplomacy to those of us who are more familiar with its finer distinctions.'

'Captain Okatai!' barked Roo Ling, banging a fist on the table and standing up. 'You have shown no such knowledge thus far. Your underling has, at least, shown the courage to answer my question honestly. If you profess to understand the machinations of diplomacy then you will recognise the need to use honesty in place of deception from time to time.

You may be a captain of your army, but while you are a guest in my house I will judge for myself who among you are worthy of my time and who are not. Stan, please take your captain's seat at the centre. I would rather deal with an honest dogsbody than a devious officer.'

'It is the prefect's wish' said Okatai stoically, shuffling across to allow Stan to take his place.

'I'm not sure I'm the right man for the job, to be honest' said Stan. 'Okatai knows your ways better than I.'

'Precisely' said Roo Ling. 'Now, where were we? Ah yes, your clothes. Tell me, Stan, why is it that you prefer heavy, dull leather to our fine silks?'

'Well, you can't rub mutton grease from your hands on fancy silk, can you?'

'No, I suppose not. That's the first reason that springs to mind, is it? Not protection from attack? How very interesting.' He turned to Ettiket and whispered. 'This man is the key. Keep him safe.'

Jochi nudged Stan gently. 'Good luck, friend. You're going to need it.'

'Thanks for your unwavering support' said the whitening face of Stan.

'I want to show you all something' announced Roo Ling. 'There are many reasons why we should be wary of each other, not least of which is the potential for one of our empires to destroy the other. I, for one, am not ready to move on to the next life just yet and so I shall do all I can to remove that option from our futures. Your Khan may have the numbers to defeat the Jin army on open ground but, as I am sure you have seen, my city is self-sustaining. We grow our own food, enough to feed ourselves continuously, so your great leader's siege tactics will not work on us.' He stroked his hair thoughtfully as if considering his next move. 'Stan' he said at last. 'What would you do if you were the great Genghis Khan?'

Every member of the Mongol Horde, including Stan and Jochi, had considered such a question, despite its daunting nature. For anyone but Genghis, being the Great Khan would mean a drastic recalculation of their life expectancy, but even a man drowning in honey is tempted to lick his fingers once in a while.

'I would besiege the city, master.'

'Have I not already shown how futile that method would prove to be?'

'No. You have explained how you can prevent your people from starving. That is only one possible method of victory in siege warfare.'

'Then what else would you have your army do?'

'I would sling sheep heads over the walls, master.'

'Would you, indeed? And does every idea you have involve sheep?'

'No.'

'Tell me, how would sheeps' heads help you defeat such a robust city?'

'If done with enough venom, and perhaps a little slurry, we would spread disease throughout the city. The first target would be the slums, where disease spreads more quickly and where the victims are more numerous.'

Roo Ling stared at the overweight Mongol in grubby clothes that jutted from his chest and wondered at the unpredictability of fortune.

'Do you consider yourself an honest man?' he asked.

'Yes, master.'

'Then I have something to show you. Come here.'

Roo Ling pulled an enormous sheath of parchment from a hidden gap below the large, stone table and rolled it out in front of him. It showed a birds-eye view of Rhizun in such detail as to send Stan's mind into a spin. He had never seen anything so exquisite before, and he was a man who had watched Tishock stitch her husband's face into a jockstrap.

'The regiments please, Ettiket.'

Ettiket disappeared into a shadowy corner, returning with a fistful of coloured stone discs. He poured them out onto the flat surface and slunk back to his perennial place at his master's side.

'Each of these discs represents a hundred men or a single catapult' said Roo Ling. 'These green ones are the archers, the red ones are heavy ballistics and the blue ones are foot soldiers.' He placed about a third of them at various points around the city. As you can see, we have a substantial army, but that is nothing in comparison to our estimations of the Great Horde.' He arranged the remaining discs outside the city walls. 'Here is your army; archers, ballistics, cavalry, and infantry. Far superior numbers than my great army. So why, you may wonder, am I not preparing my people for a desperate war we have no hope of winning?'

After a moment or two, Stan realised the question was not rhetorical.

'Because you can sustain your people for longer than we can feed ours.'

'And the diseased sheep...?'

'You would only have to remove the catapults, master.'

'That's enough' snapped Okatai. 'We did not come here to help you in the destruction of our nation. What is your move here, Roo Ling? Are you recruiting us to spy on our own people, or have you something worth negotiating for?'

'Spies are a resource I have in abundance. Captain Hie Ding is the busiest man in the city, I can assure you of that. My goal here is peace, Okatai. Peace between our two great empires. Our strengths negate each other like worms in manure, so we must find a better way to exist together.'

'You sound concerned, master. It is most unlike a Jin prefect to be so open with his enemy.'

'And it is uncommon for a Mongol to speak our tongue, yet here we are, holding a competent discourse on the benefits of sheep entrails. Let me be absolutely clear; I have no need to fear your army. There are many roads of opportunity ahead of me, and if you do not cede to my will on this one I will simply choose another. This road, at least, ends at your survival.'

'You said there would be a feast' said Stan. 'My stomach thinks my throat's been cut.'

'It may be if you keep that up' said Okatai quietly.

'What road did you have in mind?' asked Jochi, keen not to be left behind as the conversation veered from one direction to another.

'Stan is correct, of course' said Roo Ling. 'Let us not travel too far so soon. Ettiket, inform Captain Merang we will be ready shortly.'

Etikket slid into the darkness and disappeared.

'Now, gentlemen, before we eat I must keep my promise. Stan here has stolen my thunder a little, but nevertheless I will reveal our greatest weakness to you, our hated enemy. No offence.'

'None taken' said Jochi, earning himself a kick under the table from Okatai.

'If time was the battle we would defeat you with ease; that much is clear to us. We have the resources to wait out a siege of such lengths you could count every bump of every stone in our walls and still have time for tea. Stan's observation is significant, however. There are many ways to skin a pig, and it is likely you have techniques to mitigate against our perfect patience. Equally, if our confrontations were to take place on the open steppes you have the numbers and the ammunition to make such scything wounds in our army as to send us blubbering back to our mothers with our thumbs in our mouths.' He slid a red disc back and forth on the map distractedly. 'Our failure to defeat you, however, is not a guaranteed precursor to your success. You are yet to find a way through our walls, so it is reasonable to assume that you have considered Rhizun a defence too far in your rampage across the land. I am here to propose a compromise. One that will lead to the betterment of both of our great peoples.'

'Then you are already defeated' said Okatai. 'You would not offer such a thing if there was a tactic you trusted enough to implement.'

The prefect stood up and rounded the table to loom over the seated Okatai. 'You are a pure Mongol' he said, placing his hand firmly onto Okatai's shoulder. 'Never let it be said you wavered from your people in times of great peril.'

Roo Ling turned on a heel and strolled around the room with an exaggeratedly slow gait, clasping his hands behind his back. 'I lead a great city, captain. Possibly the greatest in the entire Jin empire. We produce the finest turnips in the land and trade them with those neighbours who do not offer decapitation services in return. We grow flowers of such prettiness that grown men must hide the saltwater they coax from their eyes. The education of our young is peerless and the invention it spawns is unquantifiably valuable to us. We hold The Tests each spring to sharpen the minds of our greatest thinkers. I have advisors who counsel me on everything from the management of the latrines to the positioning of the parchment on my desk. We are living in the future while you gurgle in the slime of the past. My people move forward with every rise of the sun. If our world is to be prosperous and happy then we must work together to live beside each other in harmony, not hostility.'

'Bugger that' said Okatai, standing to meet Roo Ling's eye. 'All you have listed are your strengths. If the Great Horde was to cede to your concept of the future then we will have surrendered our advantage to yours. We are the finest warriors in the world, a great swarming mass that will destroy Rhizun and all within her walls at a time of our choosing, should we decide to do so.'

'This is your attempt at diplomacy, is it?' asked Roo Ling, glad to have hit a nerve at last. 'Within Rhizun, we like to be a little less crass. We prefer to talk and debate, not stalk and cremate. I was under the impression you came here with more to offer than a Mongolian chest-puffing. Where is your love of language, of nuance and peace?'

Okatai sagged a little, gazing past Roo Ling at the dark, grey wall.

'Please forgive our captain, master' said Stan, startling Okatai from his reverie. 'We have travelled long and hard to pass through the walls of this great city with an offer of friendship and we are all in need of rest. Perhaps we could continue our discussion after we have refreshed ourselves with food and sleep?'

'Now listen here!' said Okatai instinctively, before gathering his wits. 'Ah, yes. Indeed. Forgive my regression to our old ways, master. They are hard shackles to splinter and the forging of a new relationship between our peoples will require great strength of mind.'

'That's more like it' said Roo Ling cheerfully. 'Come, let us feast.'

CHAPTER EIGHTEEN

'Mud' said Bataar.

'Mud?' parroted Sulki.

'Mud.'

'You may have somehow, inexplicably, misunderstood the extraordinarily simple question' said Sulki. 'I asked what your favourite colour was.'

This was the depth to which Sulki had sunk to find some conversational traction.

'Mud best colour' said Bataar.

'Of course it is.'

Sulki considered not asking his next question, but the intermittent silence of the last few hours only served to make them longer and any distraction was welcomed, relatively speaking.

'Why is *mud* your favourite colour?'

'It colour of floor when I walk hard at grinding stones. I look at mud for all day.'

'I see' said Sulki, reluctantly acknowledging Bataar's unique logic.

'My favourite colour is black' said Sulki. 'It can hide the deepest of secrets yet exaggerate the brightest of hues.'

'Black' said Bataar.

'Right, well that's that then.'

They trudged on slowly along the undulating steppes, with Sulki suffocating in the silence once more and Bataar staring straight ahead in neutral contentment.

'There' said Sulki at last. 'Those woods will give us cover for tonight. Come, we should reach them before the light fades.'

Mekki rubbed his ankle again. He was grateful that the pain was now only noticeable while he walked, but less so that his time was filled with such an activity. He cursed his past self again for not stealing a horse as he left. In the countless days of travelling he had hidden in bushes, lain flat against the ground in long grass, pressed himself against rocky outcrops, and climbed several trees to ensure his quarry did not sight him. The *countless days* were, in fact, very countable indeed. He had been sneaking around the steppes for just two days, but the effort required to make it through each one had stretched his perception out considerably. Time is a fair-weather friend, and the meteorological systems in Mekki's consciousness were like a hurricane smashing through floodwaters. Had he been asked, he may have said he had been on their trail for a month, but as it was he had done well to keep them within his reach and without their knowledge.

He peered through the swaying branches at the figures below him as they continued their trek through the woods and out of sight. It was still early but the light was already fading in the gloom of the forest and Mekki hoped, as he always did, that they would stop soon for the night. He clambered down gingerly from his perch, steadied himself on the trunk of the tree, and set off in the same direction. After a few minutes, he saw the flickering orange of a campfire. He climbed again then, strapped himself between a thick branch and the main trunk, and settled down for the night.

Or at least, that was the plan.

Captain Sulki tethered his horse to a sturdy, low hanging branch, untied his bag, and slumped to the floor, fatigued. He ripped some leaves from a nearby plant and stuffed them into his starved mouth. Bataar arrived a short time later, showing no signs of exertion.

'That was nice walk' said Bataar, still standing.

Sulki opened one eye and looked up at his travelling companion. 'Nice? We've just...' He paused, shook his head, closed his eye, and fell asleep.

Bataar circled him and wandered off into the woods. All around him were the sounds of forest life; birds were chirping and leaves were rustling with the movement of small creatures in the undergrowth. He didn't notice any of these things, but then Bataar's senses were not compatible with such subtleties. He did, however, notice the weighted net that landed on his back, followed a moment later by a man.

'That not nice' said Bataar, utterly unfazed. 'Me at end of long walk and you heavy.'

'And why, one might ask, are you walking so long?' said the man.

'To be good at *executing*' said Bataar, happy to be able to use his best word again.

'I could show you a thing or two about that' said the man, now doubting his decision to jump. 'I am something of an expert when it comes to that line of work.'

'If you help me why you on my back?' asked Bataar.

Lo-Ki wracked his brain, balanced his options, and came up with a plan. 'I was watching you from the trees and thought to myself *now there's a man who would make a good executioner. Perhaps I'll help him*. And here I am, helping.'

'It help if you not on my back' said Bataar. 'Take net too.'

Lo-Ki dropped silently to the floor and, rather reluctantly, removed the net from around Bataar.

'There' he said. 'Now I can help you. The first thing to remember is to always be aware of your surroundings. I could have been a dangerous assassin and you would be dead by now.'

'I not afraid of donkeys' said Bataar. 'I make them flat.'

'An *assassin* is someone who is paid to kill men' said Lo-Ki.

'Are you ass ass?'

'Details, details' said Lo-Ki, waving a dismissive hand. 'Tell me why you are here so I can help you.'

'I here because I walk long way with Captain Sulki.'

'*The* Captain Sulki?' asked Lo-Ki with false deference.

'No. He just Captain Sulki.'

'Right. Well, I would very much like to meet him. Will you take me to him?'

'He asleep.'

'Is he, indeed? How fortuna... disappointing. Then I will leave you to your wander and perhaps sleep myself while there is shelter above me.'

Bataar trampled on through the forest, forgetting the man almost immediately. The juxtaposition of the man's presence in the forest and his unexplained motivation was not a notion that came within a hundred paces of Bataar's consciousness.

Lo-Ki climbed back up his tree and watched Bataar crush his way through the woodland detritus until he was out of sight. He tightened the strap of his bag and began crisscrossing through the forest canopy. He hadn't gone far when he heard the unmistakably spluttering noise of a middle-aged man in the deepest of sleeps. He clambered down to the floor, drew his dagger, and crept up to the sleeping captain.

'Good afternoon' he whispered threateningly into Sulki's ear. 'Don't move, I have a blade at your neck and a nervous disposition. I wouldn't want to accidentally slit anything.'

Sulki's head twitched in the uniquely pre-snore way before letting out a guttural din of incompetent laziness.

'Oh, for Khan's sake' muttered Lo-Ki. He loved a good whisper, he considered it his signature move and it had a way of cranking up the menace levels a notch or two. He reluctantly raised his voice a little.

'Good afternoon! Don't mo...'

'Schnggghhuhuhumff' said Sulki's snore.

Bugger this, thought Lo-Ki, and nicked the captain's cheek.

Nothing.

'Now listen here, Sulki! I'm a bloody good assassin, but I can't just walk up and slit your throat. There needs to be a little showmanship, not just a knife in the shadows. Come on, play along a bit!'

Nothing.

Lo-Ki hauled Sulki up and leant him against the tree stump. He gave him a slap. Then a harder one.

Nothing.

Not even a snore.

His eyes darted around the small camp, searching for something flat and hard to use on the captain's head. He stopped suddenly and stared at a long-forgotten tool of his trade. He rubbed the leaf between his gloved fingers and raised them to his nose.

'Chuanspu' he whispered aloud. 'Well, that's one way to get the job done.' He prised Sulki's jaw open and saw the remnants of his leafy meal.

He rummaged through Sulki's bag, picked out a small metal brooch with a sheep's head design, and stuffed it into his inside pocket. He tilted the corpse's head a little and poked his fingers around the mouth and cheeks to give a suggestion of perimortem anguish before stepping back to study his work.

Now for Bataar, he thought.

'Thank the Great Khan I've found you!' called Lo-Ki as he stepped animatedly through a thicket of ferns. 'There has been a great tragedy at your camp, come!'

Bataar's expression didn't change. His array of facial expressions was much the same as those of a cliff face. 'Is captain dead?'

'He was still alive when I left him, but he has ingested... eaten a poisonous plant and needs help soon if he is to survive.'

Bataar pushed past Lo-Ki and stomped on towards the camp. Lo-Ki skipped along behind him.

'There is only one thing that can save him now' said Lo-Ki as they made their way through the irregular terrain. 'I can make an antidote but I need your help.'

'You say help me be good *executioner*, not help fix men' said Bataar. 'I fix captain then you help me.'

'Yes, yes! That is exactly what we will do. I will take you to the greatest executioner in the nation when we have *fixed* the captain.'

'What me do?'

'I need you to chew some of the plant that may have cost dear Captain Sulki his life, but do not swallow. That was his mistake – it will not be ours too.'

As they arrived at the camp Bataar stared at the lifeless body propped against the tree.

'He dead.'

'Not yet' said Lo-ki. 'He is quite alive, I can assure you. It is just a deep sleep. If we do not act now, however, then he will be dead as surely as the moon chases the sun. Here, chew these and make them as moist as possible. Do not swallow!'

Bataar took the bunch of leaves and stuffed them into his mouth unquestioningly. He chewed the leaves down until they were a sodden lump and pulled the dripping ball from his mouth, spitting out the residue energetically.

Lo-ki stared in disbelief.

'Now fix!' said Bataar.

Lo-Ki took the green lump and looked at it for signs of a mistake. He didn't make mistakes, though. He made death. He sniffed it, then wished he hadn't.

'Fix!'

The rate at which nothing happened was balanced perfectly by the activity in Lo-Ki's brain. He needed a plan. Another one. Better than his last effort or it may end up as his *last* effort.

Bataar's mind was working at an altogether different speed, but when consequence and probability are not involved in the process, sometimes the slow ones get there first. He grabbed Lo-Ki by the neck with one hand, pulled the green slime from Lo-Ki's hand with the other, and relocated it into the assassin's throat.

'You chew. Fix captain.'

Lo-Ki thrashed wildly, lashing out pointlessly at his soon-to-be killer. Bataar closed the assassin's mouth and scanned the area casually as if out on a spring walk.

Lo-Ki had one last plan. He stopped moving and sagged his head. After a moment he used what energy he had left to prise open one eye and take in his killer. Bataar hadn't noticed, as if ending the life of the greatest killer in a nation of warriors was no more than an itch on his arm.

The second best executioner in Genghis' Great Horde closed his eyes for the last time and sagged a little further.

Bataar turned back to Lo-Ki, then craned his neck to see past him to a figure emerging from behind a tree.

'Mekki' stated Bataar, pointing.

'Hello, Bataar. I was just about to step in and help, but it seems my timing is a little off.'

'Not off. Bad' said Bataar. 'Food off.'

'Yes, right. Well, it seems you have killed this sneaky little man here. That's one less thing to worry about, I suppose.'

'Not kill. He making green to help captain.'

'I'm afraid not' said Mekki, nudging Sulki's jaw. 'Both men are dead, don't let that get you down. They weren't good people.'

Bataar cast what would have been a doleful look at the two corpses, had he the ability to either feel or express such a complex emotion. As it was he simply stared.

'Let's check his pockets' said Mekki. 'A man like that is sure to carry some interesting items. Pass his bag over, Sulki's too.'

Mekki pulled the bag from Lo-Ki's back, took Sulki's from Bataar, and settled himself on the floor. The unexpected contents did not surprise Bataar, but then surprise was an emotion felt more often by mountains than this enormity of a man. It did, however, surprise Mekki. It surprised him a lot. He pulled out one of the ravens and fastened the sheep's head brooch to its leg. 'Hold this' he said to Bataar, passing over the bird.

He took out ink, parchment, and reed pen from the assassin's bag and stared at them thoughtfully. 'A letter is expected' he said.

'Bataar not good at letters. Big rocks better.'

'I'm not much of a writer myself' admitted Mekki.

He drew a crude picture of a man with a selection of weapons at his feet. In place of the eyes, Mekki scratched two 'X' shapes. He drew another man lying next to him with a bird pecking at the belly.

'That should be clear enough' he said. 'I don't know who sent him, but they will soon know his fate, and that of Captain Sulki.'

Mekki tied the note to the raven's other leg, unstrapped its wings, and threw it into the air. The bird darted through the gaps in the trees and disappeared. He reached back into Lo-Ki's bag, being careful not to loosen the ties on the remaining raven. He pulled out an old, torn scroll and studied it.

'Well bugger me' he exclaimed to the woods. 'It seems there is a prince among the pigs.'

'Then he farmer. Or cook' said Bataar. 'Not prince. Prince is fancy man.'

'Forget I said anything' said Mekki, stuffing the scroll into his pocket and looking about for a distraction.

Tradition dictated that the bodies of the recently deceased should be taken to the highest point in sight and left there in the open for the Lord of the Sky. Unfortunately for Lo-Ki and Sulki, the highest point around was underneath a thick forest canopy and even the Lord of the Sky would struggle to spot them before the rodents did. Bataar lifted both men - one under each arm - and made the journey to the top of a gentle hill, laying them out flat beside each other. He turned back to their camp without ceremony.

'We should rest' said Mekki as Bataar returned. 'We have a long journey ahead of us.'

'Rest not make walk shorter.'

'No, but we are not all made like you, Bataar. I must rest my ankle.'

'Bataar carry you to edge of Rhizun. Mekki sleep on back. Sulki horse set free. Easy.'

Mekki played out the range of scenarios in his mind. There was none he would choose voluntarily, but he was long past the point where he was in control of his own fate. He came up with something approaching a plan. It certainly gave him a chance to survive long enough to learn if it was the right one.

'Agreed. We will arrive as one.'

CHAPTER NINETEEN

Jin Empire

The imperial convoy found the gentlest of paths through the fluvial valleys of the Jin empire with the practise of centuries. The chief navigator had also been assigned a personal motivator from the Emperor's own *Special Persuasion* team, which was quite conducive to completing the journey with near-perfect efficiency. This combination resulted in a marginal improvement in the Emperor's mood, though not enough to stop him complaining incessantly about the poor suspension of his carriage.

There were five capitals in the Jin empire and Emperor Aizong had been positioned in Kow Tow, the closest of them to Rhizun, when Roo Ling's letter had been delivered. An unexpectedly early arrival was precisely the sort of action that pleased the emperor. Expected arrivals yield expected results, but when those you rule think they have another couple of days to sweep the poor people from the streets and the rats from the kitchen then the experience is an altogether more realistic one.

'When will this jarring hell be over?' asked Aizong of his aide.

'I expect a sighting of the city walls in no more than two days' time, your Highness' said Bow Lo.

'Instruct the...' said Aizong before trailing off in ignorance. 'What propels this carriage?'

'Horses and wheels, oh Imperial Majesty.'

'Right, then instruct the horses and wheels to move a little faster. The earlier we arrive the more reality we will see.'

Bow Lo nodded deferentially. 'I will see to it that the oscillating joints of your Highness will be kept as steady as your most honourable reign.'

Aizong sighed. He was the most powerful man for as far as the eye could see, and often further, yet he could no more de-fluff his aide's speech than he could push back the wind. Still, Bow Lo was exceptionally good at his job and people like him were hard to find, particularly when the life expectancy of one of his aides was more comparable to the waxing of the moon than the frequency of the vernal equinox. Bow Lo had been at his side for almost a year now, a new record.

The movement of the carriage settled in tandem with the whipping noise coming from ahead. Bow Lo returned.

'I trust that your Imperial Highness will find the rest of the journey more comfortable.'

'Never trust' said Aizong. Bow Lo wasn't sure what that was supposed to mean, but then he rarely did. It wasn't his job to understand. Had he been in a position to reply to the question frankly, Bow Lo would have said that his job was entirely focused on keeping a lid on the emperor's volatility and no more. The reputation of Aizong's temper was based entirely on conjecture, however, since nobody had allowed it to bubble to the fore. It had been reasonably assumed that any emperor currently holding the position did not get there by making the nicest cakes. There was usually a little more fratricide, regicide, and any manner of -cides involved in the process.

'I will take your gracious advice and hold it close to my mind at all times, oh Imperial Majesty' said Bow Lo.

'You have no idea why I said that, have you?' said Aizong.

'But of course, your Highness' said Bow Lo's nervous system while the rest of him scrabbled for a strategy that would keep his limbs connected.

'And…?'

'And… and I am humbled that one so wise as your Imperial Highness would deem me a suitable vessel for your knowledge.'

'Nonsense! Step out of the subservient shadows, Bow.'

'Your Majesty was offering sage advice to this humble servant, for which he is eternally grateful, on the best approach to take when dealing with the frailties of men.'

'So you trust my advice?' asked Aizong.

Bow Lo's head swam. With just a few well-chosen words the emperor had tangled him up into an inescapable web. His brain hijacked all bodily systems as the frantic chaos of his internal struggles mirrored the petrification of his physical self. Aizong watched on, amused.

'Aha!' he said at last. 'I will forever hold your advice close when dealing with men of the empire. Your Highness is not comparable to those lesser beings. You are the chosen one, an infallible guide, sentience in human form, a pure celestial light among us mere mortals. You can be trusted just as the sun can be relied upon to lighten our days, our wise and peerless Majesty.'

Aizong clapped his hands slowly. 'That was almost impressive.'

'Oh, thank you' said Bow, caught off guard for a moment by the uncharacteristic compliment.

'Now, get out of my sight. Is an emperor to starve for the want of an aide that can fetch a chicken leg?'

Bow Lo nodded and scurried off gratefully to find the imperial dinner.

CHAPTER TWENTY

'I'm as hungry as I was when we got here' said Jochi, flopping onto his bed with a thump.

'You should have tried some of the food then, shouldn't you?' said Stan. 'You missed out on a real experience.'

'An *experience* is not something I look for in a meal. All I need is a full belly and an absence of leaves on my plate. What do they have against meat anyway? I'm amazed they can stand upright on such minimal sustenance.'

'They have a saying here; *variety is the spice of life*, they say.'

'I don't want spice though, Stan. I want a sheep's leg dripping with grease. Wait, how do you know they have a saying?'

'One of the cooks told me.'

'Lord of the Sky, Stan. Is there anything you won't do for food? We're supposed to be diplomats, not recipe hunters.'

'If you seek the secrets of your enemy you should talk to the lowest rank' said Stan with pomp.

'Any other Jin proverbs you'd like to share?'

'That's one of mine, actually. Makes sense too. Nobody pays any attention to those without power. Tongues loosen more the nearer they are to wine, so who better to befriend than a lowly cook?'

'We haven't been here a day and you're already turning into one of them' said Jochi.

'That's no bad thing' said Okatai, stepping into the room. 'The more we think like them the more information we can gather.'

'I'm not sure we should be part of plotting their downfall' said Jochi. 'I mean, they seem like a nice bunch of people, all things considered.'

'You obviously haven't been attacked in the street by rotten fruit and a crazy dwarf.'

'Apart from that, though' said Jochi.

'Apart from that?' said Stan, raising his voice a fraction above a polite level. 'That's like saying we're a thoroughly pleasant horde, apart from the odd bit of pillaging and civic annihilation.'

'I just think we should learn more about them before we go razing their walls, that's all. They may be a useful ally.'

'For when?' asked Okatai. 'Can you imagine Genghis working with another nation? It's more likely the world is round.'

'Well, maybe they have a better way to approach the whole *war* thing' said Stan. 'We may learn something from them.'

Okatai rubbed the bridge of his nose before raising his eyes slowly to meet Stan's. 'That is the very reason we are here.'

'Ah yes. So it is' said Stan. 'So I was right then?'

'Only in the way a sheep would be right if they were asked to prove they couldn't talk. Now, let's get out of these ridiculous outfits. My chest is so itchy it thinks I have fleas.'

Okatai pulled his pale blue shirt over his head and threw it into a corner of the room, just as a knock came at the half-open door.

'Men!' called Tsensible as he strode into the room. 'I hope I'm not imposing?'

'Imposing? You're a full head shorter than me' said Jochi.

'Perhaps I chose the wrong word, I meant that I am sorry if my visit is badly timed. I have been asked to keep you entertained this evening and was hoping to show you some of the things we do to while away the darker hours in Rhizun.'

'I'd rather you didn't' said Stan, nudging Jochi mischievously. 'Can't we just play dice instead?'

'You play dice?' asked Tsensible, missing the innuendo. 'Marvellous! You must show me. It is my favourite pastime, though I'm sure there are different rules in your version. How many points does a pen score?'

'A pen?' asked Stan. 'There is no pen.'

'Then how do you defeat a double flower?'

'I think our version is a little more... *physical* than yours' said Jochi tactfully.

'Don't tell me you throw dice at each other!'

'Now hang on, we're not animals' said Stan.

'Gentlemen' said Okatai with his arms outstretched placatingly. 'I believe there has been a misunderstanding. Remember, men, that Tsensible here is not speaking his natural tongue. We must think before we attack.'

'That's the whole point of us being...' began Stan before a demonic glare from his captain stunted the sentence into surrender. 'I mean, yes. Of course. My apologies, corporal. Come, I will show you our game then you can show us yours.'

Stan bent down to his own, proper trousers that were still crumpled on the bed, and fished out his dice. He sat cross-legged in the centre of the floor and laid them out in a neat line. He gestured for Tsensible to join him.

'There are two different types of dice...'

'Die' said Tsensible as he sat down beside Stan.

Okatai raised a calming hand before Stan could react. 'He is correct, Stan. It is one die, two dice.'

'No it isn't' said Stan. 'I should know, I've lost enough money playing them.'

'Nevertheless, die is correct, though unimportant.'

Stan took a deep, compromising breath. 'So, there are two different types of dice... *die*; one for the military unit and one for the terrain. The units are a Horse, an Archer, a Sword, and three Foot Soldiers. The terrains are; a Hill, a Swamp, a Forest, and three Plains. Each player rolls two *dice* and the winner is determined by the symbols they roll. Two High Horses – that's when you roll Horses and Hills –

beats anything, for example, while a Foot Soldier in a Swamp is almost useless.'

'That sounds very similar to our game' said Tsensible, 'aside from the rules and the symbols, of course. Let's play.'

'How much?' asked Stan.

'How much what?' said Tsensible.

'For winning the game? You can't play dice without money.'

'Ah. I'd rather learn the rules first, if it's all the same with you.'

'Well, it isn't. Playing dice just for fun is like roasting a wild boar and then throwing it into a river.'

'I'm not sure that's a very good comparison' said Jochi. 'Just play him. It'll do you good.'

Stan drew in a deep breath, slowly and animatedly to ensure everyone in the room knew he wasn't happy about the idea but he was going along with it because he was a team player. 'Come on then, I'll start.'

He picked up the dice and rolled them onto the floor. A sword, a Horse, and two Forests showed on the upturned faces. Stan scooped them up. 'Now, your turn' he said to Tsensible.

The Jin watchman rolled the dice, noted the result, and turned to Stan to learn whether he had won or not. One glance at the Mongol's face was enough to tell him he had. 'So, a Double Archer on a Hill and a Plain beats a Sword, a Horse, and two Forests then?' said Tsensible innocently.

'Yes, yes' snapped Stan. 'Beginner's luck.'

'It all seems a little complicated. In Rhizun we have numbers for each symbol on the dice. Whoever rolls the highest total wins.'

'Where's the fun in that? I'd far rather beat you with an archer on a hill than a silly number.'

'Numbers are important here' said Tsensible. 'They are in everything we do.'

'Between your numbers and Okatai's letters we'll all be scribbling each other to death before the turn of the season' said Stan petulantly.

'Perhaps that is enough culture sharing for the moment' said Okatai. 'What else do you do to pass the time, corporal?'

'I will take you to the walls' he said at last. 'There are views there that would make an old warrior's heart soften.'

'Sounds like a riot' said Jochi.

'Oh no, the watchmen do not fight. They are there to alert the military captains of any unusual activity outside the city' said Tsensible.

'The wall. Great' said Okatai. 'Let's do that.'

'Marvellous' said Tsensible, grateful to have something to do. 'This way please, gentlemen.'

The Mongols were not used to these kinds of steps. They clambered up them like chickens on a roof until at last they reached a high path near the base of a watchtower. Jochi leant against the crenulated wall and peered over the edge.

'Stone the goats! It's higher than I imagined' he said, staggering backwards a pace.

'It is all part of our impenetrable defences' said Tsensible. 'It helps to keep our enemies without and our people safe.'

'So we're not enemies anymore?' asked Stan. 'This diplomacy nonsense is easier than I thought.'

'I wouldn't go that far' said Tsensible. 'You are here at the pleasure of the prefect. If he wanted your heads on a decorative spike in the walled garden you would be sliced at the neck and dressed in geraniums before you could blink.'

'Well that's comforting to know' said Jochi. 'I always said I'd like to go with flowers on my head.'

A figure approached them in the gloom.

'Announce yourself!' called Tsensible.

'Lah Fing of the Watch' came a voice.

'Hello again, watchman.'

'Giving our visiting dignitaries a grand tour, I see. Be sure to show them all the sights, now' said Lah Fing, winking out of habit, despite the dusky light.

'Perhaps we'll go this way' offered Tsensible, turning away from Lah Fing and towards the watchtower. 'Follow me. We may just catch the sun dipping below the hills. It is quite something to behold.'

The group headed through the tower and out onto an identical path. Tsensible walked briskly at the front, leading them through another two towers as the wall curved further to the west. The occidental sun had already disappeared when they stopped, a faint grey-yellow glow in the distance being the only clue as to its hiding place.

Tsensible sighed.

'My apologies, gentlemen. It seems I have timed our little tour rather badly.'

'Is it always this thrilling here?' asked Stan.

'Your intentions were honest, corporal' said Okatai in a friendly tone. 'I am sure we will have the opportunity to see it tomorrow. For now, we would like to rest. It has been a long day and we are weary.'

'Of course' said Tsensible. 'I will reflect on our day and prepare more entertainment for tomorrow.'

'*More* entertainment?' said Jochi. 'Now I won't sleep with the anticipation. What could be better than Rhizun Dice and a missed sunset?'

'Forgive Jochi' said Okatai. 'He is tired, as we all are, and will be more amiable with a good sleep behind him.'

'He is correct, despite his mocking tone' said Tsensible. 'This is no way to treat guests in this great city. Tomorrow will be a lavish feast of culture and merriment, I give you my oath. Come, I will see you to your quarters.'

The group headed back towards the centre of the city as the sky darkened above them. Flickering pockets of orange light appeared then danced in the distance.

'What are they?' asked Stan.

'The evening fires' said Tsensible. 'They help us find our way through the streets at night.'

A shadowy figure emerged from a laneway ahead of them, scuttling past and across to the opposite side of the street. A wall-mounted torch blossomed into life with a faint whooshing sound, casting shadows in the gloom.

'You people are crazy!' exclaimed Jochi. 'We'll burn to death in our beds!'

'It may surprise you to learn that we have already considered the risks' said Tsensible. 'Torches are only permitted when mounted on stone and can only be lit by those trained in Flame Management.'

'Training? To light a torch?' said Jochi. 'I'm bloody well right. You Jin *are* crazy!'

'With respect, I would rather trust a trained man with fire than an untrained one. It has also reduced crime by half.'

'*You need a bit of crime to keep you on your toes*, that's what my dear Aunt Petunia used to say before she passed on' said Jochi. 'Keeps people honest, she said.'

'And how did she die, if you don't mind me asking?' said Tsensible.

'She fell out of a tree she had climbed to escape a thief.'

'Well there you go' said Tsensible. 'She was a victim of crime.'

'Not really' said Jochi. 'She was blind drunk at the time and was hoping they would follow her for a bit of nookie. She lost her balance taking a swig from her drinking pouch and landed on a sack of stolen belt buckles.'

'Ah' said Tsensible. 'This way please, gentlemen.'

CHAPTER TWENTY ONE

Ulfred hated those three words.

No Mongol captain of such importance as he should have to deal with the fall out from them. His immediate future would change for the worse and his plans would be suspended until he unravelled the inevitable mess they would create. Genghis repeated himself, something that only amplified whatever consequences were tumbling down the hill towards its victim.

'I said, I've been thinking.'

'My apologies, Lord Khan, my mind was elsewhere.'

'The matter of my succession will be resolved this moon, one way or another.'

'It will?'

'Where is Captain Paat? If he dithers any longer the army will only have time for a delicate nibble and a light doze before they're packing up again and marching with their Khan.'

'I will send out men to bring the latest news of their progress.'

'Do. When they arrive, ready them for a great confrontation. There are formative days ahead for our nation.'

'Your will, my Lord' said Ulfred, backing out of the yurt and cursing his master's ability for free thought.

Genghis twirled a wooden figure through his fingers absent-mindedly. Ulfred returned a few moments later. 'They are approaching from the west, my Lord.'

'Of course, they are. It is hardly likely they would arrive from any other direction. Do you have any useful information to deliver?'

Ulfred was unusually flustered, in much the same way that a wobbling mountain would be *unusual*. He was a man used to navigating through life at his own rhythm and was a master at nudging the variables to his favour. Now Genghis was beginning to make decisions for himself and Ulfred's lack of control was most unsettling.

'They will be here within the hour, my Lord. I have taken the precaution of ordering them to remain two catapult distances from the general population.'

'And why, may I ask, would you do that?'

'I thought it would be a prudent measure, my Lord. Returning soldiers can be a little… unpredictable.'

'What is wrong with you, Ulfred? I am the last person to require a basic lesson on the behaviour of a returning army. You are intelligent enough to know that, too. I was referring, as would be obvious to a fully functioning version of yourself, to your decision to give an order without first consulting your khan.'

Because I rarely do, thought Ulfred. 'I thought the decision was below your station, my Lord. My humble apologies.'

'So now you think that my opinion on which orders I should give and which I should not *lower myself to* is imperfect? Should I not be the one to pass them to my own army? Perhaps I should let you make all the decisions from now on. Hah! What a mess we would be in then. You are reliable, but you are not a director. You would do well to remember that.'

'Forgive my misjudgment, oh Great Khan. It will not happen again.'

'Now I know you're up to something. You would never address me in such a way unless you were retreating from the discussion. Spit it out, man, and do not test my patience any further. I am, as you say, the Great Khan, and as such, I may wield as much or as little power as I see fit. You might say that I could choose to *order* whatever takes my fancy.'

Ulfred knew his master well enough to hear the threat. 'If you will allow it, my Lord, I will return to my yurt and make arrangements for the men to join the people on their arrival.'

'Ah, so now you think the men should join the horde? Have we not just discussed the consequences of you taking liberties with your limited power? I have not ordered the men to join the horde. Why would you think I would do such a thing? Returning armies can be so unpredictable.'

Ulfred's brain was beginning to hurt. Perhaps Genghis was beginning one of his long-winded, and often torturous, ramblings that usually ended with outlandish orders for men who could not disobey.

'I have a lot to learn' he said at last. 'I made the mistake of assuming there were only two options. It is clear to me now that you have a more cunning plan.'

'Have the men join up with the horde' said Genghis. 'On *my* orders.'

'Your will, my Lord.'

Genghis turned back to study the figure in his hand. Ulfred remained where he stood.

'Was there ambiguity in my dismissal?' said Genghis.

'Forgive me, my Lord.'

'Again? Don't push your luck. What is it?'

'I have learned of the death of Captain Sulki. It seems the sensitive information he held has expired with him.'

'Had he reached the Jin city?'

'I do not believe so.'

'Interesting. Wait there.'

There was an inference in Genghis' order that Ulfred should wait while he left to complete some task, but the Great Khan simply intensified his focus on the small, wooden foot soldier between his fingers.

'Order the returning soldiers to pass through the horde and camp a full day's march from here' he said at last. 'Every man we have will follow them.'

'*Every* man?' asked Ulfred instinctively.

Genghis gave him a look of purest power. 'Did I say *every* man, captain?'

'You did, my Lord.'

'Then it would be reasonable to assume that is precisely what I meant.'

'As you wish, my Lord.'

'Oh, and to avoid any misunderstanding, you *are* a man of my Great Horde, Ulfred. Have my travelling equipment readied and meet me in my Tactics yurt at dawn.'

'Where is that captain with my breastplates?' shouted Genghis as the sun broke cover behind the hills.

'He is helping with the distribution of armour, my Lord' said Ulfred with more patience than he felt.

'Good. And the weapons?'

'Captain Weeeee is on top of the ballistics and the men are already equipped with their close combat tools.'

'Tell him to stop messing about and get down from the catapults. Lord of the Sky, do none of our captains have the ability to remain focused on the task at hand?'

'Perhaps I was not clear. I meant only that he is in full control of the ballistic preparations. He is not physically *on top of* the ballistics.'

'Then you should be clearer in your speech' said Genghis tetchily. 'What good is your head to me if everything that comes out of it is ambiguous?'

'My humble apologies, Lord Khan. I will be clearer.'

'Yes, you will.'

'I believe we are set, my Lord. Shall I order the captains to ready their men for the first step?'

'You will do nothing of the sort! *I* am the Great Khan, am I not?'

'You are.'

'Then it is *I* who will order them when the time comes.'

Ulfred answered Genghis with a tightening of his lips and a shallow nod.

'Good. I am ready. Go to the captains and tell them my orders.'

'Which orders, my Lord?'

'Which orders!?' roared Genghis. 'What is wrong with you today? The order to advance once I have taken my place at their head. I do not lower myself to delivering my own orders, that is for people like you. I give them, you deliver them. Now, if you don't mind, I must take my nation to the limits of Rhizun.'

It'll be nice to have the company, thought Ulfred.

Genghis sat proudly on Lavender as he trotted back and forth in front of his army. It was an impressive sight; row after row of shining spears pointing in precisely the same direction. Now was the time for a rousing speech, a call to arms from the great leader of this nation of warriors. He took a deep breath and opened his mouth wide. It was at this exact moment that the sun chose to reflect off the infinite spearheads and directly into Genghis' vision. He squinted harshly, shading his eyes with a sheepskin-covered wrist, and cursing his misfortune. He pretended to adjust his sleeves, as if everything he had shown them thus far was intentional, cleared his throat, and took another breath.

'Men of the Great Horde! Today we march on the pitiful Jin empire. Today we begin the Great Expansion. Today we take their city of Rhizun!' He paused. 'Well, not today as such. It will take some time to reach the city walls, but maybe in about four or five days, we will take it. Prepare yourselves for a feast at their tables, for a celebration of their death, and for a cleansing of your souls at the altars of their false Gods.'

An infantryman whispered to his neighbour from the corner of his mouth. 'I'm not cleansing anything. I've heard they deliberately sink themselves into rivers to wash themselves. All of them, if you can believe it.'

Genghis searched the front line for the offending man. 'Who was that? Come on, I know it was one of you here' he said, waving an arm to indicate the soldiers nearest to him.

'Right, that's it. Ulfred! Have these men take five steps forward. Ten men wide, ten deep.'

Ulfred trotted forward on Maizhi, his chestnut mare. He counted ten men wide and deep. 'You! Forward... FIVE!' The century of Mongol warriors stepped out of the perfect line and into the petrifyingly unstable space in front of their khan.

'Now, this is your last chance' said Genghis. 'Which one of you here deemed it appropriate to speak while the Great Khan of your nation was delivering his rallying call?'

Nobody moved.

'Right, you leave me no choice. I'll have all your heads spiked with your own spears before you can spell insubordination.'

'We should live a long and happy life then' said the whispering soldier.

'Aha!' cried Genghis, pointing a finger at the man standing next to the culprit. 'You!'

The culprit looked at Genghis, then his endangered neighbour. 'With all due respect, my Lord, it wasn't him' he said bravely.

'Do you doubt me, catapult fodder?'

'Not as such, my Lord, no. It's just... it's just, I doubt his ability to speak.'

'So disrespecting your Great Khan isn't enough for you, is it? You have to have a go at this poor, soon-to-be-spiked soldier too? I'll have your head off for your treachery.'

'I only mention it on account of the fact that he doesn't have a tongue.'

'Ulfred' said Genghis, nodding to the man who may or may not have a tongue.

Ulfred stepped up to the man, grasped his jaw, and opened it. He thrust his fingers into the cavity and rotated them all around the man's mouth.

'He is without tongue' he announced.

'Interesting' said Genghis. 'Since I can't identify the offender I will have all of your tongues cut out at once. Ulfred, bring Captain…'

'Neknik?'

'Yes, bring Captain Neknik to me at once.'

'May I suggest another solution, my Lord?'

'Go on' said Genghis dubiously.

'Show mercy and have these men forever in your debt.'

'They are already in my debt, I'm the Great Khan!'

'Yes, but they could be your personal guards. They can prove their loyalty to you by putting their bodies in harm's way for you when the time comes.'

'I was thinking' said Genghis. 'I should make these men my personal guards. They can prove their loyalty to me through the protection of their Khan.'

'That is an excellent idea, my Lord.'

'I know. Now, they will need a name. Something intimidating.'

'How about the Tongueless?' offered Ulfred.

'I think I will name them the Tongueless. It will be a constant reminder of my mercy and my power. You can tell them. I wouldn't want to be seen to converse with common foot soldiers for too long.'

'That is a very solid name. History will see the Tongueless as a fighting force like no other.'

'History is of no concern to me. The future is all that matters now, Ulfred.'

'The future is history' said Ulfred. 'What we do now will reverberate through time.'

'That's the spirit' said Genghis, missing the correction and kicking his heels into his horse's rump. 'Now name the Tongueless, we ride at once!'

CHAPTER TWENTY TWO

'Good morning, men!' called an unusually cheery Tsensible as he opened the door. 'I hope you've got your adventure trousers on because I have planned a day of unbridled entertainment for you all.'

'Bggruff' said a rumple of wool pressed against a wall.

'I'm sorry?' said Tsensible. 'Didn't quite catch that.'

'He said bugger off!' snapped Stan. 'Now is no time to be waking up men of the Great Khan's army.'

'But the sun is almost up?' implored Tsensible. He had a set of ranks to rise through and he wasn't going to let his tickets to power flutter away because they were lazy. 'Come, there is much I wish to show you.'

'I'll show you my knuckles if you don't sod off' said Jochi.

The throaty sound of someone stretching came from under a blanket in a dark corner of the room, then a husky cough. 'Gentlemen, please' said Okatai, raising himself onto his elbows and squinting at the scene. 'We are here at the grace of the prefect, and he has entrusted Corporal Tsensible here with our care. Please show him the respect his position warrants.'

'He's a bloody corporal, not a captain' said Jochi.

'And can we tone down the language a little. No day should start with such vulgarity.'

'Fine, but I'm not going anywhere until I can see the bottom of the sun.'

Tsensible bristled. This wasn't part of his plan. He had a full day of activities all ready to go and set to a strict, if a little challenging, timetable.

'I will wait outside while you dress. The prefect will be glad to hear you are being so well looked after.'

Okatai stared at the two young men as Tsensible left the room. 'Be men, not boys.'

Jochi peeled himself off the floor and picked up his pants with a petulant swipe. Stan let out a deep sigh before snatching his shirt and pulling it over his head.

'This had better not be like yesterday' said Jochi. 'I need a good fistful of mutton soon or there's no telling what I'll do.'

'Stop complaining' snapped Okatai. 'We're here on the Khan's orders. I'll take any more complaints as being directly disobedient of those orders. Keep your heads and you'll keep your heads.'

'Come on, Jochi. We should make the best of it' said Stan.

'That's the spirit' said Okatai. 'Now, let's see what our corporal has in store.'

'This way gentlemen' called Tsensible. 'The first stop of our day is just up here.'

'Is it another garden?' asked Jochi. 'Because if it is I'm going back to bed.'

'It is better than a garden' declared Tsensible. 'If you can believe such a thing.'

'Oh I can believe it alright' said Jochi. 'I have extensive experience in seeing things better than gardens.'

'Jochi!' snapped Okatai.

'If there are no objections, we will pass by Crescent Fountain for the moment' said Tsensible apologetically. 'It forms a crucial part of the fourth section of your tour.'

'Fou...' began Jochi before reigning in his emotions. 'Four? Marvellous. I was so hoping there would be more than a couple of parts to this exciting day.' He turned to Stan and whispered from the corner of his mouth. 'Sarcasm without its inflection, my friend. That's what will get us through this interminable day.'

The peal of an enormous bell boomed into their ears. Tsensible froze.

'Shhhhh!!' said the Jin corporal, holding a rigid finger in the air as if it could halt a herd of stampeding oxen.

Another boom.

And another.

Tsensible sagged with relief. 'Relax, men. Everything is fine. Three bells... phew!'

'What does that mean?' asked Stan.

'Three peals signals the start of...'

BOOOOM!

Tsensible's jaw dropped. He stared up at the bell tower above them. 'Come on five, come on!' he pleaded to the world in general.

'What's five?'

'Five signals there has been a great hunt. It means a hearty meal this evening.'

Jochi and Stan joined Tsensible in his attempt to force another toll of the bell by staring ferociously at the tower.

Silence.

'Bugger' said Tsensible.

None of the Mongols asked what four meant.

A tall Jin man careered around a nearby corner pushing Okatai out of the way before hurtling on towards the city gates. The bell's echo dissipated and was replaced by the unmistakable sound of dozens of people scurrying to get where they were supposed to be two minutes ago.

'What's happening?' asked Okatai.

Tsensible twitched one way, then the other, as he tried to prioritise his actions. His mouth opened, then closed.

'Ah, I see' said Jochi. 'Well, that clears things up nicely.'

'F... fo...' said Tsensible.

'Four?' offered Jochi.

Tsensible's expression steeled suddenly. 'This way men. I'm afraid your grand tour will have to wait.'

He took two long strides away from them and towards the Great Hall, then turned back towards the Mongols, grabbed Stan by the sleeve and dragged him along with him.

Lah Fing scratched his elbow, or at least what he had always thought of as his elbow. He had been told so often that he couldn't identify it that he had begun to doubt that it was, in fact, his elbow.

'Do you think birds can scratch themselves?' he asked Mord Lin.

'What?' asked Mord. '*Can birds scratch themselves*? Is that really your question?'

'Well they don't have hands, do they? Maybe they don't itch at all. That doesn't seem likely though, does it?'

'It may come as a shock to you, Lah, but I have not yet considered the matter. I prefer to fill my time here with musings of a more... *intelligent* nature.'

'Who's to say it isn't intelligent' continued Lah. 'Perhaps they don't itch at all. If that were true we could work out why and apply it to us. Can you imagine a world where no one ever gets an itch?'

'I have an itch to punch you in the mouth' said Mord Lin. 'You should tell the prefect at once. I'm sure he will act upon your *intelligence* with all haste.'

'What would you say if you were placed in front of him?' asked Lah, moving effortlessly on to another rumination.

'I'd ask him when he plans to rotate the Watch shifts. I'd also suggest he pair men up with those whose interests are more closely aligned.'

Lah Fing didn't react. His gaze was fixed at a point on the horizon.

Mord Lin rolled his eyes patiently. 'Fine' he said. 'What would *you* say to him?'

Lah Fing slowly raised his arm and pointed into the distance. 'I'd tell him the emperor is here.'

'I must see the prefect at once' said Tsensible.

The radish continued to stare stoically at an arbitrary point in the distance.

'I'm not sure you understand' pleaded Tsensible. 'The future of the city is at stake!'

'Is that so?' said the radish.

'Yes, yes it is. Now, I must insist you alert the prefect of our presence.'

'Oh, you insist, do you? And what have you seen in my demeanour that would lead you to the conclusion that I would take your orders over those of the great Roo Ling?'

'Because if you don't you'll be consigned to privy cleaning duties before you can say the bloody emperor is on his way and we are giving his enemy a guided tour with free buns and a change of clothes!'

'There are buns?'

'Not now, Stan' said Okatai.

'Would that be the guided tour that our prefect requested you provide?' asked the radish.

'That was before he knew the emperor was going to stroll through the gates.'

'I have an idea' said Stan, gesturing to the corridor behind them. 'Come on.'

The group followed Stan down the dark passageway and around a corner. They huddled close together, unnecessarily as it happened, and stared at Stan.

'There's no way we can convince the guard to let us through' he began.

'Good start' said Jochi.

'So we'll have to use an alternative technique. One that plays to our strengths.'

Go on said the group's body language.

'If we can't persuade him to move aside then we should just kick him in the family jewels and push him over.'

'That's your plan, is it?' said Jochi. 'Kick the giant guard in his nomads and hope he isn't wearing a codpiece?'

'Yes.'

'That might actually work' said Tsensible. 'He won't be expecting that.'

'That's because only a fool would even attempt it' said Jochi.

'Precisely!' said Stan. 'We'll have the advantage of surprise.'

'And he'll have the advantage of being twice our size and armed with more than a pointy shoe.'

'I'll do it' said Stan, surprising everyone. 'I'm the last person he'd think would try so I should be the first.'

'The first?' said Okatai. 'May I remind you that some of us have seen many moons since our fighting days. Let's do it, but do it once.'

'Fine. Get ready to run.'

They approached the radish with all the nonchalance of a group of amateur troublemakers. They whistled softly to themselves, casting glances around the guard's area as if seeing it for the first time.

'What are you lot up to?' asked the radish.

'Up to?' said Tsensible innocently. 'I have no idea what you mean.'

'I'm a guard of the prefect' said the radish, 'not some butcher's assistant. Now, tell me what's going on or you'll feel the blunt end of this lance. And that's me being nice.'

Stan stepped up to the guard. The rest lingered to the side, readying themselves for a sprint through the doorway.

'Well, it's like this' said Stan. 'We're rather keen to get to the other side of those doors on account of us needing an urgent audience with the prefect. So...' He leaned in to the guard's personal space, inviting the radish to do likewise. 'So, we thought it would be a good id...'

Thump!

The guard looked down at his waist, then down further to the writhing Mongol clutching at his foot.

'I'm sure I mentioned I am a guard of Roo Ling. Do you think I come to work dressed with frilly undergarments and scented shirts?'

Okatai, Jochi, and Tsensible looked at each other, nodded slightly and threw themselves at the radish, sending him tumbling down the stairs and giving his head a painfully brief encounter with a stone pillar. They hauled Stan upright and burst through the large doors, sprinting the length of the great room, and through the door, Roo Ling had exited through the previous day.

'Which way?' cried Okatai.

'I have no idea' admitted Tsensible. 'This is the prefect's private residence. I've never been here before.'

'Marvellous' said Jochi, trying the handle of a door.

'He's in here somewhere' said Tsensible. 'Come on!'

The group bumbled through a maze of corridors, trying the handles of each door they passed.

'Here!' cried Okatai as he stumbled through an unexpectedly open doorway. 'Wait, no.'

'What is it?' asked Stan.

'Never mind, boy. Some things are best left unseen. Suffice to say we should be braced for some... *unfamiliar* visions.'

Tsensible stopped in front of a door, larger and more ornate than the others.

'This must be it' he said. 'Ready?'

'No.'

'Good, let's go.'

He turned the handle slowly, as if the punishment for interrupting the prefect uninvited was inextricably linked to the speed of entry, and pushed. Inside was a space that seemed larger than was possible without having its own postal system. The group shuffled in nervously. At the far end was a figure, presumably the prefect but impossible to tell from so far away, dressed all in red with an impossibly large hat balanced precariously on its head. The figure turned towards them.

'Ah there you are' it said. 'You took your time.'

'We took our...?' began Tsensible before his survival instinct reasserted itself. 'Apologies, master. We were delayed by one of your zealously professional guards.'

Tsensible gave a look to the group that said *I don't bloody well know either*.

'Well don't just stand there gawking like a Mongol with a book, come here! Ah. No offence.'

They ambled awkwardly across the vast room, each trying their surreptitious best to arrive last.

'Well?' said Roo Ling as he tied a band of red fabric around his redshirt.

Tsensible cleared his throat. 'I have brought the Mongols to you, master.'

'Have you indeed? Then where are they?'

'They are, erm, right here, master.'

'Of course they damn well are, now tell me something that isn't as obvious as a tree on a roof before I send you to Captain Spi Khi's *Room of Special Persuasion.*'

Tsensible swallowed. 'I thought it prudent to bring them to you so they may be placed in a suitably discreet location for the duration of the emperor's visit.'

'What makes you believe I wish them to be held discretely, corporal? You are a corporal, are you not?'

'I am, master' said Tsensible firmly, hoping the prefect would respond and save him the torture of working out if the former question was rhetorical.

'Are you familiar with the nuances of our military rankings, corporal?'

'Nuances, master?' said Tsensible noncommittally.

'Yes, *nuances*' said Roo Ling. He let the vagueness of his question hang in the air for a moment before piercing Tsensible's anxiety with an elaboration. 'There are certain rights that come with the higher ranks. A sergeant may take an apple from Sie Duh's orchard every second Thursday, for example, while a private may not. Did you know that, corporal?'

Tsensible did not know that, but that didn't help him to identify which answer he should give the prefect.

'It is a great symbol of your generosity.'

'Don't flatter me, imp. I can't bear sycophants' lied Roo Ling. 'Now, tell me this. How much do you know of the trappings of captaincy?'

'I have much to learn, master.'

'That's more like it' said Roo Ling. He clasped his hands behind his back and strode deliberately back and forth in front of the group, something only those with too much power and not enough entertainment are capable of doing without looking like a latrine guard. 'A captain receives many gifts' he began. 'Not least of which is a private room in Captain Snu Zhi's residence. They are given two fulsome meals each day and several hours each week to do as they please. Does that sound like something that would appeal to you, *corporal*?'

It did, but that wasn't important. What was important was whether Roo Ling wanted him to say it did or to say that he was grateful to be where he was in the pecking order. *Bugger it*, thought Tsensible. Now or never.

'It would appeal to me greatly, master.'

'Then you may be interested to hear that a loftier rank brings a greater responsibility, and a greater responsibility allows accountability.'

Tsensible wondered at Roo Ling's use of the word *allow*.

'Do you understand me?'

Tsensible did. Do what I command or have your head chopped off like a cabbage in Ul-suh's vegetable garden. 'I do, master.'

'And does this knowledge dampen your enthusiasm for a captaincy?'

'No, master' he lied.

'Then you will be keen, I am sure, to learn of my views on your delivery of our enemy to my private residence.'

Tsensible responded by staying petrifyingly still.

'It takes a certain type of man to rise through the ranks in my city, corporal. A man of courage, of conviction and of intellect.

Tsensible wondered if he was any of those things. More pertinently, he wondered if Roo Ling thought he was any of those things.

'The problem with that' continued the prefect, 'is that you can spot a high ranking officer faster than a hippo in a cup. What I need is a captain who doesn't *look* like a captain. Someone who *shouldn't be* a captain.'

No, you don't thought Tsensible desperately. Accountability, it turned out, was a powerful dampener to his dream of promotion.

'Do you think you should be captain, corporal?'

The impossibility of correctly answering the question swam through Tsensible's head and sent his wits into a plummeting spin. To the eternal gratefulness of the part of his brain in charge of decision making, the part in charge of self-preservation chose this precise moment to faint.

CHAPTER TWENTY THREE

'Captain?' came a voice, dim and distorted. 'Captain, are you feeling alright?'

Tsensible's consciousness glooped back towards him. Every bit of him felt vague. He kept his eyes closed as his memories jogged to catch up. He was giving the Mongols a tour of the city. Then what? Another memory caught up. The bells! As he grappled with their significance he processed the sound that had woken him. Captain? Perhaps he was in Snu Zhi's quarters.

'Captain Tsensible?' came the voice again.

Bugger, thought Tsensible. *Accountability.*

He cracked open one eye and immediately regretted it. Looming over him was a Vegetable, dressed all in orange and wafting a shirt in an attempt to bring Tsensible round.

'The prefect will see you now.'

He was hoisted up by his armpits and on to his seemingly boneless feet. He staggered into the chest of the Vegetable and gave him the kind of hug usually experienced by mothers of sick children.

'On your feet!' commanded the guard. '...captain' he added diplomatically.

'I think you may have me confused with someone else' said Tsensible desperately. In all the time he had spent coveting the idea of a captaincy it had never occurred to him that it may shorten his life expectancy so efficiently. 'I am Corporal Tsensible of the Watch. Perhaps it is Captain Sikhing you are looking for.'

'No' said the guard flatly. 'You are Captain Tsensible, by order of the prefect. He insists on an audience the moment you wake. Which is now, by the way.'

Tsensible fainted.

'No silly games now' said the guard, slapping Tsensible's face gently. 'I didn't get to be Privy Guard of the Private Residence Privy Council by allowing petty captains to run amok in here.'

'That's a lot of privies' said Tsensible groggily. 'You should speak to the cook, get him to change his menu.'

The guard slapped him again, harder this time. 'Sorry' he said with false concern. 'Didn't realise you were already awake.'

Tsensible rubbed his cheek and gave the guard a disapproving look, then one of resignation as he took in the sheer bulk of the man.

'Fine, help me up' he said, raising an arm.

'Captain Tsensible' announced the Vegetable as they entered another oversized room.

'Ah, you're awake. Marvellous. Please, sit' said Roo Ling from behind a large wooden desk.

Tsensible took a few paces towards it and sat down on an uncomfortably carved chair.

'Do you think this should be here' said Roo Ling gripping a large metal jug, 'or here?' He moved it to the other side of the desk.

'There' said Tsensible, pointing to a spot to the prefect's right.

'And what makes you say that?'

'You are right-handed, master.'

'Indeed I am' said Roo Ling with what Tsensible considered to be a disproportionate level of thoughtfulness.

'Sit' said the prefect, before looking up from the desk. 'Ah, you are. Good, I have something of great importance to relay to you. You are to take up a key position in my ranks; a pivotal role in the greatest offensive in the history of the Jin empire.'

Tsensible swallowed. 'But I am a mere corporal, master. I could not hope to repay your faith in me.'

'You doubt my judgment, *captain*?'

A high pitched bell trilled somewhere behind the prefect. 'Come!' he called.

A green Vegetable entered the room and stood to attention.

'I said come, not step inside and linger at the doorway like a man who doesn't have a message for his prefect that is urgent enough to interrupt him!'

The Vegetable crossed the room nervously and bent low to the prefect's ear. Roo Ling's eyes focused intensely.

'Leave us' he ordered.

Tsensible watched the prefect as he raised himself from his seat and began to pace back and forth again. He stopped and turned to Tsensible, then looked away. Nothing in the prefect's behaviour helped ease Tsensible's feeling of utter dread. He wondered how he could have lusted after such progression for so long.

'Captain...?' asked Roo Ling.

'Tsensible, master.'

'Tsensible, eh? That's a peculiar name. Doesn't seem to fit somehow' said Roo Ling. 'Rather a mouthful.'

'Indeed' said Tsensible diplomatically.

'I have just received news that Major Arturhi was taken ill this morning and has, unfortunately, succumbed to his ailment.'

'I am sorry for your loss.'

'It is no loss' said Roo Ling. 'He was too old for this mission anyway.'

'Mission, master?'

Roo Ling shook the reverie from his head. 'Hold your questions, *Major* Tsensible. There is much for us to discuss.'

Bugger.

'You seem to have developed a bond of sorts with these Mongols, according to my reports at least.'

In a single sentence, Roo Ling had given Tsensible several issues to wrangle with. Firstly, he wasn't sure whether he *should* have formed such a bond, or whether that would be considered fraternising with the enemy. Secondly, the prefect clearly had some form of surveillance on him, giving Tsensible a hitherto unconsidered appreciation of the importance of his task. Fortunately for Tsensible, the prefect's question was hidden inside a statement, allowing him an arguable justification of his decision to remain stock still and deathly silent.

'Well?' asked Roo Ling. 'Would you consider that to be a fair assessment?'

Tsensible gulped. 'Yes, master.'

'Then you are in a unique position to assist me, major. There is an urgent matter of great importance to the city. To the empire, even. As you will have heard, the emperor is at the city gates and will be here shortly.'

'Here as in *here*?' interrupted Tsensible, swirling a finger around the room. 'Or here as in *here*.' He cartwheeled his arms widely in an attempt to indicate the entire city.

'I'm not sure that matters' said Roo Ling. 'The emperor is always here, wherever *here* may be.'

'That doesn't make any sense, here could be anywhere' said Tsensible with an instant feeling of regret.

'Here is always here, just as my dungeons are always there' said Roo Ling pointing at a doorway. 'Perhaps you believe your new rank gives you a certain amount of credit with me, but please remember that the neck of a major is as easily sliced as that of a corporal.'

Tsensible did remember that. He remembered that very well for the rest of his life.

'Now, enough pleasantries' said Roo Ling. 'Captain Tran has the Mongols safely in his room. I wish to bargain with them over dinner. You may tell them there will be meat on the table, thick with grease, in case they fear a repeat of yesterday. I could see their culinary reticence from a hundred paces. Stan is to sit at their head, and their captain is to be given a dozen sheaves of paper. That should close his impertinent mouth long enough for...' he paused. 'Long enough.'

Two caterpillars sine curved their way along a thin branch.

'Do you know something?' said one. 'I'm beginning to think he didn't leave us at all.'

'What do you mean?' asked the second.

'Well, it seems unlikely he would just up sticks and head to the top of the tree without so much as a goodbye wink.'

'Who?'

'Daiv. You know, the one with the spot on his back' said one.

The second caterpillar looked blankly at the first.

'He fell off a leaf that time and was nearly picked off by a passing bird, remember?'

'Oh, him?' said the second. 'He's gone, has he? Another taken too soon.'

'What do you mean?'

'Well, there's been a lot of it recently, hasn't there? There's always someone disappearing into the trees these days.'

'Old Bert says it's because they're going to turn into butterflies' said one.

'That's just a story they tell the young ones. They've probably been eaten by a frog.'

'That's not what he said. He said it'll happen to all of us. We'll have a nice big sleep, he said, and when we wake up we'll be able to fly as fast as we like with wings like rainbows.'

'He was nearly right' said the second. 'But it's called the *long* sleep. There's no coming back from that.'

'Well, I believe him, even if you don't.'

A brightly coloured butterfly landed in front of them. 'There you are!' it said. 'I've been looking for you for days. How have you been?'

The two caterpillars looked at each other in surprise, then at the butterfly, then back to each other.

'You've been looking for us?' said one.

'Of course, I have!' said the butterfly as if the reason for his search was as obvious as the ground. 'I'm afraid the whole thing caught me by surprise and I didn't get a chance to say goodbye.'

'Listen' said the second caterpillar, 'I don't mean to cause offence, but I'm sure we haven't met before.'

The butterfly looked up at his wings. 'Ah, these' he said. 'They're new. It's me, Daivyd.'

'You can't be Daivyd' said the first caterpillar. 'He hated being called that, said it was too fancy. He preferred Daiv.'

'Well I'm different now, aren't I? More refined. It's amazing what a good cocoon and some wings can do to a caterpillar.'

'If you are Daiv – and I'm not saying you are – then you'll know how many times you... *Daiv*... fell off the Sleeping Stone.'

'Aha!' said Daivyd. 'Trick question! I fell off a leaf, not the Stone.'

'You must have seen him do it' said the second caterpillar.

'Perhaps, but if I wasn't Daivyd then how would I know that you have a thing for...

'Alright, alright!' called the second caterpillar. 'I believe you.'

'A thing for what?' asked the first caterpillar.

'Never mind about that. Now, Daiv, tell us all about the big sleep. Is it painful?'

'There's one thing you need to know. One thing that would have saved me an awful lot of pain and heartache. I wish I knew beforehand, it would have given me time to prepare myself for the shock.'

'Yes?' asked both caterpillars at once.

'Well, the really important thing to know is that you should not, on any account, neglect to keep your...'

A small bird swooped into Daiv, clasped him in its beak and wobbled him down its throat.

'Keep your what!?' cried the first caterpillar. 'Keep your what!?'

'Eyes open for birds?' offered the second caterpillar.

'I trust today's offering is more pleasing to your pallet?' said Roo Ling. 'Captain Merang has been crafting tirelessly all day to create a table worthy of your position.'

'I hope not' said Jochi. 'Our positions are usually next to the latrines.'

'It is a delight' said Okatai. 'Please send our gratitude to the captain.'

Stan swallowed the last of his mutton. 'Why are we here, prefect?'

Roo Ling looked curiously at Stan through narrowed eyes. 'You are the ones who knocked on my door, perhaps *you* could tell *me*?'

'You know what I mean. Why are you now feeding us meat instead of flowers? I would not expect a Jin prefect to be so crass as to pander to the desires of the enemy unless it was part of some grand plot.'

Jochi's meat-knife nicked his gaping jaw as it fell with a clatter onto the table. Okatai's eyebrows furrowed, unsure whether to be proud, mystified or worried. Only Roo Ling held his expression.

'You are a curiosity, Stan. Here you sit, a mere... whatever it is you are, at the table of the most powerful man in a great and imposing enemy city. Yet you act as you would with a common worker.'

'Why would I act any differently?' asked Stan honestly.

Roo Ling paused. 'Well, you just shouldn't. I'm the bloody prefect!'

'Yes, but you're not *my* prefect, are you? If the great Genghis Khan was feeding me well-roasted mutton I might agree with you, but you're not him, are you?'

'I suppose not, but may I remind you of the terror that lives in my dungeons?'

'No' said Stan. 'You can tell me for the first time though, if you like.'

The others present in the room could have been a thousand miles away for all the ability they had to interject, so staggered were they at Stan's behaviour.

'What is your game?' asked Roo Ling. 'It is clear to me that you are more than you seem to be, for no man of your stock would behave in such a way.'

'Let me educate you, prefect. I am tiring of our time here; there is too much confinement and not enough wind, too many covert performances and not enough honesty. I will speak plainly. It is clear to *me* that you are too far removed from the lives of the common man to be in any position to cast aspersions. That's the trouble with leaders, too much to live for, and not enough life to use. Common men – men like me – live for each other as well as themselves and are rarely more than they seem. We may lack the sophistication of your ruling peers, but that does not make us any less valuable. What we lack in chicanery and deceitful distraction we more than makeup for with our sense of belonging and worth to each other. Also, I don't know what stock you are referring to, but I would be surprised if your spies gathered such specific information during their surveillance of us. To ease your curiosity, my preferred type is that of the chicken.'

'I am going to ignore your mention of chickens for now' said Roo Ling, 'mostly because I have no idea how they came to be involved in our conversation. I think it would be prudent for us to move on to the pressing matter of your stay here, since it appears to be something of a grievance to you.' He stood again, pacing the room with practised deliberation. 'Major Tsensible, my patience has run dry and your time has come. Take these Mongols back to wherever it is they call home. I will give you horses enough to make it a pleasant journey and a message for the great Genghis Khan, leader of sheep.'

'Maybe that's why he's so successful' thought Tsensible out loud.

'I beg your pardon?'

'I said that's why you're so successful, master. It's a wonderful idea! What kind of leader needs sheep, eh?'

'A successful one?' offered Stan.

'Shut up, Mongol' snapped Roo Ling.

'Can I finish this before I go?' asked Jochi, joining in the bravery.

A door opened at the far end of the room. A blue Vegetable approached the prefect and bent to his ear, whispering something inaudible before retracing his steps.

'Gentlemen!' announced Roo Ling. 'I'm afraid I must suspend my hospitality. Ettiket, bring guards for our guests. And be ready for fresh orders.'

'How many watches are there on the wall?' asked Lah Fing.

'Four at a time, as you well know' said Mord Lin.

'And how many shift changes are there?'

'Three per day. I know that because I spend my days waiting for them to give me a break from your incessant personality.'

'So that means there are...' Lah screwed up his face in concentration. '... twenty-four Watchmen who could, in theory, be a *principal discovery individual*.'

Mord raised a single, surprised eyebrow at Lah's use of handbook terminology. 'Indeed.'

'Why, then, is it always me?'

Mord followed Lah's outstretched arm to the dark blot on the landscape.

Bugger, thought Mord.

CHAPTER TWENTY FOUR

Ulfred trotted his horse up to Genghis as they made their way up a gentle hill.

'There is a small matter I wish to discuss, my Lord.'

'Go on' said Genghis.

'I received some interesting news as we left this morning.'

Genghis waited for an elaboration. 'Must I request each line from your mouth in turn, or are you going to string two or three together?'

'My apologies, Lord Khan, I do not mean to sound hesitant.'

'Well, you have failed spectacularly, Ulfred. Honestly, I don't know what's wrong with you these days. Your stoicism is what keeps you in your position, don't let it fail you now.'

'Of course, my Lord.'

Genghis glared at him. 'This is my final prompt. Spill all that is in your head and leave it to me to reassemble.'

'Your will' said Ulfred, bowing his head slightly. 'Captain Sulki's emblem has reached me. A sheep's head brooch attached to a raven.'

'You have already informed me of his death. Do I need to ask the significance of this development?' said Genghis. 'Or would you prefer to become an example to the Tongueless?'

'He does not involve himself with ravens, my Lord. Nor would he give up his brooch. I fear he may have been intercepted by a shadow, one with a very specific skill set and an unhealthy affiliation with birds.'

'And by *intercepted* you mean…?' asked Genghis with unexpected patience.

'He has fallen to the shadow.'

'Lord of the Sky, man! Spit it out.'

'Sulki is dead, as is the secret he holds. A drawing was sent with the raven, one depicting two dead men. It is clear from this that Sulki and an assassin have expired. I have no information on the whereabouts of Bataar, nor the status of the unexpected assassin.'

'Come now, Ulfred. Do you expect me to believe that you do not maintain a line of communication with the man you sent to silence Captain Sulki? You do me a disservice.'

Ulfred swallowed hard. 'There is a certain level of knowledge that a Great Khan should not hold, my Lord. Such information would make him vulnerable to blackmail and ambitious usurpers.'

'I will be the judge of that. Tell me what you know and let me decide whether or not I should know it.'

'Erm…' said Ulfred dubiously. Now was not the time to question the logic of Genghis Khan. 'My working hypothesis is that the assassin was killed by an unknown individual and that Bataar has colluded with them to rescue his brother.'

'Because…?'

'I have no doubt that the assassin completed his mission successfully, he is a man of unmatched efficiency. Bataar is certainly stupid enough to befriend Sulki, rather than take a spiteful dislike to the man, and it is possible that he lashed out at the assassin on witnessing Sulki's killing. That would leave Bataar on his own with the raven and the brooch, but without the wit to identify their meaning. If all of this is true, then there can be only one conclusion drawn; another man was there with them, one with the guile and motive to send a message to me.'

'Who is to say that the assassination was not completed as instructed? It seems to me the killer succeeded in his mission, sent a message back to you, and continued about his business. He's probably still out there studying the local ornithological sights.'

'A message *was* sent to me, as I said. The artistry is beyond Bataar's skills.'

He pulled a strip of parchment from his cloak and passed it to Genghis.

'I see' said the Great Khan curiously. 'I assume you have concluded who sent it?'

'Not precisely, my Lord. It is a difficult conundrum. There is no-one who knew of the additional personnel, not even you, for the reason I have already given. The only other mission in that direction is, of course, Okatai's reconnaissance of Rhizun. If we assume they followed your orders to keep their operation clandestine, then there is but one person who knows of its existence.'

Genghis angled his head and strengthened his glare as if challenging Ulfred to play a guessing game in return for his head.

'One of Okatai's group was involved in an accident as they were setting off. He was too injured to travel and they were forced to leave him behind.'

'Does this man have a name?'

'Mekki.'

'He was not mentioned on the scroll' said Genghis.

'No, my Lord. He is a friend of... of your son.'

'Then it is not a *conundrum* at all. He is the assassin's assassin and is protecting his friend with courage and wit.'

'Therein lies the problem, I'm afraid. He is not an individual who would naturally come to mind when considering candidates for high end strategic thinking. He is more of a... well, not that anyway.'

'Or' began Genghis, 'he is exceptionally good at it. Do not judge a sheep by its wool, Ulfred. Beneath the soft, warm exterior is a plump side of meat that would keep a dozen men fed for a week on the battlefield. What of the bodyguard?'

'I believe he is still alive. He is the brother of one of Mekki's friends.'

'Then he *is* alive. A man who kills as Mekki does is more than capable of keeping a beast like Bataar alive.'

'If I may be so bold, my Lord, I believe you are overestimating his talents.'

'Just as you have overestimated my patience.'

'Quite so' said Ulfred anxiously. This was teetering ominously close to one of Genghis' dangerously unpredictable rambles. 'We must gather our strength and hurl it at the city. If Mekki is muddying the waters then it is vital we reach the city before he can do too much damage.'

'Damage?' said Genghis. 'As far as I can tell, all he has done so far is to outmanoeuvre you at every turn, remove an experienced assassin from the field, and have the courage to protect his friends in the face of all logic. He does not sound like a man to be trifled with. We would underestimate him to our peril, Ulfred. No, we must give his strategy a little time to play out. Order the men to continue at the same pace.'

'Ah' said Ulfred flatly. 'Just to be sure I'm understanding this correctly, my Lord. With all of the information we now have, you would like me to order the men to continue with their current orders?'

'That's what I said, was it not?'

'It was, my Lord.'

'Then see to it, and see to your nerves while you're at it.'

CHAPTER TWENTY FIVE

Bataar's relentless march was finally punctuated by an increasingly imposing shape on the horizon. There was no change to his gait as the sight morphed into the Rhizun city walls, and his arrival at the enormous wooden gate came as no surprise to him, despite the clamour on the other side.

'That's what he said, I'm telling you' said Koo, the first gatekeeper.

'Captain Khi would not allow a Mongol warrior of that size inside the city, no matter how many turnips the prefect promises him. Our concern is the safety of the city, not whether the prefect has allowed one, two, or a thousand enemy parties inside.' said Kye, the second gatekeeper.

'We must carry out the orders as they have been given to us.'

'Then what was the point in all that interminable training? They took the best years of our lives to teach us the intricacies of decision making and how to conduct an effective risk analysis with a spear at our throat and a dog chewing at our ankles. They may as well have handed us a key and said *turn it this way to open and that way to close. Everything else is just heavy lifting.*'

'If it's all the same to you, can we follow our orders and let the Mongol in now?'

'You want to open the gates to a monstrous specimen of a man with nothing but ten paces and a stern glare between us and certain death? That's our glorious destiny, is it?'

'Ours has got to Rhizun, Kye. Ours is now two, do or die' said Koo.

'Don't start that again. The gates are no place for bloated philosophy.'

A marching sound came from behind them. 'Why are the doors still closed?' cried a man at the front. Kye turned at the call.

We are just beginning the opening protocols now, master' said Kye, pushing his poetic colleague towards the cranking handle.

A great creak erupted from the old hinges as the first shaft of sunlight revealed waves of dust, dancing in the glow. They disappeared again as Bataar stepped into the opening and cast his enormous shadow over the entrance. The two gatekeepers exchanged nervous glances as Roo Ling stepped forward.

'I am Roo Ling, prefect of Rhizun and ruler of the most loyal and supplicant city in our Emperor's undying empire etc., etc., You are welcome within our walls, stranger.'

'Me Bataar.'

'Right, well. That's the formalities out of the way' said Roo Ling. 'Captain Snu Zhi here will show you to your room. You may change into your feasting clothes there... or not, actually. Anyway, we have prepared a great banquet in your honour. I will see you again at the tables.'

He bowed low, turned towards the group of captains behind him, and walked back through them to his private residence.

'Bataar!' called Jochi, as he strode towards his brother. 'It is good to see you. When we get to your room you can tell me why you have travelled so far alone.'

'Me not alone' said Bataar. 'Captain Sulki and donkey with me sometimes. Bataar carry…'

'Not here, brother. Come.'

Jochi waved Snu Zhi away and headed for the sleeping quarters.

'What happened' said Jochi as the door closed behind the Mongols. 'Why are you here?'

'Great Khan send me to not make Captain Sulki dead' said Bataar.

'Genghis himself? Well, well' said Okatai, pacing slowly around the room like a poet with a new muse.

'Where is Sulki?' asked Jochi. 'And the donkey?'

'Both dead.'

'Didn't do a great job, then' said Stan. Jochi gave him a look. 'Fine. What happened?'

'Donkey make dead captain. I make donkey dead' said Bataar.

'The donkey killed Sulki? What did he do, slobber him to death?' said Stan.

'He make captain eat poison.'

'So the donkey handled some poison and fed it to Sulki?' said Jochi with disappointment. Even he was struggling to make sense of what his brother was saying. 'How did he make it?'

'Me not see him make poison. Sulki dead when I got back from walk. Donkey gave me poison but it not make me dead. I make man eat poison to help captain and now he dead.'

'The donkey was a man?'

Bataar felt a rare emotion; confusion.

'Yes. He say he was ass-ass. I like donkey better. More nice to say.'

'Assassin!' cried Stan. 'The donkey was an *assassin*.'

'Yes. That what he say. Hard word for Bataar. Donkey better.'

Okatai's thoughts spilled out. 'So Sulki is sent by Genghis to follow us, with Bataar here as a bodyguard. Then an assassin is sent to silence them both. It doesn't add up. Why would he go to so much trouble? Sulki must have understood the... something best left in the shadows. That doesn't explain why he would use espionage, though. Why introduce more moving parts if the mission was so sensitive to begin with?'

'You are looking at this from the wrong hilltop, Okatai' said Stan, surprising everyone. 'You are assuming that Bataar's intervention was unforeseen. What if our Great Khan wanted the spy removed from the board as well as Sulki? Bataar may be dull-witted, no offence, but it would take more than a single assassin to bring him down, given the right prevailing conditions.'

'*Prevailing conditions?*' blurted Okatai. 'Since when have you been a master military tactician?'

'It was around about the time our little reconnaissance mission began involving prefects, emperors, and unexpected assassins.'

'Assassins tend to be unexpected, it's something of a pre-requisite in their line of work.' said Jochi.

'Alright, just your standard, every day assassin then. I stand by my theory though, there is no way Genghis would leave anything to chance.'

'Genghis might' said Okatai, 'but Ulfred wouldn't.'

'Now would be a good time to tell us more than we already know' said Jochi. 'Whether you would wish to or not.'

'My dear Jochi' said Okatai. 'My wishes are an irrelevance. Time will reveal all you need to know. In the meantime, I suggest we ready ourselves for the feast. Here, put this delightfully pink shirt on, it might distract you for a while.'

'Is there room for one more?' called Mekki as he threw off Bataar's cloak and jumped off his back.

'Mekki!' cried Stan and Jochi as one.

'How did you get here?' asked Jochi.

'That's your question?' said Stan. 'He turns up on the back of your brother with a bad ankle and a furtive cloak and you ask how he got here?'

'Bataar carried me' said Mekki unnecessarily.

'So, is it true?' asked Okatai.

'Which bit?'

'Sulki and the donkey. The orders from Genghis. All of it!'

'All true' said Mekki. 'Turns out I didn't need my new writing system after all. Sulki spent all his time between the sheep and his yurt - not at the same time I should add - until Ulfred arrived one day. As far as I can tell he arrested Sulki there and then. The next day Sulki was given Bataar for protection and they began their journey here. I followed them as best I could, hiding in the shadows for fear of being caught in the open with my treacherous ankle. I finally caught up as Bataar was putting the finishing touches to the assassin. Sulki is dead, but his secret lives on.'

Okatai received a knowing look from Mekki. 'Perhaps now *is* the time to share a little information with you, after all' said the captain.

'I didn't think you had it in you, Bataar' said Jochi.

'Shut up!' cried Stan. 'He's about to tell us something at last.'

'Me not mean to kill' said Bataar. 'It was axy... ack seed...'

'Accident' said Jochi.

'Yes. That. Me try to help Captain Sulki. Me not do that good.'

'For the love of all that's green! Would you all just shut up for one minute. Sulki was a bad man, now he's dead. So is the man who was trying to kill him. Marvellous, lots of bad people are dead. Now, Okatai here is finally letting us in so if you wouldn't mind keeping your mouths closed for longer than it takes Jochi to mount a horse that would be very much appreciated!'

Okatai opened his mouth. A knock came from the door, followed by four enormous Jin guards. Major Tsensible stepped awkwardly in front of them.

Mekki slipped quietly behind the door.

'Sorry about this' he said timidly. 'I tried to persuade him against it, but there was just no telling him. Rest assured I'll be working around the clock to have your sentence reduced.'

'What's a clock?' asked Jochi.

'Our sentence?' said Okatai, who clearly had a greater handle on events than his companion. 'We haven't done anything!'

'That will form the basis of my argument' said Tsensible. 'Now, I'm afraid you must go with these guards at once.'

'Where are they taking us?' asked Stan.

'Captain Spi Khi's dungeon, I'm afraid. Don't worry though, the prefect has ordered him to ready his rooms but he is to leave his tools manacled for the moment.'

'Well why didn't you say so?' said Jochi. 'Who doesn't enjoy a little trip to an enemy dungeon to take in the sights and sounds. I'm sure it will be a joy.'

'Is that a joke?' asked Tsensible innocently. 'I'm never quite sure where the line is when it comes to you Mongols and your approach to death. Sometimes you're like bees on a flower and other times you're like wax on a pond.'

'And you think *we're* the confusing ones?' said Jochi.

'Wait' said Tsensible. 'Guards, I need a moment alone with our prisoners. Wait at the far end outside.'

'So we're officially prisoners now, are we? This is all getting a bit out of hand.'

'Shut up Jochi' said Tsensible in a tone that warned against further debate. He turned to the guards. 'I said out! I am a major of the prefect's own regiment, don't test my patience.'

The guards retreated to the corridor outside. Tsensible closed the door, locked it with a heavy beam and pressed his ear against the wood. Once he was content that the guards were far enough away he turned back to the group.

'So you're a major now. We *have* been good for your career' said Jochi.

'But not for my life expectancy. Now, there is bigger news here than my promotion. Who is this, and what is he doing in your room.'

Mekki stepped forward from behind the door.

'This is Mekki' said Stan. 'He's a friend from our home.'

'And what, may one ask, is he doing here?'

'That is a very good question' said Okatai. 'Mekki?'

Mekki swallowed. 'Well, it's like this' he began.

He gave a redacted version of events, enough to convince Tsensible but not so much as to rouse more suspicion than was already there.

'It seems we must rely on the stupidity of guards' announced Tsensible. 'Take your place beside your friends here. Let us hope, for all our sakes, that little enough attention has been paid to your numbers.'

Two bricks remained motionless in the city walls of Rhizun as the sun broke cover on the horizon. This was not unusual. The sun rose each morning, and bricks are, more often than not, slow-moving. Particularly so at dawn.

'Morning Nik' said Rik. 'Looks like it's going to be another lovely day in the Rhizun city walls.'

'Only if we make it to sunset in one piece' said Nik.

'Don't be like that' said Rik cheerily. 'We've survived this long, why would today be any different?'

'Because there's a shadow on the hills. Look.'

'Oh they're just birds, or sheep or something.'

'With their own private army of Mongols?' said Nik

The sky darkened as he finished speaking, covering them in shadow. A moment later it was dawn again.

'Morning Nik' said Rik. 'How do you know they're Mongols?'

'Well, stands to reason, doesn't it? How long have we been here now?'

'Oh, a couple of hundred years, give or take.'

'Right, and how many armies have besieged the walls?'

'None that I remember. Oh, there was that aerial assault a few years back.'

'That was just a stunned eagle. And all it did was smack into Pik and fall to the floor. Hardly an assault.'

The sun sank. The sun rose.

'Morning Nik' said Rik. 'Alright. Not counting the violent and dangerous avian attack, none. Ish.'

'Precisely! Now, if we assume there are a finite number of days, then everyone that passes makes it more likely that today will be the day we're attacked.'

'Or' offered Rik, 'we're never going to be attacked.'

'Come off it' said Nik. 'You heard what the humans were saying when they were repairing Fik's section last summer. Those Mongols are bloodthirsty imperialists, they said, bred to desecrate cultural treasuries on account of their voracious appetite for indiscriminate destruction.'

The darkness came. The light came.

'Morning Nik' said Rik. 'Well they would say that, wouldn't they?'

'Why?'

'They went to all the trouble of putting us bricks into an impenetrable formation for the good of the city. They wouldn't do that if they thought they'd be playing three rounds of *Fancy Bumpkins* with any armies that happen to pass by.'

'That's exactly my point!'

'Is it? Well, you might be right then' said Rik.

'I'm telling you, today's the day. Mark my words.'

Dark. Light.

'Morning Nik' said Rik. 'Not yesterday then? Maybe it'll be today. We'd better tell Tik. Is he back yet?'

'No, he's still down there with Hik. Feels like he's been there since the wall went up. You know what he's like when he gets going, though. His stories go on longer than two dogs fighting over a rabbit.'

'Well, he'd better get back up here quickly, here they come!'

'Bugger' said Nik. 'Positions everyone!'

CHAPTER TWENTY SIX

Genghis stopped sixty thousand men with a half-raised arm. He also broke a man's leg, caused another to headbutt the soldier immediately in front of him, and sent dozens of Captain Kupcayk's famous creations to the muddied floor.

They were almost at the very peak of the last hill between his nation of warriors and the most formidable city he had yet encountered. The warm, comforting prospect of imminent bloodlust mingled nauseously with the unique distraction of this confrontation. A short walk over the brow was his fragile legacy, a solitary point of life between immortality and irrelevance.

'We cannot throw everything at the walls' he thought aloud.

'We can't?' said Ulfred, lingering at Genghis' left shoulder.

'My successor is in there. We cannot besiege my apprentice.'

'He's your apprentice now?'

'I need answers, not questions, Ulfred. Wake up, man! How can we take this city without unleashing our usual hell upon them?'

'We could negotiate with them, my Lord. Perhaps they will release him in return for some small token.'

'You assume he is in a position that requires a release. What if he is performing his reconnaissance with perfect diplomacy? Our actions may put him in a position that does, in fact, require *release*. No, that won't do.'

'So we cannot negotiate, nor unleash our flames. I cannot see another way, my Lord.'

'I do not pay you to find paths we cannot take, Ulfred.'

'You don't pay me at all.'

Genghis gave Ulfred a sidelong glance. 'I will let that transgression slide, given the special situation we find ourselves in. Do it again and I'll cut your head off myself.'

'My apologies, oh Great Khan.'

'That's better.'

'We could show ourselves and see how they react' said Ulfred desperately. 'Their reaction would give us some clue as to their opinion of our little advanced party.'

'I will not cede control to my enemy. To do so would be to give up the advantage of surprise.'

Ulfred felt like he was trying to wrap an elephant with a fig leaf.

'We will break cover at the very zenith of the hill and not a pace further. Order the men to stand three deep right across the hills. If we cannot attack them with force we will use cunning in its place. They will see our warriors fill their vision, crumble under the sight, and meet our demands faster than Paat's men can empty a barrel.'

'And what are our demands, exactly?' asked Ulfred bravely.

'Details, details. We will recover him and assess our options then. All that matters for now is the safe recovery of my son.'

Ulfred winced a little at the use of the word. It was one thing to have incendiary knowledge secreted away in the dark part of your brain that looked after clandestine schemes, but quite another to hear evidence of it from a key protagonist. Doubly so when you have lost control of the timeline.

'We will see him kneel at your feet before we leave, my Lord. I give you my oath.'

'Well that's a relief' said Genghis. 'It is heartening to know I can rely on the support of a greying elder with no capacity for lateral thinking.' He adjusted his fleece jacket, checked his reins, and trotted his horse forward. 'Order the men, captain! It is time to roll our dice.'

'Feng!'

Roo Ling's Public Relations Office sidled into the prefect's private room. 'I see you have changed the tapestry, master.'

'Is that a problem?' asked Roo Ling. 'The flowers were giving me a headache.'

'No problem' said Feng diplomatically. 'May I ask why you chose a pig?'

'I would have thought that was obvious. It may surprise you to hear, however, that I did not summon you to discuss my taste in soft furnishings. There are many moving parts in my city, some more pressing than others. I need a sharp mind to cut through them and you have shown admirable skill in that regard. Now, are you listening with both ears?'

Feng nodded.

'Good. Untangle this. We have four Mongol enemies in the dungeon, having arrived in two parties. The emperor is sighted shortly before Genghis chooses to crest the brow of our lands and scupper the foundations of my great plan. One of my trusted majors chooses to leave this world without so much as a *by your leave*, and to top it all off my head of Public Relations is questioning my choice of decor. What do you make of that?'

'It seems to me that there is one rather elegant solution, master.'

'Go on.'

'As I understand things, you are afraid… no, conscious of an attack from Genghis Khan and how that would play out with the arrival of the emperor.'

'I didn't invite you here to state the bleeding obvious, captain. I want solutions.'

'Indeed, master. The problem does not lie with the captives in the dungeon. You can detain or release them at your leisure. The real issue is how to prevent a conflict between the Mongol army and the emperor's entourage.'

'The next sentence from your mouth had better be a solution or I'll put one of Captain Bun Sen's special solutions down it.'

'I suggest we allow both elements to reach close enough to the city walls for us to manage any sudden changes in dynamic, but with a buffer between the two, or all manner of bloodshed would befall us.'

'I will not draw answers from you like sap from a tree' said Roo Ling.

'Then may I suggest, when the time comes, that you send Major Tsensible out with our band of curious Mongols. Perhaps a little buffering will be all that is needed.'

'And what then? Are they going to single-handedly bring peace to our empires with a firm handshake and a polite request to stop marauding?'

'I will need more time to crystallise a plan, master.'

'You have five minutes.'

CHAPTER TWENTY SEVEN

'Funny how things turn out' said the radish. 'Doesn't seem that long ago since we passed this door before.'

'Yes, thank you for the reminder' said Tsensible. 'Nothing like an unfair imprisonment to get the memories flooding back.'

'I thought you were in charge of this lot? Why are you going in with them?'

'Roo Ling's orders.'

'I suppose it'll teach you not to do whatever it was you did again' said the radish unhelpfully.

'I didn't do anything, that's the whole point! All I did was follow the orders of the prefect, and look where it's landed me.'

'Then you did do something. You can't just go around following orders willy-nilly. What kind of a state would the city be in if everyone went around ordering people about?'

'That doesn't make any sense' said Tsensible. 'You follow orders for a living. And it was the bloody prefect, not some two-bit gutter cleaner with a big broom.'

'Oh, it was the prefect, was it? That's different then. Got to follow the orders of the prefect. You'd be a fool not to.'

Tsensible looked intently at the radish for signs of sarcasm but found none. 'You really are quite strange, do you know that?'

'Well this is cosy' said Jochi as they entered the room. 'I like what he's done with the place. Nothing like having spiky balls hanging from the ceiling, that's what I always say. Oh, and that table over there is stunning. The chains go right through the middle of it. Very clever.'

'Not now, Jochi' said Okatai. 'I need silence to concentrate.'

'I wouldn't bother if I were you. There's no escape from this. Look at the size of that lock.'

'Keep your comments to yourself, some of us are trying to save our skins.'

'Yessir, captain sir!' said Jochi.

'And no mock deference either.'

'I wasn't mocking, captain. I was just giving you all the credit you deserve for leading us to this fine example of a Jin torture chamber. Imagine! Me, the son of a common washerwoman getting to experience all the Jin empire has to offer in the very latest pain dispensaries.'

'That's it! I've had it with you. Cease your incessant ramblings at once.'

'Or what? Are you going to try your hand at Dungeon Master and then have to sleep next to a corpse for however long we're stuck here.'

'Maybe.'

'Oh shut up you two' said Stan. 'Our predicament is not ideal, I'll grant you, but we won't get out of here with talk like that. Now, may I suggest that we each take a few minutes to come up with the bones of a plan and we'll see if there isn't a little nugget of something buried in the middle of them? Good, now keep the noise down.'

Each of the group settled down in their own space. Any attempts to focus their thoughts by staring blankly at a wall were hampered by the myriad of pointy bits of iron attached to it. A side-effect of this, however, was that while their efforts to concoct an escape plan were a little sporadic, they were, in fact, coming up with ideas rather more quickly than if there had been a large window with a nice view instead.

'We could uncouple that mace from the wall and smash our way out' offered Tsensible.

'And the guards?' said Stan.

'We could… we could smash them too.'

'You'll do that, will you, *major*? Or will you develop a penchant for delegation this early in your tenure?'

'I thought you Mongols were masters of all things military?'

'So it's *you* Mongols now, is it?'

'Mean Okatai. Mean Jin man' said Bataar. 'Be nice. Lots to do to… to…'

'Escape?' offered Jochi.

'Yes. Out. Quiet, Bataar thinking.'

'Oh, well that's fine then. We're all going to be saved, men' said Okatai, standing up and waving his arms energetically. 'The lump of a man with brains the size of a chicken's eyeball is going to come up with an elaborate scheme to see us out of this heavily guarded, frighteningly stocked torture chamber. Well I, for one, am relieved to hear that!'

'I think he's losing it' whispered Stan to Jochi. 'I have to say, I didn't think he would be the one to break first.'

Jochi didn't react. He was looking intently at Bataar.

'What is it, brother?'

'Bataar has plan. We out soon.'

'I have a plan, master' said Feng.

'It had better be a good one' said Roo Ling.

'I believe it will suffice.'

'I don't want one that will suffice, captain. The fate of our city is at stake and suffocation is not conducive to victory.'

'Suffocation is not an extension of *suffice*, master. I believe you may have misunderstood the etymology.'

'Or perhaps you were unclear in your ramblings?'

'Yes, that must have been it' said Feng. 'I will be clearer in future.'

'Maybe I should rethink your appointment as Public Relations Officer' said Roo Ling with genuine consideration.

That would be thunderously fortuitous, thought Feng. 'I am here to bend to your will.'

'Perhaps after the imperial collision. Now, tell me of your non-suffocating plan.'

'There is information you should be aware of before I begin. There are no longer four Mongols in Captain Spi Khi's room.'

'That's to be expected, I suppose' said Roo Ling. 'You can't expect a man of his disposition to stay his hand when there is so much entertainment to be had.'

'It is rather the opposite, I'm afraid.'

'Come now, Feng. I know they breed like rabbits but even they couldn't increase their numbers so soon.'

'May I respectfully suggest that the time they have spent there is a secondary obstacle to population growth when one considers the notable absence of women.'

'Cease your chicanery' snapped Roo Ling petulantly.

'It seems there were two men at the gates.'

'You are treading a fine line here, captain. I welcomed the man Bataar personally. I would have noticed if there were two of them.'

'With respect, master, he has enough bulk to hide a smaller man in his cloak. I believe that is how they smuggled him in.'

'I can see why the Mongol military mind is held in higher regard than their discretion, for they have smuggled him directly into a room of *special purpose*.'

'Indeed, master. It means there are now five troublesome rats in the cellars, plus Major Tsensible.'

'That's more like it. You should use more of that kind of language when you are addressing the armies.'

'*When*, master?'

'Of course. How else are we to do it? Now, your plan.'

Feng swallowed hard. 'How many sheep do we have?'

'Not this again. I will not use sheep on the battlefield, how many times do I have to tell you? Do you have a plan that does not involve sheep?'

'Not as such, master, no.'

'Then we must go with my plan instead.'

'You have a plan?' said Feng with instant regret.

'I am the prefect of Rhizun, I always have a plan. We will send the four Mongols… *five* Mongols out onto the plain. Major Tsensible will accompany them to ensure a little composure is present when the worlds collide.'

'I'm not sure I follow, master.'

'Stan will lead the Mongols, on my orders, and the meeting of the world's two great empires will be bloodless and civil.'

'Forgive my frankness, master, but why would you trust such men in this most critical of moments?'

'They are just like Captain Merang's plum puddings' said Roo Ling. 'My people may be lions, but when the battle is to see who can make the best cake it is better to be the worst cook in the city than the fiercest lion on the steppes. Stan appears to be the least of their kind, yet he has a keen military mind. What makes it so perfect is that he has absolutely no idea. He will not raise so much as a pointy stick to the emperor while there is an army at his back. There will be no option available to him than one of diplomacy and discretion.'

'His clothes don't even fit him! Have you gone mad?' said Feng, now losing the run of himself.

'Still your tongue! I am the pinnacle of Rhizun. Do my bidding or I'll have the Mongol giant sit on your ears. Bring them all to me at once, there is much I wish to discuss with them.'

'So that's it, is it?' said Okatai. 'We wait for a guard to open the door with our dinner then hit him with something hard and heavy.'

'Yes. I hit hard' said Bataar.

'I'd say you do, but there is one rather obvious flaw in your plan.'

'I stand on it. No problem.'

'No, no. *Flaw*, not floor.'

'I stand on it' repeated Bataar.

'What Okatai is trying to say' said Jochi, 'is that there is a problem with your plan. The guards may not open the door, perhaps because they do not intend to waste any food on us, or because they could slide it through the gap under the door. Either way, we don't have anything to hit them with, in any case.'

'We use this' said Bataar, ripping an iron pole from its bracket on the wall.

'Well that's one problem solved' said Stan. 'All we need now is for someone to open this heavily locked door wide enough for us to drag them in and whack them over the head.'

'Yes. Bataar plan good. Very clever. See, door open now.'

The group turned as one in surprise to the opening door. Three guards stepped in and, seeing Bataar and the metal pole, raised their hands in a frantic but placating gesture.

'We have come to bring you to the prefect' said one. 'He sends his apologies for leaving you for so long in a place like this. Come!'

Jochi lowered Bataar's arm and took the pole from him. 'Looks like your plan was half right, brother.'

'Ah, gentlemen!' said Roo Ling cheerfully. 'Please, sit. I'm afraid my War Chamber is not the most welcoming of sights, but it will serve its purpose well today.'

The five Mongols and Tsensible each took a seat at the large square table.

'I don't believe we've met' said the prefect, extending a hand to Mekki. 'I am Roo Ling, prefect of this great city and warden of your immediate future.'

'Nice to meet you' said Mekki. 'Sorry about the nature of my arrival. Had I known the hospitality that awaited me I would have stood proudly in the open before your gates. You have some remarkable items in the lower rooms.'

'I will assume, for the moment, that you are praising our approach to weaponry and not hiding a disparaging remark within a compliment. My assumptions have a habit of reversing themselves, however, so I would counsel you to tread very carefully when you address me. Feng, the plans, if you would.'

Feng placed a large sheet on the table, fished out the counters from a box on the floor, and placed them in a neat pile in front of Roo Ling.

'This' began the prefect, 'is my great city. Some of you have seen this map before. For now, I will use these red counters to represent our emperor and his approaching army and the blue for our key fortifications within the city. Now for the interesting part.' He placed a single green counter at the very edge of the map. 'This, it may surprise you to learn, is your glorious leader. The great Genghis Khan.'

'It not him. Bataar walk hard for long time. That only one step.'

'It is a map, brother' said Jochi. 'Like a smaller version of the real thing.'

'Why they have two cities? Small one no good for living in.'

'I'll explain later' said Jochi, turning then to Roo Ling. 'My brother is more suited to heavy lifting than mental agility. Please accept my apologies.'

'There is a time and a place for every talent' said Roo Ling. 'As I was saying, this is your khan. He has crested the hills and approaches the city as we sit here. A battle is in neither of our interests, so I have masterminded a strategy worthy of this pivotal moment in our two empires. One that will see us all survive long enough to feel the warmth of summer on our backs.'

Tsensible and Feng shared a look of fearful anticipation.

'I propose a diplomatic sortie be sent out to greet the two armies as they converge, with a member of each faction acting as leaders in this most delicate of meetings.'

'I will not be a pawn in your war games' said Okatai. 'If the Great Khan is indeed approaching your gates then you would do well to barricade yourselves as best you can and hope his temper lasts long enough for you to find a way out.'

'Which is precisely why you will not be leading, *Captain* Okatai. This mission is too important to trust to an old head, no matter how much that head professes to prefer peaceful actions. What is needed here is youthful vision and a fresh perspective, which is why Stan will lead your party. Major Tsensible will lead ours and Ul-suh will accompany him.'

'Ul-suh' blurted Feng. 'He's no more than a trumped up cook. What use will he be on the other side of the wall?'

'You see, this is why you should stick to mass communication. He has done more to mend the rifts between our two people in a single conversation with Stan on the best way to cook a goat's leg than you have in a lifetime of service.'

'How do you know about that?' said Stan.

'Please, Stan. Eyes and ears cover my city with utter completeness. Nothing happens here without me hearing about it before the sun darkens.'

He stood up then, beginning his familiar meandering around the room, hands clasped behind his back.

'You will go out and act as a buffer between the two forces. Once a certain *stability* has formed you will prevent any bloodshed and instruct the Mongol horde to return home. The emperor will be allowed in, army and all, and peace will reign in the region once more.'

'That's your great plan, is it?' said Jochi. 'Send us out there and hope we have the diplomacy skills to prevent two salivating armies from knocking ten types of turnip out of each other? Perhaps if we ask Genghis politely enough he will appreciate our good manners and send his marauding army back to play peek-a-boo with the babies.'

'Not quite' said Roo Ling. 'Captain Okatai will remain here as you tread the tricky path between life and death.'

'Tricky!? It's a bit more than tricky' said Jochi. 'It's like asking the moon to pop down for a quick rendition of *The Dancing Tiger* and a nice cup of yak's milk.'

'Hang on!' said Okatai. 'I won't be held hostage while my men are sent to their deaths.'

'I'm afraid my mind is set. Rest assured you will not be harmed once *your men* follow their orders. I hope you trained them well.'

'What orders!?' cried Jochi, anger rising through his fear. 'This is madness.'

'Bataar make Jin man flat?' asked Bataar.

'Not yet' said Jochi, locking Roo Ling's eyes with an iron glare.

'Then it's settled' said Roo Ling. 'I wish you the very best of luck, and may the winds of favour blow your way.'

'They'll blow you away if Genghis isn't in a merciful mood' said Jochi. 'I'm not convinced you know what you're dealing with here. There is nothing to your plan, nothing to bend the iron will of the great Genghis Khan.'

'You will find a way' said Roo Ling. 'Okatai's life depends upon it.'

'Do you think they still make those fruit parcels?' asked Emperor Aizong as they rounded the last great hill. 'They were just to die for.'

'I do not believe they were mentioned in the reports, your Imperial Highness. I will have a scribe go through the records at once.'

'Oh do stop it, Bow Lo. Just because I make a passing comment doesn't mean you need to throw every resource in the empire at it. It was merely an insignificant rumination.'

'As you wish, oh glorious Emperor. Please accept my humble apologies for any offence caused to the Light of Heaven on his majestic journey.'

'Roo Ling was right, there is no place for such flowery language. I decree it has become old fashioned, please desist at once.'

'…' said Bow Lo.

'That's better. Now, how much longer must the imperial backside suffer the bumps and bouncings of this infernal carriage?'

'I expect the city to be sighted presently' said Bow with effort. 'I will see to it that the imperial b… that your comfort will be restored to a level befitting… sorry… that you will be comfortable once more.'

'Well done, Bow. Much better.'

The carriage continued its excitable motion along the track as the first crenellations of Rhizun's city walls came into view on their left. Bow excused himself from the presence of the most exulted emperor of the glorious Jin empire, Light of Heaven and Keeper of the Imperial Slipper, and zigzagged his way back down the convoy. The line of carriages slowly gave way to a wider line of pedestrians before ballooning out into a vast, solid swathe of the Jin Imperial Army. He approached an important-looking man whose enormous headwear seemed to be defying several laws of physics simultaneously.

'Angs Ti, the city has been sighted. Have your men readied for our arrival?'

'How many times do I have to say it before someone takes notice?' said Angs Ti. 'I am General Ti. First names are of no concern while a *General's* hat is on my head.'

'I can have that removed if you prefer' said Bow Lo. 'Your hat, naturally. It would be unfortunate indeed if your head was to be caught up in the act.'

'I will ready my men, you look after the emperor.'

'Lovely to chat with you, as always.'

Bow retraced his route back to the emperor's carriage with a lightness to his step he hadn't felt for some time. They had made it to lodgings and a proper dining table at last and only a few inconsequential infantrymen were lost to the aftermath of their gambling games along the way. It was a successful journey, all things considered. He reached the imperial carriage as it crossed the last expanse of land in front of the city, grabbed a support pole and swung himself up onto the ledge that ran around the outside. He took deep, contented lungfuls of the cool breeze as it flicked at his hair. He then coughed them back up as he spotted the dark smudge on the distant hills to his right.

'Your Imperial Majesty, Light of Heaven and ruler of the eternal Jin Empire!' he shouted as quickly as he could. 'Stop the horses! Enemy approaching!'

Emperor Aizong stepped down from his ornate carriage and put a shading hand to his brow. A line of Mongols, impossibly wide, straddled the hill to their right.

'They are weak' he said.

'Weak, your Highness?' said Bow Lo. 'Their army fills the horizon. Many hundreds of thousands of men. We have not travelled to war and have but forty thousand at our backs.'

'It is fortunate you are not in my position, for the empire would have scuttled away in fear at the flap of an eagle's wing. The Mongols have pulled themselves taut to give the impression of enormity, but there are gaps that betray them. There, look. The line is three or four men deep at best. They do not have *hundreds of thousands*, as you put it, they are of a similar size to our small brigade. There is little to fear from an enemy who must rely on trickery and illusion before blunt force. Come, we will ride to the gates and invite their cowardly Khan to some friendly conversation. Let's see how many of his men turn and run when they see the fullness of our numbers.'

'It seems they may have seen through our ingenious plan, my Lord. The enemy advances.'

'Yes thank you Ulfred. It may come as something of a surprise to you to learn I have two eyes of my own. However, they are attached to a more cunning mind than yours, so you may stop stating the obvious and ready yourself for orders.'

'Your will.'

Genghis studied the battlefield.

'Height' he mumbled.

He studied a little more.

'Ready the archers, Ulfred. No, wait. As you were.'

Genghis squinted his eyes as if it would help his concentration.

'Foot soldiers won't work' he said quietly. 'The horsemen might. No, they'll be too quick.'

'*Too* quick, my Lord' said Ulfred.

'What?' said Genghis distractedly.

'You said the cavalry would be too quick. The speed of our victory has never been a problem before. The faster the better, in fact.'

'Are you able to see into my thoughts?' asked Genghis icily.

Ulfred chose not to answer.

'Well? Can you?'

Ulfred wished he had answered. 'No, my Lord. I cannot.'

'Of course, you can't!' screamed Genghis. 'So if you cannot see my thoughts, how would you have any idea what the success of this attack looks like? Damn fool!'

Killing them all as quickly as possible usually does it, thought Ulfred. 'My most humble apologies, Lord Khan.'

'Better.' Genghis watched the Jin army restart their march towards the city walls and coalesce into a defensive formation on the plain.

'Interesting' said Genghis. 'They have seen through your charade, Ulfred. Bring the troops back and follow me down. I wish to learn this emperor's thoughts with the whites of my eyes in his vision.

My charade? thought Ulfred. *He's finally teetering on the edge of insanity.* 'We are to negotiate before the battle?'

Genghis answered Ulfred with a fiery glare, kicked his heels into Lavender, and rode down to meet Emperor Aizong, Light of Heaven, Emperor of the imperial cities of blah, blah, etc., etc.,.

Ulfred watched his khan shrink into the distance towards the enemy army. He thought he knew him better than any living man, Genghis included, but the predictability of warlords is not something to be relied upon for too long. He turned to face the soldiers at his back. 'Form up!' he roared. 'Follow your khan with sheathed weapons. Yah!'

CHAPTER TWENTY EIGHT

The six men stood at the gates of Rhizun like a bucket of fish preparing to be emptied into a piranha pond.

The gates creaked.

The gates opened.

As did Mekki's stomach.

'Pull yourself together' said Jochi. 'This is no time for weakness.'

'Was it you who just said that, Jochi? You sound like one of the military men, all you need now is to sort out your aim and you'll be ready to serve the Great Khan on the battlefield.'

'May I respectfully suggest we leave the bickering until after we have resolved this little dispute between warring empires?' said Tsensible, now close to fainting with nerves. 'Does anyone have any idea what we're supposed to be doing?'

'As I understand it' said Stan, 'we are to stride out into the no mans' land between the fierce Mongol army there, and the terrifying Jin one over there. We then persuade them to lay down their arms, shake hands, and play a nice friendly game of dice until the sun goes down.'

'That not sound like good plan' said Bataar.

'It isn't' said Ul-suh, 'but at least you lot have some idea as to why you've ended up here. I was boiling a pig's head one minute and the next I'm being summoned to the prefect's private chamber for a quick chat and a promotion.'

'You were promoted?' asked Tsensible. 'So sorry to hear that.'

'To a bloody captain, too. I mean, a corporal would have been fine, but *they don't have accountability'* he said.

'Did he say why he picked you?' asked Stan guiltily.

'He said I had a *special relationship* with our guests that may prove useful in a delicate situation. I don't know what he expects me to do here.'

'You cook' said Bataar. 'Need cook for big feast after.'

'After what?' asked Jochi.

'Flame and death.'

'No, brother. We are not going into battle, or at least I hope not. We are going to talk to each side and try to diffuse… stop the men being angry at each other.'

'That not sound like fun. Bataar good *executioner.*'

'You are, brother, you are. Just don't go and show off your skill until this whole thing has blown over please.'

'We should probably get this over with' said Stan. 'Everyone's looking and we haven't taken a single step forward yet.'

The group sagged as one, then lifted a leg with visible reluctance. They were on their way.

'See, it isn't so bad' said Stan. 'It's just a nice stroll on a crisp day.'

'If you don't count the armies on either side and the almost certainly fatal negotiation ahead of us' said Tsensible.

'Exactly.'

'What you cook after' said Bataar.

'A slow-roasted boar would be perfect' said Ul-suh.

'With a bit of sage' offered Stan.

'For the love of all that's green!' cried Tsensible. 'Now isn't the time for culinary chit-chat. We're heading to the most dangerous speck of land in the world without even knowing why we're heading there, let alone with any sort of plan, and all you lot are concerned about is what type of animal we won't get to eat because we'll be dead.'

'Perhaps now would be a good time to think of one' said Stan, pointing.

The armies were separated by no more than a hundred paces. Just enough space to fit the fates of six men.

Roo Ling shivered slightly in the whipping gusts of the watchtower. He swung his hair forwards over his shoulder and fidgeted with it as his newly formed diplomatic corps was about halfway there.

'Where is your money?' he asked.

'My money, master?' said Ettiket.

'How do you think this will play out? Genghis has brought his army to the very gates of our city, with an enemy in range, and not a single Mongol weapon has been drawn. Meanwhile, our emperor has trotted up to meet him with an army at his back and a refuge within an arrow's flight. He could attack or seek shelter, yet has done neither. There is no precedence, Ettiket. No precedence at all.'

'Then I will place my money on a new outcome. There will not be a battle, for there is no longer an advantage on either side. Genghis will not retreat, just as the sun will not burst into flame. Our Imperial Highness, likewise, will not back away in the sight of so many of his subjects.'

'So that's what you think will *not* happen. Now tell me what you believe *will* happen.'

'To make such a prophecy would require information given to men more consequential than I, master.'

'You would give Feng a good run for his money, Ettiket. Still, you are correct in your assumption and even I am not in possession of enough. That honour, I believe, lies with the Great Khan.'

'Major Tsensible, Stan' said Ul-suh, spreading an arm out towards no mans' land. 'I believe you are the leaders of our little band. We should give you the pleasure of introducing us.'

'How kind' said Stan, bowing low in mock gratitude. 'It will be a pleasure to have my life extinguished before you all. Saves me watching my friends' heads bounce on the grass.'

'Keep it light, Stan' said Mekki. 'It might not come to that.'

'Ah yes, our great plan may step nimbly between the cavernous diplomatic pitfalls and bring peace between two violently ambitious empires.'

'We not plan' said Bataar unhelpfully.

'Exactly!' cried Stan. 'We're almost within earshot and the sum total of our plan is comparable to Bataar's knowledge of pig herding, no offence.'

'Yes fence' said Bataar. 'No fence makes pig run away.'

'Well isn't that just perfect' said Ul-suh. 'Even Bataar has a better chance of making a career change than we do of surviving the afternoon, no offence.'

'Why no one want fence. Pigs good meat.'

'You're very quiet, major' said Jochi. 'I hope it's because you're formulating an ingenious scheme to get us out of this mess.'

Tsensible dragged his attention back to the group. 'Not as such' he said. 'I was wondering where I'd like my body to be left when I die.'

'Keeping positive, then?' said Ul-suh. 'I think I'd like to be laid in a chicken coop. It seems appropriate.'

'I'm more of a hilltop man myself' said Stan. 'Let the hawks take me into the skies.'

'I have an idea' said Jochi. 'How about we all stop planning our funerals and start planning a way out of this?'

'There is no way out' said Tsensible with effortless melancholy. 'We are the expendable pawns sent to ignite a great battle.'

'Not necessarily' said Stan.

Go on, said four facial expressions in unison. Bataar remained emotionless.

'On one side we have the fierce Mongol horde, and on the other a ruthless Jin army. Genghis has given up the option of besieging the city by presenting himself in front of the emperor. The emperor, on the other hand, has given up the element of surprise by rounding the hills and marching to the gates of his city. The armies are of a similar size, so any direct attack by Genghis would leave both sides with a decimated army. There wouldn't be enough Mongols left over to then mount an attack on the city, and Genghis would know it.'

'The emperor would not allow such a scything of his army in view of the city' added Tsensible, glad to have a splinter of convenient logic to cling to.

'Indeed. Neither would choose to give up so many men, so a stalemate is the most likely outcome. If we approach our mission with the knowledge that violence is less probable than diplomacy, then there is a chance we can talk our way back into the city with the same number of ears.'

There was a fragile silence as the group digested this improbable vestige of hope.

'Let's say your assumptions are correct for the moment' said Mekki. 'So we walk up into this gap between two pacific armies, offer our warmest compliments of the day to Genghis Khan and the Emperor, and ask them… what?'

'We could explain how any form of combat would be self-destructive and that a much better course of action is if we all say our goodbyes and think no more of it' offered Ul-suh.

'That best plan yet' said Bataar with striking accuracy.

'I'll think of something' said Stan, surprising everyone. 'Come on, let's get this over with.'

He pulled at Tsensible's sleeve as he widened his stride. 'If I'm putting my head in a noose then you're coming with me.'

The six men stood in an inverted 'V' formation a few paces back from the very centre of no man's land. Stan and Tsensible took a symbolic step forward and raised their chins.

'Bring your envoys!' roared Stan in what he hoped was a confident tone.

Genghis trotted his horse forward. 'Which of you is Mekki?' he asked. 'Bring him to me. Then we can begin.'

Stan looked behind him nervously to see Mekki peering furtively from behind Bataar. He gave him a supportive look before asking him to approach with a flick of his head.

'I am Mekki' said a wobbly voice.

'Come here where I can see you.'

Mekki surprised himself by successfully placing one leg in front of the other several times until he was within dagger-lunging range of the Great Khan.

'You are a surprising man' said Genghis. 'You appear to be a common dogsbody, with talent enough for latrine duties and little else.'

'Thank you' said Mekki.

'You see, that is the beautiful nuance of someone of your persuasion. Every action, no matter how trivial it may appear, is considered carefully yet instantly. A thousand imperceptible actions give birth to the grandest of schemes in your soul.'

'I see' said Mekki with more flailing desperation than he had ever levered into two words before.

'Tell me, how did you kill the assassin?'

'I didn't' said Mekki honestly.

'What do you mean you didn't? Who did?'

'He killed himself, in a manner of speaking. He poisoned Captain Sulki, then Bataar used the same tactic against him.'

'So you didn't kill him?'

'No, my Lord.'

'And you didn't kill Captain Sulki?'

'No.'

'So all you have done thus far is to hobble across the steppes and be caught by the Jin?'

'Bataar carried me most of the way.'

'Where is this Bataar?'

'Here, my Lord' said Mekki, turning his body and pointing.

'Bring him to me at once.'

Mekki sagged visibly as he escaped the glare of his khan and returned to the relative safety of his recently assembled band of panickers.

'Me Bataar' said the bulk as he placed himself in front of Genghis.

'Well stone the hills you are an unexaggerable specimen!' said Genghis. 'What do you do for the good of the nation?'

'I best *executioner*' said Bataar proudly.

'I can imagine. Stay here with the Tongueless, I could do with someone of your skills in the coming hours.'

Ulfred cleared his throat diplomatically.

'Yes, Ulfred?'

'You should promote him, my Lord. If he is to be a personal guard of the Great Khan then he must be ranked captain or above. *National Regulations*, I'm afraid.'

'Right, yes' said Genghis. 'What is your rank, Bataar?'

'No rank. Bataar is Bataar.'

'Great, well now you're a captain. If anyone tries to harm me, you are under orders to... to do whatever you think necessary to neutralise the threat.'

'...' said Bataar.

'The Great Khan means you are to hit anything that tries to hurt him' shouted Jochi.

'Am I *executioner* now?' asked Bataar.

'If the need arises' said Genghis.

A wonky grin appeared on Bataar's face, revealing his cornucopia of irregular brown teeth.

'Seems like promotions are all the rage these days' whispered Ul-suh from the corner of his mouth. 'Poor bugger.'

'Who said that?' said Genghis. 'Here, now!'

Ul-suh cursed inwardly and stepped forward.

'And who are you, Jin man?'

'I am Ul-suh, oh Great Khan.'

'Great Khan, eh? How would your emperor feel about you saying such a thing? Am I *your* Great Khan?'

'You are *the* Great Khan. My emperor is his Imperial Majesty, just as I am Captain Ul-suh.'

'And what is it you do, *Captain*? Why has your prefect seen fit to send you out with my men?'

'I have no idea' said Ul-suh honestly. 'One minute I was boiling a pig's head and the next I was marching out to meet you.'

'Why would a captain be boiling animal parts?'

'Pardon me, but I wasn't a captain then.'

'You implied you were cooking only recently. Do not take me for a fool, captain, or it will be *your* head bubbling before the day is out.'

'I can assure you I meant no disrespect. I was, as I say, a mere cook earlier today. My master deemed me worthy of promotion and immediate deployment for reasons best known to himself.'

'I see, so you have a part to play here it seems. Or at least, you have a part to play in your prefect's grand plan. I will not accommodate his advantage. Go back to the city or there will be a siege so monstrous as to echo through history. Starting with your head.'

'Yes, oh Great Khan' said Ul-suh thankfully.

He passed by his new friends as a grin spread on his face. 'Good luck, gentlemen. I'm off the hook' he said, clicking his heels together and skipping back to the city gates in blissful confusion.

'Now, who else do we have?' said Genghis.

Emperor Aizong, ruler of the vast Jin empire, Light of Heaven on Earth, and owner of more names than an escaped convict, called over to his aide. 'What are they saying, Bow? All I can hear are roughly hewn noises.'

'I believe they are discussing the best way to boil a boar's head, though my translations may be a little off.'

'They are a strange folk indeed' said Aizong, stroking his moustache thoughtfully. 'Now there is only one of us left in their little band of diplomats. Bring him to me, he can translate for us.'

Bow Lo called out to Tsensible, just as Genghis did the same. Tsensible looked between the two, decided choosing one over the other would be more fatal than he would have preferred, and stood squarely between the two.

'If I may offer my services as translator' he said, once in each language, with arms raised in a peaceful gesture.

'Good' said Aizong.

'Good' said Genghis.

'What did he say?' asked Aizong.

'He said *good*, your Imperial Majesty' said Tsensible.

'What did he say?' asked Genghis.

'He said *good*.'

'And after that?'

'He asked what you had said.'

'And what did you tell him?'

'I said you said *good*.'

'Good.'

'What is he saying now?' asked Aizong.

'He asked what you had asked me' said Tsensible.

'And what did you say?'

'I said that you had asked what he said.'

'And the last thing he said, what was that?'

'He just said *good*.'

Tsensible rubbed the bridge of his nose patiently and turned to Genghis. 'May I suggest that each leader make a statement in turn, which I will then translate into the other language? The opposing leader can then respond with a statement of their own and we can take it from there.'

'Agreed' said Genghis.

He repeated the suggestion to his emperor.

'What did he say' asked Aizong.

'He said he agreed.'

'Then I agree.'

Tsensible gave a shallow sigh of thanks. 'Marvellous. Now, as His Imperial Majesty is hosting this little get together, he may make his statement first. Your Highness' said Tsensible sweeping an arm as he backed away from the centre ground.

Emperor Aizong stepped forward and looked at Tsensible. 'Name and rank, officer?'

'Major Tsensible, your Imperial Highness.'

'Major, indeed. You don't look like a major.'

'Thank you.'

'Are you ready?'

No, thought Tsensible. 'Yes, your Highness.'

'So the famous Genghis Khan has finally breached the boundaries of my empire. It would seem natural that I would welcome you with the same respect I would give to a rat in a cooking pot, yet I am reluctant to be so obtuse. You have journeyed far to be here, but without the numbers needed to defeat me. A crazed warrior you may be, but a fool you are not.'

Obtuse, thought Tsensible. I'm not even sure what that means in my own language.

'I believe you are here for another reason' continued Aizong. 'And I would wager it has something to do with this peculiar collection of vagabonds. Tell us your true motivation, or go down in flames.'

As Tsensible translated as best he could, Ulfred leaned in towards Genghis and whispered. 'Okatai is not here, my Lord. May I suggest restraint?'

'Your Imperial Highness' began Genghis. 'You are wise indeed, for I am not here to raze your city to the ground, though you are wrong to suggest we would not succeed in that regard. With the chop of an arm I would unleash a hell never before seen in your prim and pretty lands. An unparalleled volley of ferocity to melt the legs of your hardest soldiers.'

Ulfred gave him a discreet kick.

'But, as I say, that is not why I am here. I wish to collect something that is mine. Something of great importance to me.'

Tsensible cursed the uncommon language as he translated.

'It must be important indeed if you come to retrieve it personally with thousands of men at your back' said Aizong.

'One can never be too careful when it comes to family' said Genghis.

'*Family*, indeed?'

'Yes, family. Do not think I am so clumsy as to unknowingly give away information that strengthens your hand. I know you will think me more malleable if my family's interests are on the negotiating table, but let me be clear. My army is my family. My land is my family. My horses, my catapults, my arrows are my family. You cannot barter with them, for they saturate this land. You have a choice to make, oh Imperial Highness. Stand aside as I hold an audience with the prefect of this city, or bury your dead where they fall as I take control of it myself.'

Tsensible began his translation with a brief eulogy on the importance of remembering he was just a messenger.

'Your threats do not concern me, khan. My men know these lands like their own mothers and would protect them with the same vehemency.'

'These lands?' scoffed Genghis. 'We're on a flat, open expanse beside a city wall. Do you think this is the first time we have found ourselves in such a position? Major Tsensible, here.'

Tsensible translated quickly, then approached Genghis.

'You are from this city?' asked the Mongol leader.

'I am.'

'Then I would like you to describe the location of somewhere within those walls where a flaming arrow can land without causing damage.'

'There are gardens that are seldom used. I would say they are five hundred paces in and just to the right of the bell tower.'

'Pikspot!' roared Genghis.

A tall, lithe man scurried forward through the crowd and bowed low at the feet of his khan.

'Tell him, Tsensible. Then tell your emperor. We will show our might without snipping the hair of a single Jin.'

Pikspot selected an arrow from his quiver, loaded his bow, and drew back his arm.

'Wait!' cried Tsensible. 'I haven't finished telling him yet.

'Well hurry up then' said Genghis. 'He can't hold his arm taut all day.'

Tsensible rushed through the translation.

'He can't do that' said Aizong. 'The city will think they're launching an attack.'

'That's what I said. We need to get a message to Roo Ling.'

'Tell that to Genghis.'

Tsensible jogged the few steps between the two men. 'We need to get a message to Roo Ling.'

'And how, Major Tsensible, do you propose we do that?'

'Let's start by relaxing that man's arm.'

Genghis nodded to the archer.

'I think I may be able to help' said Jochi, stepping bravely up. 'He is doubtless watching us. We could write a message in large letters in the ground.'

'They would never be able to read it from this distance' said Genghis.

'With respect, khan, we have experience in this regard. I believe it will work.'

'Fine' said Genghis. 'But if it doesn't work I'll have your legs chopped off.'

Tsensible took the arrow from Pikspot and began tearing at the ground. When he finished he looked at Jochi. 'That about right?'

'That should do it' said Jochi. 'They're bigger than mine and we're closer to the watchtowers.'

'What does it say?' asked Genghis.

'It says: The Mongols are about to fire a peaceful arrow at the garden. It is not a declaration of war. Ring bell to confirm understanding. Stand by.'

'Stand by is bad idea' said Bataar. 'Might get arrow in face.'

'It gets to the point I suppose' said Genghis, nodding his approval of the message.

'That why it bad idea' said Bataar.

The bells rang once, confusing most of the population who were unaware of the message and took it to mean a ferret had been executed in the dining hall.

'When you're ready, Pikspot' said Genghis.

The archer drew another arrow, loaded it, and pulled back his arm. He glanced at the assembled crowd to be sure there were no unexpected developments this time, aimed, and released his grip.

CHAPTER TWENTY NINE

O ne of the downsides of locusts' inability to speak more than one language is that they have been unable to pass on their hard-earned secret of immortality. For thousands of years, they practised reincarnation, almost to the point of perfection, and tried myriad ways to share their knowledge, but no one ever seemed to take the hint.

'We tried to let the humans know first' said Flinch to his current son, Minch, 'but they were more interested in themselves to pay any attention to our efforts. We even summoned every locust in the known world and crammed ourselves into the land around those big pointy buildings in the desert they seem to be so proud of, but they were too busy worshipping a giant cat. They're an odd bunch, those humans.'

'What do you expect from a species that haven't even noticed your basic planetary curvature?' said Minch. 'There's no hope for them. At least, not until they work out the intrinsic relationship between cosmology and navigation. Poor buggers still think your common or garden solar radiation is just a sign of the...'

'Then there were the birds' interrupted Flinch.

'Oh yes, the birds! Took us forever to get so many of us up into the clouds and all they did was pick a few of us off for dinner as we fell to the ground. They learn to fly and all of a sudden they think they're above us insects. Arrogant buggers.'

'You're right, son. They've no class, none at all' said Flinch supportively.

'And another thing' said Minch, now firmly on a roll. 'Those mayflies go on about the *circle of life* and how they're the most efficient creatures in the universe because they circle back to where they started – which is dead – after just one day. Someone should tell them it's a dotted line of life, not a circle. How is an animal supposed to make the most of life if it gets snuffed out before the bats come out?'

'I think their point is that we don't evolve because of reincarnation' said Flinch. 'We just keep coming back as locusts.'

'Fair point' conceded Minch. 'If we could evolve a little each time we're reborn then eventually we'll be able to communicate with other species and stop them spending most of their time searching for meaning in their life.'

'Do you know something, Minch? I think I know how to do just that. Yes! That's it! I have the answer.' cried Flinch, hopping from leg to leg.

'Well spit it out then!' said Minch.

'This is going to change life as we know it' said Flinch with a giddiness reserved for those who have just worked out how to remove the question of the meaning of life for all living things. 'All we have to do is get a great, big...'

An arrow whistled through Flinch's head, preventing him from sharing history's greatest moment of inspiration since one unusually evolved amoeba realised it could blink.

Ferrets, thought Smahtarz as he wandered through the gardens. *Haven't had that one for a while.*

He was making his way back to the Lu Hen Cha with some bakery supplies from the great storage halls. As he passed the unappreciated flora he didn't hear an arrow as it passed through most of his chest.

Bugger, he didn't have time to think.

Thud.

'Nice shot, I assume?' said Genghis. 'How do we know if it fell true?'

'Ah' said Tsensible. 'Hadn't thought of that. Hang on.'

He picked up the arrow again and scratched frantically at the ground. 'There' he said at last.'

'What does it say?' asked Genghis.

'It says to ring the bell twice if the arrow fell peacefully into the garden' said Jochi.

'Now is not the time for false showmanship…'

'Jochi.'

'…Jochi. Now, Major Tsensible, tell me what it says before I… before I do something almost fatal to you.'

'It says to ring the bell twice if the arrow fell peacefully into the garden' said Tsensible nervously.

Genghis stared at Jochi. 'There is more to you than meets the eye, young Jochi. We must discuss your future when this has all settled down.'

'Yes, my Lord' said Jochi, furiously hoping it didn't involve a promotion.

A silence descended heavily onto the group. No bells tolled.

Ettiket sprinted down the smooth tracks in the road towards the garden. He ran wide as he hurtled through the archway and into the immaculately manicured landscape. His eyes scoured the area until they fell upon a prone figure lying on his back with a Mongol arrow protruding casually from his chest. Ettiket bowed his head respectfully before reaching to close the man's eyelids. He stopped short as he took in the identity of their owner.

'Well, well, well' he said aloud. 'If it isn't the peach thief of Rhizun. Looks like Captain Merang's fruity parcels will be back to their old selves again.'

He pulled the arrow from the man's chest as if plucking a chicken and rubbed it into the dirt. He dragged Smahtarz's body against a wall behind a nearby bush and headed back to the watchtower.

'You must find this a little awkward' said Emperor Aizong.

'There is time yet' said Genghis.

'Perhaps we should do a countdown' offered Aizong. 'There's nothing quite like a countdown to build the tension, wouldn't you say? We could start at ten.'

'How about forty thousand?'

'Ten is a most gracious offer, khan. Your time is already up, but I am a fair man. I am also a man with a penchant for thrills, so we will have a countdown and it will begin at one hundred. Major Tsensible, if you would be so kind.'

'One hundred' began Tsensible with near-catatonic reluctance.

Genghis stared at the tower as if his glare alone could move the enormous iron bell.

'Ninety-nine.'

'Ninety-eight.'

'Perhaps you could just say every fifth number' suggested Stan.

'What did he say?'

Tsensible quivered. 'Ninety-six. He said perhaps I... ninety-five... could just say every... ninety-four... fifth number... ninety-three.'

'Ah, but where's the drama in that? Every number is a nail in the Mongol coffin. Wouldn't you agree, major?'

'Ninety... your will, your Imperial Majesty. Eighty-nine.'

'My Lord?' said Stan weakly. 'May I make a suggestion?'

'Eighty-seven.'

'Why not?' said Genghis.

'Well, I was thinking. Assuming your strategy is dependent on sending our emissaries into the city, and that if the bell tolls then we will be free to do so, then all we need to cover off is how to get them beyond the walls without the help of a bell. It will cost many men to reach that far if we simply set off without a word, but why wouldn't we make our way there now? We could talk the emperor into an oath that he will not attack while Tsensible's countdown continues.'

Genghis looked at Stan properly for the first time. He studied his eyes and his mouth, his ears, and his nose. 'Does the name Takkan mean anything to you?' he asked at last.

'No, my Lord.'

'No, I don't suppose it would.'

Genghis sank into thought.

'Seventy four.'

'My Lord?' asked Stan.

'You do it' said Genghis. 'I would like to see how you deal with those in power.'

'Me? But I am just *your general dogsbody*. Captain Okatai said so himself.'

'Did he, indeed. All the more reason to prove him wrong then, wouldn't you say? Don't ask the emperor for an oath, though. It will only serve to rouse suspicion. Find another way.'

'Your will, my Lord.'

'Sixty-seven.'

Stan crossed the no man's land and gave a deferential bow to Emperor Aizong and his aide.

'Your Imperial Highness. Please forgive the short nature of my address, but time is of the essence and I have come to make a simple request.'

Tsensible translated between counts.

'Go on' said the emperor.

'If the bell does not toll I would like the opportunity to release my captain from his bonds within the city before the carnage begins. He is only there to prevent an all-out assault on the city, but we both know that a single man would not prevent such an outcome. All I ask is that you allow us enough time to spare one life.'

'Sixty two.'

'And how would a... whatever you are... prise an enemy soldier from the talons of the mighty Jin empire?'

'We will release Major Tsensible in exchange for Captain Okatai.'

'*Release?*' said Aizong. 'He is a free man.'

'Fifty-six' said Tsensible in a squeakier voice than before.

'For now' said Stan. 'Allow me to take a small band of men into the city and he will not be harmed.'

Emperor Aizong looked admiringly at this matted bundle of misshapen leather and wondered at the incongruous nature of the evidence before him. 'You are a curious people' he said. 'Your military minds are well-honed, yet you cannot bring yourself to maintain a basic level of hygiene. How oddly your priorities lie.'

'Fifty.'

'With respect, your Imperial Highness, our priority now should be to prevent an all-out war, not to pass comment on the cleanliness of my undershirt.'

'*Our* priority?'

'My apologies, I was working on the assumption that you were as keen as I to maintain the current numbers in your army.'

'Forty-six.'

Stan's head was swimming, or rather it was flailing at the waves in wild desperation. Next time he would keep his ideas in his head where they belonged.

'What is your rank, man?'

'I do not have a rank, your Majesty. I am more your general do… diplomatic envoy.'

'No rank, eh? Interesting. I can read you well enough, *man*. You are more powerful than you would have me believe, of that I am sure. It would be enough to know the Great Khan has sent you to negotiate on his behalf, but you have tried too hard to hide your true position. I am not inclined to poke a wasps' nest for the sake of learning your place in Genghis Khan's horde of creatures. Attempt your rescue, if that is the cost, and I will silence you and your captain on your return.'

'Forty-one.'

Stan bowed low and shuffled backwards.

'Well?' asked Genghis.

'We may take a party of men into the city for an audience with the prefect' said Stan.

'At what cost?'

'*Cost*, my Lord?'

'What did you offer in return?'

'Thirty-seven.'

'Nothing' said Stan.

'Nothing? You asked the Jin emperor to hold his fire while we waltz up to his city to have a quick chat with its prefect, and he asked *nothing* of you?'

'Yes, that appears to be the case. It seems Okatai was right, words *are* our future. Who would have thought it? He had doubts as to my standing in your army, thinking me to be more important than I am. I simply leveraged that to our advantage, nothing more.'

Genghis clasped Stan's shoulder and shook it. 'He did no such thing. Come!'

'Thirty-two.'

'Mekki, Jochi, you are with us. Bataar, stay here with the Tongueless and watch the emperor. If he moves, hit him over the head.'

'I would rephrase that if I were you, my Lord. Bataar has a habit of taking orders a little too literally.'

'Good' said Genghis. 'Now, gentlemen, we ride! Oh, sorry. I ride, you jog beside me.'

'Twenty-eight.'

As the four men began their journey to the city gates a powerful metallic boom assaulted their ears. Genghis spun his horse around and faced down the Jin emperor.

'It seems we have negotiated our way into your city twice, *your Majesty*. How's that for a show of power? Major Tsensible, you will come with us now. Your skills will be required once more.'

Ul-suh stepped through the narrow opening in the huge gates and skipped the first few steps inside to be sure he wouldn't be pushed back out. His relief was tempered a little by the sight of Captain Khi, arms folded and scowling like an ill-treated yak.

'You are lucky that Roo Ling has asked for you directly' said Khi.

'That's lucky these days, is it?' replied Ul-suh.

'It is when you've just made me open our gates with a Mongol Horde pressing against them.'

'It just took me ten minutes to get here, they're hardly *pressing*' said Ul-suh defensively.

'Well they're closer than they were this morning. What are you doing here, anyway?'

'If it's all the same to you, captain, I'll leave that information between me and the prefect. Now, if you'll excuse me, I have an appointment to keep.'

Ul-suh strode past the gatekeeper with a confident gait that offered precisely the opposing message to that of his current emotional stability. He made his way to the prefect's quarters, nodded to a guard, and waited.

'He's in the watchtower' said one of the guards without unlocking his gaze from a captivating brick in the opposite wall.

'Which one?' asked Ul-suh.

'Watchtower' repeated the guard unhelpfully.

'Great, thanks.'

Ul-suh ran now, along the labyrinthine corridors to the nearest tower. He careered up a spiral staircase and burst out onto the parapet.

Lah Fing turned casually to take in this latest development. 'Afternoon, Ul-suh. How are the pigs?' he said as if there was nothing in the cook's actions to warrant any other question.

'Where is the prefect?' asked Ul-suh, panting.

'Over there' said Lah, pointing. 'Fourth one along.'

'Thanks. Pigs are fine, by the way.'

Ul-suh ran along the path and through the series of towers until he reached the fourth. He knocked on the door and waited.

'Come!'

He opened the door and stepped inside. Roo Ling was leaning on a windowsill with a cylinder of fingers pressed against one eye.

'What did he say?' asked the prefect without turning to greet his visitor.

'Who?' asked Ul-suh.

'Who? *Who*!?' cried Roo Ling. 'Genghis bloody Khan!'

'My apologies, master. I thought you may have meant the emperor.'

Roo Ling lowered his hand, turned with exaggerated slowness, and bore into Ul-suh's eyes. He spoke in a menacingly slow voice. 'I did not mean the emperor. I meant the warlord leader of our greatest enemy, with whom you have just held a conversation, the contents of which would be of great use to *your* prefect as he hones his final strategy.'

'He held a short question and answer session to establish who was who, then asked why I was promoted.'

'And what reason did you give?'

'I said I had no idea.'

'Good. Was that all?'

'Forgive my ignorance, master, but do you mean *was that all* as in *you're dismissed*, or as in *did he say anything else*?'

'Ettiket, how easy is it to demote a captain?'

'Easier than you might imagine, master. You need only say the word' said Ettiket from a shadowy corner.

'Good. Now listen to me, *captain*. I'll have you demoted to corporal faster than you can peel a turnip if there's any more insubordination, do you understand?'

'Oh yes, I understand perfectly, master. Just one minor query, if you don't mind? Does a demotion come with any… *physical consequences*, or just the demotion itself?'

'Right, that's it! I've had enough. I hereby…' Roo Ling paused for a moment before turning to Ettiket. 'How formal does this need to be?' he whispered.

'Not at all, master' said Ettiket.

'I see. Captain Ul-suh, I demote you to your previous rank of…'

'Cook' said Ul-suh helpfully.

'…cook.'

A smile creased Ul-suh's face. 'Is that all, master?'

'Yes. Bugger off out of my sight.'

'Yes, master. Thank you, master' said Ul-suh as he slinked out of the door. He almost collided with an incoming Lah Fing who swerved acrobatically around the departing cook and straight into Roo Ling's watchtower.

'He's coming!' he cried. 'Genghis is marching on the gates!'

'Bloody typical' said Roo Ling. 'How long have I been watching them, Ettiket? I turn my back for one minute and the emperor lets Genghis stroll up to our very door. Sums up my day. What's your name, watchman?'

'Lah Fing, master.'

'Well you are now Captain Lah Fing of the Watch. Well done on your fine work and enjoy your weekly apple. Tell Sikhing he may look for his pants elsewhere from now on.'

'Yessir, thank you sir!' said Lah. 'Will that be all? Only, my watch partner is a cantankerous stick-in-the-mud and I'm sure this news will cheer him up no end.'

'Yes of course, see to your men captain' said Roo Ling. 'Ettiket, we must leave too. We can't have Genghis Khan brought into the city without me being there to check his stride.'

CHAPTER THIRTY

'**D**o we knock?' asked Genghis. 'I've never invaded a city this way before. There's usually a little more fire and iron.'

'They will open it for us, my Lord' said Stan.

'Right. It's that easy, is it? They just open the gates and we walk through?'

'That is the most likely scenario, yes.'

'So that is why you were so keen to have us reach the walls, eh?' said Genghis wagging a finger at Stan. 'What a mind you have.'

Stan was spared having to find an appropriate response to the ill-founded compliment by a loud creaking noise.

'You were right!' said Genghis, as if seeing the sunrise for the first time. 'Incredible.'

Stan, Genghis, Mekki, Jochi, and Tsensible crossed the threshold of Rhizun and into the cool shadow of the gatekeeper's courtyard. Roo Ling stood proudly in a solitary sunbeam and his hands clasped the top of an ornate staff in front of him.

'I am Roo Ling, prefect of Rhizun and loyal subject of His Imperial Highness, Light of Heaven, blah blah, etc., etc.,. Welcome to my city, Great Khan. Come, we have much to discuss.'

Several guards fell in behind Roo Ling as he walked off towards a squat tower at one corner of the courtyard.

'Should I not introduce myself?' asked Genghis, now utterly lost in the mystery of this new approach to warfare.

'I think he knows who you are' said Stan.

Jochi and Mekki walked side by side as the most polite invaders in history followed Roo Ling through the winding city streets.

'What's going on with Stan' said Jochi. 'Everything he says is the greatest idea ever concocted, and he's negotiating with emperors now too!'

'Time will tell' said Mekki knowingly. 'Meanwhile, I may as well be on latrine duty for all the notice anyone is paying to me.'

'I wouldn't complain' said Jochi. 'The more *you* get noticed, the more your neck does too. I'll be quite happy if this all blows over quietly and we return home with nothing more than an above-average anecdote and an increased dislike of bright clothing.'

'Not much chance of that' said Mekki. 'On the scale of *things to do to go unnoticed,* heading into a meeting between Genghis Khan and a Jin prefect is right next to *setting fire to the emperor's pants.*'

'Let's keep our mouths shut and an eye on the door.'

Inside the stout building was a single room, entirely unfurnished. It was large enough to fit a good-sized table and perhaps even a small desk, but the space was devoid of such features. Any features, in fact. Except, that is, for the large hatch in the centre of the floor and a single, wall-mounted torch. Ettiket pulled at a heavy iron hoop and lifted the wooden panel away, revealing a stone staircase that led down to a blackness that had clearly been practising its portentiousness. He took the torch from the wall and stepped into the hole.

'Hold!' shouted Genghis. 'You don't expect us to go in there?'

'But of course' said Roo Ling, opening his arm to indicate Genghis should do so at once. 'How else are we to get to my dungeons?'

'This is your idea of hospitality, is it?' asked Genghis.

'No. It's my idea of security. Your reputation is not one of a washerwoman.'

'I should hope not' said Genghis defensively. 'I sacked three cities last year. I didn't do that for the good of my health.'

'Indeed. I hope, then, you understand my moderate precautions. It is the safest place in the city, for both of us.'

'Have you *seen* the size of my army? It is not I who needs protection, prefect.'

'You're quite right, of course' said Roo Ling. 'Which is why I must insist you accommodate mine, part of which is to hold our meeting in a secure location. Now, if you don't mind?'

'Only if you promise to keep the hatch open while we're in there' said Genghis.

'Fine.'

'Promise?'

'I said so, didn't I?'

'No, you just said *fine*. Your people are strange in many ways, Roo Ling, but you understand an oath well enough, I'm sure. Full-sentence, please.'

'I promise not to close the hatch while we're inside' said Roo Ling in a tone that wouldn't have been out of place had it come from a spoilt child.

'You are a wily one, I'll give you that' said Genghis. 'Come on now, properly this time.'

'I said exactly what you wanted me to say. And you call us strange?'

'I know you will not close the hatch, you'll be in my line of sight the whole time. I need an oath that the hatch will not be closed, whether by your hand or another's.'

'I promise the hatch will remain open, and not be closed by any man…'

'Or woman…'

'…or woman while we're inside. There, does that satisfy you?'

'It will have to do' said Genghis.

'You wouldn't be afraid of the dark, by any chance, would you?' asked Roo Ling.

'The darkness is fine, it's the enclosure I take issue with. Why would you choose to confine yourself to such a small area when there is a whole landscape out there to spread out in? I can understand building a city, from a defensive standpoint, but why make everything inside the walls so small? What if there's a flood?'

'It provides order and security' said Roo Ling. 'Why would you leave yourself vulnerable on the steppes when you can relax inside these walls morning, noon and night?'

'I am the Great Khan of the fiercest fighting men in the world, prefect. Anyone who comes within a thousand paces of our settlements without an invitation would have his head removed faster than you can fry an egg.'

'Yet here you are, afraid of a door.'

Genghis bristled.

'Anyway' continued Roo Ling, 'there is someone I would like you to meet. Follow me and no harm will come to you, I give you my *oath*.'

'Fine' said Genghis. 'But I'm not happy about it, just so you all know. Bataar, you stay with me. Bataar?'

'He is with the Tongueless, my Lord' said Mekki.

Bugger thought Genghis. He looked around at his options. 'Who is the strongest?' he asked.

'We each have unique skills, oh Great Khan' said Jochi. 'Stan has a flair for flavours, I am a fine horseman and Mekki is… is…'

'I am a master of surveillance' said Mekki.

'Bloody marvellous!' said Genghis. 'So if I want to find a lost horse so I can cook it for dinner you're the men to call. You, here.'

Mekki looked around innocently, pointing at his own chest. 'Me?'

'Yes, you. It seems surveillance is as close as I can get to security. If a blade comes for me, you are to get in the way, understand?'

'Yes, my Lord.'

'Are you quite ready now?' asked Roo Ling.

One by one the group entered the hatch, descending just a short way to a corridor that ran perfectly straight for much further than the eye could see. They reached another staircase, spiral this time, and headed back up. At the top was a room, almost identical to the one in which they had entered. Ettiket opened the only door and continued on around a series of corners until he reached the unremarkable door that hid the room of *special persuasion.*

'Some of you have been here before. Do not be alarmed by the furnishings, khan. They are meant for others. Your friend is inside, but no harm has come to him I can assure you.'

'Now I really do feel diplomatic' said Mekki. 'We're going round in circles.'

A guard stepped out through the open doorway and stood to attention as the group passed into the room. Inside was not quite as they had left it. There were fewer contraptions, and those that remained were of the less maniacal sort. The table with the ominous chains had been removed and the mace that hung on the wall had been replaced by an altogether less intimidating object.

'How good of you to come' said Okatai from his manacled position halfway up the wall. 'I mean, I was enjoying the company of that fine gentleman there, but one does need a change of company once in a while, wouldn't you agree?'

'Captain Okatai!' called Stan. 'What are you doing up there?'

'What am I doing…? *What am I*…? I'm having a bloody picnic, what does it look like I'm doing?'

'I'm afraid there was nowhere else to put him' said Roo Ling. 'It wouldn't be my first choice for our guests, but when Captain Spi Khi designed the room he had all the manacle sockets placed halfway to the ceiling. I think it was just his particular sense of humour.'

'Likes to leave a punch line hanging in the air, does he?' said Mekki.

'He does not allow punches to be thrown here' said Roo Ling. 'All contact with the guest must be made by a designated implement.'

Mekki sighed. 'Are we going home yet?'

'Nearly' said Jochi. 'We just have to rescue this prisoner from an enemy torture chamber and negotiate a lasting peace between two warring empires.'

'Any peace only needs to have enough integrity to put our army between me and the city walls. Anything longer than that is someone else's problem' said Mekki.

'Not precisely' said Genghis. 'You will be at the forefront of any future campaigns, *Captain* Mekki.'

'Captain, my Lord?'

'Captain?' said Jochi.

'*Captain?*' said Stan.

'Him?' said Okatai.

'You have shown your worth in modern surveillance' said Genghis, 'despite your obvious flaws. I am sure you will find ways to use them to your advantage in the years ahead.'

'Captain?' said Okatai.

'Release this man at once' said Genghis.

'I'm afraid I can't do that' said Roo Ling. 'I intend for us to have an amicable meeting, but only a fool would remove such a leverage from his cuffs.'

'May I make a suggestion?' said Okatai from the wall.

'Quiet!' snapped Roo Ling.

'Gentlemen, if I may?' said Stan, tilting his head towards Genghis.

Roo Ling nodded.

Stan motioned for Genghis to follow him to a corner of the room, as if that would stop the others hearing their conversation.

'Are we here to sack the city or get home without casualties?' whispered Stan.

Genghis stared once more at this unusual man before him. 'We are to return home once all my men are safe. Rhizun can be sacked another day.'

Stan nodded.

'As I see it' he continued, turning back to his audience, 'there are several issues to be resolved. We have a captain of the Great Horde tied to the wall of an enemy – no offence –

dungeon. Our wish is that he be released from his bonds. Our army waits outside for our safe return, with orders to unleash the full power of the horde should we remain within these walls. If that fails to open the doors at once, then they are to besiege the city to the last man. Be under no illusion, they will take such orders literally. On your side, prefect, you have an enemy at your gates, a city that cannot survive a siege of such length, a population softened by comfort and security, and an emperor watching on in judgment.'

Mekki and Jochi exchanged confused glances.

'The options before us are limited' continued Stan. 'We can attack each other head-on, at enormous cost to both armies. We may eliminate your emperor with a single arrow, then raze the city to the ground, should we choose to do so.'

'You have forgotten those options that result in your *elimination*' interrupted Roo Ling.

'Have you seen them? The Great Horde will not be destroyed by a sweep of a prefect's arm. They are battle-hardened veterans of countless victories. We will win, of that you can be sure.'

'I was referring to you, Stan, not your people.'

'They are one and the same' lied Stan. *This is starting to get out of hand*, he thought.

Genghis nodded to himself.

'I don't believe you for a moment' said Roo Ling. 'When the time comes to choose between preserving your own life or that of your people, you will undoubtedly protect your own interests.'

'I will' said Stan. 'My *interests*, as you put it, are intertwined with those of the nation. You may test me if you wish, but need I remind you of the army awaiting our safe return?'

'Has anyone seen Stan?' asked Jochi. 'I'm sure he was with us.'

'We are not warmongers' continued Stan, 'nor are we unjust. We will offer a way out of this contorted mess you have delivered to your city.'

We will?, thought Genghis.

'I will humour you for the moment' said Roo Ling, conceding the argument despite his rhetoric.

'One; Mekki… *Captain* Mekki will conduct a thorough search of your storage facilities beside the gardens. Two; you will instruct your men within the city to stand down as we return to our army. Three; allow our army safe passage away from your territory. In return, we will resist the temptation to destroy you. I believe that is a fair and reasonable deal that will prevent unnecessary bloodshed.'

'What about me!' cried Okatai from the wall.

'Ah yes. You will also release Captain Okatai at once. Oh, and Captain Ul-suh will share with me his recipe for pork and peach dumplings.'

'Are you quite finished?' asked Roo Ling. 'Or would you like Captain Snu Zhi to reveal the secrets of a well-made bed?'

'I believe that will be all' said Stan.

'I am many things' said Roo Ling. 'I am the prefect of the greatest city of the Jin empire and maintain a level of order unseen in all the lands of the world. I have built the greatest of towers and the finest of gardens. My cook can create the most delectable fruity parcels with nothing more than a handful of plums and a small bag of flour. Yet that is not all. I have deterred the great army of Genghis Khan from attacking Rhizun for my entire reign. The horde that sweeps across the land at will remained a stranger to my city. Our defensive capabilities and self-sustainability were, to my mind, the reason behind such uncharacteristic avoidance on your part.'

'We just hadn't got around to it' said Genghis honestly. 'There are so many places to burn these days it's hard to keep up.'

'Yet I was wrong' continued Roo Ling. 'Stan showed me how an active defence against an invading Mongol horde would be fruitless. He is a master diplomat and strategist, Genghis. You would do well to keep him close.'

'He is?' said Mekki instinctively.

'Told you' said Jochi.

'I know' said Genghis, surprising everyone.

'You do?' said Mekki.

'You have chosen wisely, prefect. Your timing is also extraordinarily fortunate. Tell me, do you accept our terms? We leave each other in peace for the moment and return to our own places and customs.'

'For the moment?' said Roo Ling questioningly. 'That is a vagueness that would undermine the entire agreement.'

'Then I will cede a little more ground to demonstrate my sincerity' said Genghis. 'My Horde will not attack Rhizun while it is mine to command.'

'And do you intend to pass your mantle on anytime soon?' asked Roo Ling.

'No. I am committed to leading my men as I always have, until such time as my heir has children of his own.'

'Is your heir expecting a new arrival?' asked Roo Ling, keen to avoid any ambiguity.

'Not to my knowledge. His identity is a fairly recent revelation and I am yet to learn of his... *domestic situation.* Would you like me to ask him?'

'Ah, I see now' said Roo Ling with a wagging finger. 'There is no heir is there, Genghis? You are trapped in an enemy dungeon with an unfamiliar feeling of containment and will say anything that might see you out into the crisp air. Do not take me for a fool.'

'I cannot deny a preference for the open steppes' said Genghis, 'but I am a scholar of arms and this room is a pleasure. It has given me some rather alluring ideas to improve infantry discipline.'

'Your talk is clumsy, khan. You answer only those questions that do not diminish your position. What of the heir?'

'Oh that is quite true, I do indeed have an heir.'

'Yet you would demand, I am sure, to be released from your disadvantageous position in my dungeon to prove it.'

'On the contrary, prefect. He is in here with us.'

CHAPTER THIRTY ONE

'Don't look at *me*' said Mekki. 'I think I'd know if I was the heir to the Great Khan.'

'Me too' said Stan.

'And I wouldn't?' said Jochi. 'If it isn't one of us three then it's either Okatai, which seems unlikely given the grey hairs, or it's Roo Ling. Which it isn't.'

'Could be Major Tsensible' offered Stan. 'He gets on well enough with us.'

'Sociability isn't a precursor to inheriting an adversarial empire though, is it?' said Mekki.

'That leaves only one possible candidate' said Jochi. 'You!' he shouted, spinning to the door and pointing to the Jin guard.

'Gentlemen, please' said Genghis, raising his arms. 'It is neither the guard, nor Major Tsensible.'

'So it *is* Okatai!' announced Stan. 'How does that work then? Is it one of those *he's your nephew, even though he's twenty summers older than you* things?'

'It is not Captain Okatai, nor the prefect' said Genghis.

'Then...'

'Indeed. It is one of you three.'

'Well this is all very dramatic' said Roo Ling, 'but could we save the drama for when we step out through the gates in peace?'

'Okatai, what's your guess?' said Genghis.

'Guess, my Lord?' said Okatai from the wall.

'Your guess please, captain.'

'We're *guessing* the heir to your throne? Here?'

'Forget it' said Genghis. 'No sense of spectacle, that's your problem. I can see why you ended up in administration.'

'May I?' asked Roo Ling, keen to end the mystery and get on with earning credit with his emperor.

'Be my guest' said Genghis. 'Ha! See what I did there? I'm your guest and I said *you* could be *my* guest.'

'Are you quite well, my Lord' asked Jochi.

'I think he needs to get out into fresh air' said Stan. 'Let's get this over with. Roo Ling, your guess please.'

'There is only one who has gone unnoticed so subtly and with so much understating of his role in this whole affair. One who travelled here on his own, gained access to my city through deception, and has a skill for visual analysis – a key attribute for those looking down on the battlefields from the back of a hilltop horse. Mekki is your heir.'

'Wrong!' said Genghis.

Jochi and Stan stared at each other in panic.

'So, is it you?' said Genghis nodding at Jochi before turning to Stan. 'Or you?'

'Have you considered that it may be neither of us?' asked Stan. 'Now is not the time to draw hasty conclusions.'

'Captain Okatai, would you care to enlighten them?' asked Genghis.

'Can I get down first?'

'No' said Roo Ling.

'Then I will remain silent.'

'Spoilsport' said Genghis childishly. 'Fine, I'll tell them.'

He cleared his throat and straightened his back. 'One of you is my son' he announced. 'A son to rule the empire when the birds have picked their fill of my body. After I'm dead, of course. I want to be absolutely clear that I must be completely dead before you place me on a mountain top for the eagles. In fact, leave it a day or two from when you *think* I'm dead before you do anything irreversible, just in case I'm just having a particularly long sleep. There would be nothing worse than to wake up from a satisfying slumber to find myself in a snowy crag with birds pecking my eyeballs out.'

His eyes darted around the room. 'Ulfred! Are you taking all this in? A day or two, do you hear?'

'Ulfred is not here, my Lord' said Jochi. 'He is outside with the men.'

'Outside?' said Genghis. 'Outside' he repeated, more thoughtfully and quietly this time. 'Outside!' he roared, and sprinted for the door. He yanked it open, punched a rather surprised guard in the nose, and hurtled off down the maze of corridors.

The group careered after him.

'Your heir!' cried Roo Ling. 'Who is your heir?'

Mekki turned his head as he ran. 'Stan! It is Stan!'

Stan and Jochi slowed to a stop.

'Lord of the Sky, Stan. You're the son of Genghis!'

'Mekki, wait!' cried Stan, chasing after his friend and grabbing his sleeve. 'How do you know?'

'It was on the scroll. I found it in Sulki's bag.'

'But you can hardly read' said Stan desperately.

'It wasn't all letters. Please don't ask me to describe the pictures.'

'Look on the bright side' said Jochi, catching up. 'You'll be eating only the finest meat from here on in, and you'll have your choice of the women.'

'Bugger.'

'You'll be safe too. Nobody will target the son of Genghis Khan.'

'Bugger.'

'Actually, they might. Let's not dwell on that though.'

'Bugger.'

'Shall we talk about this later?'

'Bugger.'

'I'll take that as a yes' said Jochi, grabbing his recently well-bred friend's sleeve. 'Come on, I think that guard's waking up.'

They ran after the rest of the group, catching up with them at a dead end. Roo Ling and Tsensible were blocking Genghis' escape as Mekki attempted to talk him round.

'I know of Stan's heritage, as does he.'

Genghis' frenzied eyes slowly calmed. His breath deepened and his body relaxed.

'The quickest way out of here' continued Mekki, 'is to be guided by the Jin. If you cut a deal now we'll be riding the steppes within a heartbeat. But you must gather your wits. Deep breaths now, deep breaths.'

Genghis took in the scene and locked on to Roo Ling.

'I will not attack while I am alive. Stan will not attack until he has children of his own. That is my deal. Accept it, prefect.'

'We have a deal' said Roo Ling. 'On one condition.'

'Quickly' said Genghis.

'We ride out together to my emperor and tell him, oh I don't know, something about how you were daunted by the... by the...'

'Military defences of such an obviously well-led city?' offered Tsensible.

'Yes, that!' said Roo Ling.

'Fine. Now which way is out?' said Genghis, pushing through the blockade and striding off at an ever-increasing pace.

'Hello? Helloooo? I'm still here you know. Don't forget my writing block. It's in our room.' Okatai's head sagged. 'Bloody self-absorbed ruffians' he muttered to himself.

'Twelve years I've been doing this job and I've never seen a day like it' said Captain Khi. 'Seems like any passing imperial leader is invited in without a thought for us poor souls on the gate. *Just open the gate*, they tell us. *How hard can it be?* Well, that just shows how much they know about the mechanics of the thing.'

'They do have a point, though' said Kye bravely. 'When you boil it down, all we really do is push to open and pull to close. It isn't as complex as, for example, topiary. Now there's a skill. Imagine having to coax a geranium to grow in just the right way. It's high risk, too. One slip of a blade and a season's work is gone.'

'High risk?' said the captain. 'It's a flower, not a marauding Mongol horde or an all-powerful emperor.'

'Everything's relative' said Kye. 'I would be far happier knowing all I have to do to keep my head is push and pull every now and again. Ask me to bring a garden to geometric life and I'd be smelling them from beneath the soil before you can say *flamingo shaped privet*.'

'I'm the captain and I say you're wrong' said Khi, ending the debate once and for all. 'Now, eyes ahead men. Here they come.'

Roo Ling and Genghis strode on at the front, the Mongol khan tilting his chin upwards as he breathed in the crisp air. Tsensible walked beside Stan, and Mekki beside Jochi. The gates opened and the group headed across the open land to the opposing empires.

'Well it has been lovely talking with you' said Emperor Aizong to Bataar. 'We must do this again soon.'

Bataar maintained the silent, iron gaze he had held since Genghis had left.

'Are they all like this?' asked Aizong.

'I believe he is an uncommon example, your Imperial Highness' said Bow Lo. 'They are usually more boastful and less stoic.'

'Just as well. Ah, here they are.'

Genghis stepped lightly up to Ulfred and gave him a thunderously uncharacteristic hug.

'Good to see you, old friend. How have you been?'

Ulfred's mind staggered bravely through the confusion. 'I have been well, my Lord. I trust the negotiations were similarly positive?'

'You'll have to ask him' said Genghis, pointing at Roo Ling as the prefect presented himself to his emperor.

'Your Highness' said Roo Ling, bowing almost low enough to smell the grass. 'It is an honour of incomparable purity for your most loyal and trusted city of Rhizun to receive your grace and majesty.'

'Yes, yes' said Aizong. 'Thrilled to be here. Now, what news from within the walls?'

'Ah, right, well. The issue with the pigeons has been sterilised, and…'

'I don't care about the bloody pigeons!' snapped Aizong. 'The *negotiations*. Am I to take your presence here as evidence of their conclusion?'

'Indeed, Light of Heaven.'

'And you are in agreement, khan?'

'I can smell the air' said Genghis, passing a hand slowly through the space in front of him.

'He's a still little groggy I'm afraid' said Roo Ling.

'What did you give him? Not chuanspu, I hope. Is that how you were able to come to such a swift concordance?'

'The khan is unaccustomed to our surroundings, your Highness. He finds the indoors a little unsettling. I believe he will be back to his old self presently.'

'Shame' said Aizong.

'If it pleases you, your majesty, I will furnish you with the details of our settlement.'

'Yes, yes.'

'After rigorous negotiation, the khan has ceded to return peacefully to his homeland with his army. He has given an oath to me, committing to a suspension of military action for as long as he is alive. I was also able to agree to an extension of sorts. The oath will last beyond his death, until such time as his heir produces one of his own. I believe this is a sound declaration, and I recommend we accept.'

'Very good, prefect. It is, as you say, a sound declaration. Tell me, though, who is his heir? Is he likely to produce a child soon? If that is the case then it would only take a well-aimed arrow and we will be manning the parapets with archers before the sun sets.'

'I do not believe either events are likely, with respect, your Highness. This is his heir.' He pointed at an ashen-faced Stan.

'Goodness, he is an unlikely sort. Very cunning, khan. Very cunning indeed.'

'It is my understanding that the khan has only recently become aware of his existence and has had no influence over his upbringing. If he is to inherit the Mongol nation any time soon then we need not fear their teeth.' 'Then it is settled' announced Aizong. 'I will accept the terms, with one small addendum. You may look after the details, Bow.' He whispered his final condition into his aide's ear.

'You would like me to announce this now, your Imperial Highness? In front of the khan?'

'I see no better time to ensure it is done.'

'It would be an honour worthy of my life' said Bow Lo. 'I will ensure the spirit and letter of the declaration is maintained throughout and your name shall be emblazoned as the merciful and benevolent emperor as befits...'

'Oh do stop it' said Aizong. 'Your flowery language is giving me a headache again. I seem to recall your emperor commanding you to desist with such bloated pleasantries. Follow an imperial order or I will cast judgment upon your neck.'

'I will uphold the... I mean, I... will... do... that' said Bow, wincing at the crude informality as if a blade had already sliced him open.

'Good, be sure you do. Now, have you announced my assent yet?'

'Not yet, your Highness' said Bow, confused. 'I was waiting for you to... never mind. I will do so at once.'

He turned to Genghis and cleared his throat. 'Emperor Aizong, Light of Heaven, Emperor of the imperial cities of blah, blah, etc., etc., has agreed to our terms. You are to leave the city at once.'

'Is that it?' asked Stan.

'Not quite' said Bow, squirming a little. 'His is to be given a score of Rhizun's fruity parcels before the day is out and a warm fire lit in his room.'

'What's a fruity parcel?' asked Jochi.

'Not now' said Mekki. 'We've nearly made it through this madness.'

'He's right, Jochi. Never question the peculiarity of leaders' said Tsensible. 'While it has been a tremendous pleasure spending this time with you, I will be glad to see your backs shrink into the distance. No offence.'

'None taken' said Mekki. 'I will be glad to get home to the routine I was cursing a few short days ago.'

'I wouldn't count on that' said Jochi. 'If Stan is being pulled into the Great Khan's inner circle then you can bet a High Horse over a Foot Soldier he's going to drag us along with him. Your days of scratching your behind in the sun are over, friend.'

'Or' said Mekki, clinging on, 'I can do it more often. I might even have someone waiting on *me* for a change.'

'Let's go with that for now' said Jochi supportively.

'Did we win?' asked Genghis.

'We haven't actually fought…' began Ulfred. 'Yes. Yes we won, my Lord. We are to return home at once.'

'Where is Lavender? I need to feel the wind in my hair again. That place is enough to send a lesser man cuckoo.'

'Indeed, my Lord.'

'Lavender! Lavender!?'

'Mekki, bring Lavender to the Great Khan. We ride home at last.'

Stan, Jochi, and Mekki shook Tsensible's arm in turn, wishing him well and offering empty promises to meet up again when all this had blown over. They gave a shallow bow to Roo Ling before taking their horses' reins from a stable hand. Mekki looked up dolefully as Stan mounted his ride.

'Room for a small one?'

'Yes, but not for you' said Jochi laughing. He kicked his heels and galloped away.

'Come on' said Stan. 'Help me up and you can ride with me. I feel a little too woozy to ride alone in any case.'

Mekki mounted then hauled his friend up behind him.

'Yah! Yah!'

CHAPTER THIRTY TWO

They had been riding for two days now and the claustrophobia of Rhizun had dissipated in the wind that whipped their hair. Spirits were high, not least because Genghis was back to something approaching his normal, moderately-less-unpredictable self. Mekki, Jochi, and Stan rode at the front with Ulfred, much to their collective chagrin.

'This is more like it!' shouted Genghis as they galloped along a shallow valley. 'Walls are for conquering!'

'Yes, my Lord' came several grumbling replies.

Everyone but Genghis was ready for a break. They had been in the saddle since breakfast without so much as a latrine stop. Stan was the first to have his fear of Genghis overtaken by the need to relieve himself.

'My Lord?' he said. 'May I suggest, respectfully, that we pause for a brief time to allow the men to… to make themselves more comfortable?'

'Comfortable?' said Genghis, slowing his horse to a trot. The change in pace caused several unseatings behind him and at least one leg of dried mutton to be catapulted into the face of an unsuspecting archer. 'What could be more comfortable than the back of a fine beast like this? Our people were born in the saddle.'

Stan took a deep breath. If he was to be Great Khan one day then now was as good a time as any to test his mettle.

'They need a break, my Lord. We must stop at once.'

'At once, you say? And what gives you the right to tell me what I can and can't order my men to do?'

'I'm your son, the heir to the khanate' said Stan nervously.

Genghis trotted up close to Ulfred. 'Keep the horde on track, I want to speak to my men alone.'

He turned his horse. 'You three, come with me' he said.

They trotted off to the side of the marching army until they reached a small pocket of trees. Genghis dismounted, tied his horse to a branch, and ordered Mekki and Jochi to do the same.

'Stay there, Stan.'

'Why?' asked Stan, his trepidation drawing out the word to several times its normal length.

'Mekki, what made you think Stan here was heir to the great khanate? You should know that a predictable fate will befall you should your assertion be false.'

'I have seen the scroll' announced Mekki. 'It is conclusive evidence, I believe.'

'Is that so?' said Genghis confidently. 'Tell me, captain, how have your eyes met that which sits in my jockstrap?'

'I beg your pardon, my Lord?'

Genghis pulled a crumpled piece of parchment from his nether regions and opened it up for the men to see.

'Ulfred did underestimate you, after all' said Genghis.

Mekki reached into his pocket and pulled out the scroll he took from Sulki. 'It seems Captain Sulki made himself a copy.'

Genghis took the parchment from Mekki and compared it to his own.

'Jochi, you may give your oath first' he ordered. 'On your knees.'

Jochi knelt down in front of Mekki and looked up at Genghis. 'What oath am I to give?' he asked.

'You can start by giving it to the right person' said Genghis. 'It's not Mekki, you damn fool.'

The absolute confirmation sent Stan's head into a spin, followed by his body and finally his mood. He fell like a stone onto the floor and blacked out.

'Can I still give my oath if he's knocked out?' asked Jochi. 'Is it more important that I say it, or that he hears it?'

'Good point' said Mekki, already planning an escape from the upper echelons of Mongolian power. 'Let's wait until we get home, just to be sure.'

'You can give it now, in front of your Great Khan' said Genghis. 'That will suffice for the moment. You can swear it again at the succession ceremony with the eyes and ears of the entire nation upon you.'

Mekki swallowed hard. 'Well, that's something to look forward to.'

'May I ask a question?' said Tsensible.

'Go ahead' said Roo Ling.

'When you promoted me you mentioned a special mission. Am I to assume it was aborted?'

'You see, that's why you were perfect for the job, Major. You have chaperoned the leader of the deadliest fighting force the world has ever seen and acted as a conduit between him and our Imperial Highness. You have fraternised with the common Mongol, improving our standing with these ordinary men of Genghis' army. We will exploit this weakness when the time comes. That you have done this without exposing yourself to the gravity of the mission only serves to vindicate my judgment.'

'So you're not demoting me back to corporal?'

'Heavens above, no!'

'And you've thought this through? You're absolutely sure you don't think corporal would be a more suitable rank? I could hide in the drinking houses and gather information from the common man.'

'On the contrary, you deserve all the credit that comes with such a perfect execution of your orders. Congratulations, Colonel.'

'Colonel!? I'm a bloody *colonel*? I was a happy corporal a few days ago, with no more to think about than stopping Captain Sikhing from wearing his pants on his head and now I'm a bloody colonel.'

'Amazing how things go sometimes, isn't it?'

Mekki held out a light coloured shirt with a dark lining.

'Will this do, oh gracious Jinong? Or would you like another of your servants to stitch a new one? They could make a nice fluffy number to go with your hat.'

'Shut up, Mekki' said Stan. 'It's bad enough having to stand in front of the entire nation dressed like an overweight sheep with styling issues without having to deal with your nonsense.'

'You can call it insubordination now, you know?' said Jochi. 'Just go easy on the death sentences with us though, if you don't mind.'

'I could get your brother to do it' said Stan. 'Leaders are supposed to be inclined towards fatal irony, aren't they?'

'I can't say I've ever considered it. That's your job now anyway, oh Great Jinong Stan.'

'Shut up, Jochi.'

'Khan come' said a deep voice from outside the yurt.

'Thank you Bataar' said Stan. 'Mekki, my shirt, and quickly!'

Mekki scrabbled through a pile of clothes on Stan's bed and threw one over. Stan looped it over his head, just as Genghis entered.

'Are you ready, son?' he asked.

'Physically? Yes. Let's get this over with.'

'There will be a great announcement at the ceremony' said Genghis. 'I will not have my son suffer the same concerns over his legacy as I endured.'

'But I don't have an heir yet' said Stan with absolute certainty.

'You and Zabin can sort that out another time. For now, it will be enough to etch your name into history. I have decreed that any new lands we conquer will end with your name, Stan. It will be a fitting epitaph.'

Stan creased his eyelids in concentration. 'Like Rhizunstan?'

'Think bigger, son. We will not stop at something so trivial as a city. It will be Jinstan before the winter bites again, mark my words.' Genghis' eyes glazed over for a moment. 'Now, to today's business. You will, of course, be flanked by your two aides here. Are they also ready?'

'They are, my Lord.'

'It's like we're not even here' whispered Jochi.

'I wish we weren't.' said Mekki, who then paused for a moment with a pensive expression.

'What is it?' asked Stan.

'Just a feeling we've forgotten something.'

'Is it an ancient law forbidding hats at succession ceremonies?' asked Stan.

'I'm sure it's nothing important' conceded Mekki.

'He's Jinong now' said Jochi. 'Whatever it is can be made again.'

'You're probably right' said Mekki.

Jochi pulled on his shirttails, straightened his back, and bowed low. 'If we're all ready, your nation awaits, my Lord.'

'Hello?' rasped Okatai to the soulless room. 'Helloooooo?'

A thickset guard opened the door and peered through the opening.

'Shi!' said Okatai, using the Jin word for water. Unfortunately for him, the guard knew eight Mongol words. One of which was their word for sheep, which is precisely what he thought Okatai was asking for.

'No sheep' he said, and closed the door.

THE END

HISTORICAL NOTE

You may have realised by now that this story is not meant for students researching accurate histories of the Mongol and Jin empires. Having said that, there are one or two half-truths hidden away amongst the nonsense.

Famously, traces of Genghis Khan's genetics can be found in more people today than is healthy for someone who has been dead for eight hundred years. For this reason, I chose the dearth of a successor as the central pillar to the story. On the off chance that a scholar of Genghis stumbled across this book, I named one of the main characters, Jochi, after one of his real children. I hope there is someone out there who thought from the outset that he was the heir to the khanate rather than Stan. It was also a very satisfying play on the word *jockey*. Similarly, Okatai is loosely named after another of Genghis' sons, Ogedai.

Chuanspu is, in fact, a herbal poison used in Asia during that time, though the name has been slightly tweaked to allow me to shoehorn a pun into it.

Genghis did have coloured tents, though it will not be a great surprise to learn they were not for the purposes noted herein. When besieging a city he would raise a white tent to tell the enemy they should surrender by the end of the day. If the enemy did not cede to his demand he would raise a red tent, signifying that he would unleash the force of his army and kill all men of fighting age. If his enemy still refused to obey him he would raise a black tent to politely let them know he was going to raze the city and kill everything inside.

The timeline is not accurate. By the start of this story in 1215 Genghis had already taken the Jin capital of Yanjing and forced the new emperor to move his seat to Kaifeng. I have written out this military victory to allow for a more satirical twist.

The military ranks are, of course, entirely anglicised. This was done for almost entirely comedic reasons. The idea of a Captain Padding, for example, is arguably funnier than Jagutu-iin Padding.

There is a brief mention of a *River Tree* incident with Jochi. This is based on a formative experience of the young Genghis Khan, then Temujin. He had been captured in an enemy raid but escaped, hiding within a tree in a river crevice. This was, arguably, the beginnings of his imposing reputation.

Roo Ling was not the prefect of Rhizun in the 13th century. This is partly because he is entirely a figment of my imagination, as the name would suggest, and partly because Rhizun is also fictional.

The Jin Emperor did, as far as I can tell, enjoy a good fruity parcel.

www.ingramcontent.com/pod-product-compliance
Lightning Source LLC
Chambersburg PA
CBHW030402180626
46812CB00005B/1898